I SEE LONDON, I SEE FRANCE

Also by Sarah Mlynowski
Ten Things We Did (And Probably Shouldn't Have)
Magic in Manhattan series
How to Be Bad (cowritten with Lauren Myracle
and E. Lockhart)
Gimme a Call
Don't Even Think About It
Think Twice

I SEE LONDON, I SEE FRANCE

SARAH MLYNOWSKI

HARPER TEEN

An Imprint of HarperCollinsPublishers

HarperTeen is an imprint of HarperCollins Publishers.

I See London, I See France
Copyright © 2017 by Sarah Mlynowski
All rights reserved. Printed in the United States of America. No part
of this book may be used or reproduced in any manner whatsoever
without written permission except in the case of brief quotations
embodied in critical articles and reviews. For information address
HarperCollins Children's Books, a division of HarperCollins
Publishers, 195 Broadway, New York, NY 10007.
www.epicreads.com

Library of Congress Control Number: 2016963707
ISBN 978-0-06-239708-9

Typography by Michelle Taormina
19 20 21 22 23   PC/LSCH   10 9 8 7 6 5 4 3 2 1
❖
First paperback edition, 2019

For Todd Swidler,
on γ va

LONDON, ENGLAND

The Basics: London, the capital of England, is the perfect gateway city for your European adventure. You can fly there directly from pretty much anywhere in America, it's a five-hour time difference from the East Coast, plus the Brits speak English.

Um, most of the time. They snog instead of kiss, wear knickers instead of underwear, and spend pounds instead of dollars, so you might not always understand what they're bloody (bloody = curse word!) talking about.

I am going to Europe. EUROPE. I am leaving the country. I have never left the country, and now I'm going to at least *five* countries.

If we make it to the gate.

"Run, Leela, run! Come on! Hurry!" I yell as the two of us charge through the airport. "They just called final boarding!"

"Wait!" she calls back. "I lost a sandal!"

I turn to see her hopping on one foot. Her bright blue purse is overflowing with a black leather wallet, *Vogue, People, EW, Newsweek*, hand sanitizer, a small notepad, pencils, her iPhone, and an open metallic makeup bag the size of a microwave. She's also holding a white plastic bag stuffed with chips, a vitaminwater, and a sandwich.

"I dropped the napkins!" she says. "I have to go back for the napkins!"

"Forget the napkins," I order. "We don't have time for napkins. Put your foot back in your shoe and keep moving! I'll take your food, let's go!"

I grab her bag along with mine and keep running. Instead of a purse, I'm wearing a small black backpack that's keeping everything in place. My passport. My wallet. My guidebook. Four paperbacks—*One Day, The Paris Wife, Daughter of Smoke and Bone*, and *My Brilliant Friend*—that all take place in cities I'm planning to visit. Now that it's summer vacation, I can finally read whatever I want.

When we get to the gate there is only one person in front of us.

The board says:

London

Flight: 401

Departs: 5:00 p.m.

Final Boarding

"We made it!" I say, panting. "I can't believe it."

Our first almost-delay was when my mother nearly had a panic attack when Leela's parents picked me up to take us to the airport. She'd come to the driveway to say good-bye, but as I was getting into the car, I saw her eyes glaze over and she seemed very far away. "Mom?" I said, freezing in my spot. "Are you okay?"

"Just a bit light-headed," she answered, retreating toward the house. "Don't worry about me. Go. Have a safe flight."

I felt slightly sick as I watched her close the front door behind her. I wondered: Can I really do this? Can I really leave?

"Everything okay?" Leela's dad asked.

"Yes," I said. "Let's go."

So we went.

Traffic was miserable, costing us an extra ten minutes. Then security pulled Leela over to examine her massive makeup bag to make sure she wasn't breaking any kind of liquids rule.

"Why do you need so many lipsticks?" I asked her.

"That's a ridiculous question."

"Then why didn't you pack them in your suitcase?"

"Most of them *are* in my suitcase. But I couldn't pack all of them in there. I was worried they would melt."

The final straw was my fault. I insisted on stopping at our terminal's Fresh Market to get sandwiches. That way we'd be able to eat as soon as we got on the plane, be done before takeoff, and could go straight to sleep. But the line inched forward and we almost missed boarding.

Yet we made it. We lost the napkins, kept the lipsticks, and we made it. Now, we're here at the gate. Electricity and excitement rush up my spine—I'm seriously, no joke, actually doing this. I am traveling around Europe with my best friend for four and a half weeks. Holy crap.

"Boarding pass and passport, please," the flight attendant says when it's our turn.

"Here you go," I say, and hand over my paperwork.

"Have a good flight, Sydney," the flight attendant tells me, and hands back my stuff. She turns to Leela.

"Damn," Leela says. "My boarding pass was with the napkins."

Tip: Are you taking a late-night flight? Sleep on the plane! That way you'll be well rested when you land and ready to hit the ground running.

Otherwise you're totally going to be a hot mess by noon.

Somehow we make it. We spot the pile of napkins and the boarding pass and thirty minutes later, we're in the air. I take a final bite of my Fresh Market sandwich. "Bathroom, then sleep," I say.

"Perfect," Leela says, still chewing. "I'll watch our stuff."

Her stuff is already overflowing from her seatback pocket, and covering both her floor area and mine.

As I make my way toward the back, I can't believe I actually left. I haven't been on a plane since I was ten, over nine years ago. I feel free, like a balloon floating through the sky.

The plane rocks to the left.

Free. And slightly untethered.

I push away any feelings of uneasiness. The next four and a half weeks are going to be amazing. Incredible. Amazingly incredible.

I smile at the passengers as I pass them. Hello, little boy. Hello, little girl. Hello, too-skinny mom. Hello, extremely sweaty dad. Hello, cute guy.

At first, I don't recognize him.

Then I think: His shaggy brown hair, pink cheeks, and lazy smile look familiar.

Then I realize. MATT. IT'S MATT. *Leela's ex-boyfriend MATT.*

I have never met Matt in person, since Leela met him in Montreal at McGill University, but I recognize him from her Facebook, Snapchat, and Instagram. Selfies of the two of them on the top of a mountain (#climbedit #MontRoyal), pulling all-nighters at the library (#needcoffee), and sharing a plate of french fries, gravy, and cheese curds (#myfirstpoutine).

Leela introduced us via FaceTime, too.

He's definitely as cute in real life as he was on the phone.

He's watching something on his iPad. I make a U-turn, go back to our row, and sink into my aisle seat.

"I forgot my parents' converter," Leela says. "To plug stuff in."

"Don't worry about that. I bought one and definitely packed it. We can share." I place my hand on her arm. "But brace yourself, my friend. Matt's on the plane."

Leela gasps. "My Matt?"

"Yes."

"No," she finally says when she catches her breath. She drops the rest of her sandwich in her lap. Cheddar. Everywhere.

"Yes," I repeat.

"Are you sure it's him?"

"Ninety-nine percent sure."

"What row?"

"Thirtyish. He's wearing a McGill sweatshirt."

She buries her face in her hands. "The jackass is on my airplane. What the hell is he doing on *my* airplane?"

"Technically the airplane is owned by Delta. Yet operated by Virgin Atlantic."

She doesn't laugh, even though it was super funny. Okay, maybe not super funny, but definitely a little funny. I would have laughed if she'd said it.

"He must be in our original seats," she says. "Thank God I switched mine to be next to you. Thank God. Could you imagine if I had to sit next to him for the entire plane ride? I would die. DIE."

"Can we not talk about dying when we're on a plane over

6

the ocean? Thank you."

"He was supposed to cancel his ticket," she continues. "I told him you were coming with me, and he said he'd go home and get a job in Toronto instead. So why is he here? On my plane? Why would he fly out of Baltimore? He doesn't even live in Baltimore! I do!"

"Didn't you buy the tickets to London together? He probably just kept his. Or maybe he likes the Orioles? I don't know," I say. I look out the small window by her head. All I see is blue. "Are you going to go back and yell at him?"

"Yes! No. I don't want to see him. I don't want to talk to him. He knows I'm on the plane. If he wants to see me, he can look for me. He's an ass." She jerks up. "Crap. Was he sitting with someone?"

"I don't know," I say. "I was so surprised to see him I ran right back here. I never made it to the bathroom."

"Did he notice you?" she asks, worried. "I'm sure he'd recognize you too."

"No, no. He was watching something. I don't think he saw me."

"Please, please, please go back and see if he's sitting with anyone."

"Right now?"

"Yes. Please. I need to know." She shakes her head. "No way he's going to Europe by himself."

"He might be," I say. "Lots of people do."

"No," she says. "He's not the solo traveler type. Oh God,

I bet he's with that chick Ava. She's probably sitting right next to him. They're probably feeding each other peanuts. Peanuts! I hate peanuts! Who actually *eats* the peanuts they give you on airplanes?"

"They don't pass out peanuts anymore. Too many allergies. It's a lawsuit waiting to happen."

"Can you just pretend you're going to the bathroom and check?"

"I actually *do* have to go to the bathroom. Still."

"Perfect. Problem solved." Leela's face is desperate, pleading. Her brown eyes look crazed. Even her usual sleek brown hair is mussed, adding to an overall manic look.

I unbuckle my seat belt and stand up. We're in row fourteen. The plane rumbles beneath my feet as I carefully maneuver my way to the back. Twenty-eight. Twenty-nine. Thirty.

I look up. And there he is. Still in the aisle seat. Still watching a movie. There's an older man reading a James Patterson novel to the left of him.

Not Ava. Small miracle.

Matt looks up. Notices me staring. We lock eyes. I look away but it's too late. Oops.

"Hey," he says.

"Hello, Matthew," I say. Crap. If he didn't know who I was at first, I blew it as soon as I said his name. I'm not sure what I'm supposed to do, so I keep moving, using the backs of people's chairs to wipe off my now-sweaty palms. Luckily there's no one in the bathroom, so I quickly step in and lock the door behind me.

On my way back, I pretend he doesn't exist.

Leela is gripping her armrests like the plane is going down.

"He's alone. And he saw me," I say.

"What do I do?"

"I don't know. Go talk to him?"

"He should come talk to me! He should apologize again! He cheated on *me*! He's on *my* plane!" Her voice is a hysterical whisper.

"You're right," I say. "He should come talk to you."

"He'd better," she says.

I take a deep breath of stale airplane air and wiggle around, trying to get comfortable. It's tough, since the seat seems to be designed for a preschooler.

Leela combs her fingers through her long dark hair. "Do I look okay? In case he comes back?"

"You look great," I tell her.

"How's my lipstick?"

"Still good," I say.

"Thank you, Bite."

I slip off my shoes and try to stretch out my socked toes. "What's Bite?"

"This Canadian brand of lipstick I'm obsessed with. I'm applying for an internship there next summer. I love their branding." Leela is studying marketing at McGill.

9

I'm studying English lit at the University of Maryland.

I turn to her, realizing the implication of what she just said. "You might stay in Canada next summer?"

"Maybe," she says. "If I get the internship."

I sink back into my seat, feeling something close to relief that I came on this trip. Leela and I *need* this month together. A friendship can't survive on childhood memories alone. We have to create new experiences, or the friendship will shrivel up. Like the orchids my dad sent me for my birthday that I completely forgot to water.

She points to the screen above us. "Want to watch the movie?"

"I thought we were going to sleep?"

"I can't sleep at a time like this! Also I have to pee. And there's no way in hell I'm going to the bathroom."

Tip: You might want to get CFAR (Cancel for Any Reason) insurance to prepare for the unexpected.

If you don't, you're SOL if your boyfriend hooks up with some random girl and you want a refund on your ticket. Sorry.

Leela and I had always planned on traveling together.

We'd been best friends since the third grade. We picked matching outfits in advance and told people we were twins. Although we were both around the same middle-row-on-picture-day height, I doubt anyone was fooled; she's Indian and has dark skin and wavy long dark brown hair, and I'm pale with curly medium-brown Jewish-girl hair.

While other kids played soccer and went to ballet, Leela and I read books. *The Princess Diaries. Anne of Green Gables.* But our favorite books took place in England. *Mary Poppins. Matilda. Harry Potter. Peter Pan. Angus, Thongs and Full-Frontal Snogging.* Thongs! Snogging! Ha!

We vowed that one day, when we were older, we would go to England and have our own adventures. London would be so much more fun than Maryland. We would have tea with our pinkies up. We'd go to Buckingham Palace. We'd fly across the city with umbrellas and broomsticks. We'd get engaged in London. Okay, not really, but Leela's parents had gotten engaged in London and wasn't that the most romantic thing you'd ever heard?

In middle school, we became obsessed with the Eiffel Tower. We decided we'd go to Paris *and* London. In high school, Leela studied French and discovered stinky cheese. I read *Anna and the French Kiss, Just One Day,* and a whole lot about Marie Antoinette.

My cousin Melanie actually backpacked through Europe when she was nineteen. She went for six months. She explained that backpacking through Europe didn't mean hiking from city to city over mountains like I kind of thought it did. She took trains, and she just carried all her things in *a backpack* instead of a suitcase. We couldn't imagine. How would everything fit? I wanted to travel with all my stuff in a backpack! We wanted to backpack through Europe!

Even after Leela got into McGill University in Montreal, Canada, and I got a scholarship to go to University of Maryland—which was great because I could live at home, and I felt like I needed to live at home—our plans didn't change.

"We're still going to Europe next summer," she said.

"Of course," I told her, although unlike Leela, I didn't have a passport.

The night before she left for Canada she said, "We're still going to Europe this summer," as she hugged me good-bye.

I promised we would.

Leela met Matt on the first day of Frosh. That's the week of drunken debauchery at McGill, the week before school starts. Like in Europe, the drinking age in Montreal is eighteen.

At the start of the year, Leela and I spoke or texted every day. But as the months went by and I got caught up in classes and studying and parties and driving to and from campus in addition to running around for my mother and my sister, Addison, my response time got slower and slower.

Leela: Call me when you can. I miss you!

Leela: Remember me?

Leela: Cough, cough, this is still your number, right?

Me: I'm sorry! I suck! I'm so busy! I love you!

I missed the days when our daily lives were intertwined with school and gossip and hanging out and reading and just watching TV together.

My phone buzzed in late February.

Leela: We're still going to Europe together, right?

I didn't answer right away. I wanted to go to Europe. Badly.

A week later she wrote again.

Leela: Hello, stranger. What's the story for this summer? ARE we going to Europe or not? If yes, we have to get plane tickets.

I hesitated, my hands on my phone. Our friendship needed this trip. But I couldn't say yes. I wrote back:

I don't know.

Leela: Your mom will be fine.

Me: I'm not sure that's true.

I waited for Leela to respond. She finally texted:

Leela: But we've been planning this trip FOREVER!!

Me: I know.

I thought about it. I missed Leela like crazy, but I couldn't do it. I couldn't leave my mother for the summer. She *wouldn't* be fine.

My mother has a severe anxiety disorder called agoraphobia. People think agoraphobia is a fear of going to public places, but that's not totally it. Agoraphobics are afraid of being out in public and losing control, so they prefer to stay in places they think of as safe.

That's how my father explained it anyway.

When my little sister and I were still in elementary school, my mom always asked my dad to drive, and we were always the first to leave events, but she still came to our school plays and book fairs and teacher conferences. She worked from home since she's a children's book illustrator, but she still left the house. She didn't love it, but she did it. She and my dad argued all the time. He wanted to go for more dinners, more parties, to meet more people, see more things. She wanted him to slow down and pay attention to his family. He liked to be out. She liked to play Monopoly and watch TV. He wanted to see a marriage counselor. She refused. Her aunt was a therapist, and she thought her aunt was a total kook.

So he went without her. And then when I was in seventh grade, he moved out without her. Without us.

After she and my father got divorced, everything went downhill. She was driving us to my middle school's winter carnival when she had a panic attack. I was in the front, and my sister was in the back seat. We were at a red light when the light turned green and my mom didn't move.

"Mom?" I said, and then noticed that her face was white and her hands were shaking. "Mom, are you okay?" She didn't look okay. She looked like she was about to pass out.

The navy Taurus behind us started to honk. Once. Twice. Again. *HONNNNNK.*

What was happening?

"You have to drive, Mom," Addison piped up from the back seat. "You can't b-b-block the road!" Addison had developed a bit of a stammer. Stress, her teacher said. She was only in the fourth grade.

"I . . ." My mom's voice cracked. "I don't feel well. I think I'm . . . my chest hurts."

Was she having a heart attack? My own heart started to race.

HONNNNNNK.

"Mom? Mom?" Addison cried out.

"Pull into the Dunkin' Donuts over there," I said suddenly. I put my hand on top of her arm. It was cold and clammy.

She pressed her foot lightly on the gas, crossed the lane, and drove into the parking lot, her hands still gripping the wheel. She put the car into park.

"What are you doing?" Addison asked, her voice rising. "You guys are freaking me out!"

"Does your chest still hurt?" I asked.

My mother nodded. She continued to shake. An Adele song played on the radio.

It was a heart attack. My mother was having a heart attack. I had to do something. What could I do? I needed help. We had to go to the hospital. "Should I . . . should I call an ambulance?" I looked for her purse. Where was her purse? I needed her phone!

She shook her head no, but didn't speak.

"Mom? Where's your purse?" I asked. "I need to call an ambulance."

"No," she said finally. "Don't. I'm just . . . nervous."

What did that mean?

"Nervous?" Addison asked, and then squeaked out a laugh. "About the winter carnival?"

My mom closed her eyes. "Syd. Run inside and get me water?"

"Okay." I jumped out of the car and into the cold, relieved to have something constructive to do. I watched them through the store window as I waited in line. My mother's hands were no longer gripping the steering wheel, and her door was open slightly. She seemed to be taking deep breaths.

A minute later I got back in the car, opened the bottle of water, and handed it to her. "Do you feel better?"

She took a long sip. "A little."

"It's for sure not a heart attack?" I asked.

"A heart attack?" Addison screeched. "You think Mom is having a heart attack?"

"I'm not having a heart attack," my mother said quickly. "I'm fine. It's just a panic attack. I had them when I was younger. Just give me a minute."

We sat still, the radio continuing to play.

"Okay," my mom said after a few songs.

"We don't need to go to the carnival," I said. "Do you want to go home?"

"No!" Addison squawked. "The carnival has c-c-otton candy."

I wanted to yell at my sister but didn't want to stress my mom out even more.

My mom's lower lip trembled. "I wouldn't mind lying down."

I put my hand back on her arm. "It's okay. It's not that important."

For the next few years, my mom wouldn't drive anywhere unless I was in the passenger seat. She said she liked having me beside her. I calmed her down. Addison and I started taking the school bus to and from school, and I went along with my mom to her appointments, to the mall, to the grocery store, to the pharmacy, to wherever she or my sister needed to go. She was worried that without me there she would have another panic attack, and somehow lose control of the car. I liked knowing that I could help. That I could make my mother feel better.

When I was sixteen-and-a-half and I got my license, I started doing most of the driving. That way my mom could relax in the passenger seat and not have to worry about having a panic attack at all. I didn't mind: I felt needed. I hated that she worried so much, and that her world was getting smaller and smaller, but I was glad I could help and I liked driving and that I basically had my own car. I got to take it to school and wherever I wanted. I also had to pick up Addison after swimming and take my mom to the grocery store.

Until we stopped going to the grocery store. One minute my mom was studying a frozen lasagna in the freezer section of Safeway and the next minute her hands were shaking and the lasagna was on the floor. She was sweating and hyperventilating, and she needed me to take her out of there, take her outside right away before she fainted. I grabbed her hands, we left the groceries in the cart and the frozen lasagna on the floor, and I found a bench outside. I told her to take big breaths, that she was going to be okay, that I loved her, and she was going to be fine.

She hasn't been back to the Safeway since. You can order online from Safeway, and they deliver in an hour.

My mom was pretty sure she'd have a panic attack at our high school parent-teacher nights, so couldn't my father go to those, he didn't live that far away, and then he could tell her what they said? He liked doing stuff like that. Surely he could do at least that after moving out on all of us. He could. And he did.

He also asked her to see a therapist.

She said she'd be fine. She'd had a few panic attacks as a teenager, but they had gone away. She ordered some books with relaxation techniques.

When they still didn't go away, I begged her to at least ask her regular doctor for help. She finally agreed.

I drove her to the appointment and read Ned Vizzini's *It's Kind of a Funny Story* in the waiting room. Her doctor told her that she had to learn to relax, and prescribed an antidepressant. My mom took it every day for a month but said it made her brain cloudy, and then she still had a panic attack when she tried to take us to see a movie. So she stopped taking the pills.

That was two years ago.

These days she doesn't drive. Or go to the grocery store. Or to the movies. Or to shopping malls, or go on trains, or planes, or take cabs. She won't see another doctor, or try another medication. She doesn't want to feel drugged out. I'm not sure what else I can do to help her, but it's hard to watch her in pain. So I do what I can to keep the panic away.

My mom will sit in the backyard, and even go for walks, but she needs me to be with her when she leaves the house to keep her calm. She doesn't want to risk panicking and fainting and god forbid hitting her head on the concrete and bleeding all over the sidewalk without anyone to help her.

It took me a week to answer Leela's text about whether or not we were still on. I finally wrote back:

I'm sorry. I can't.

She wrote back immediately:

BOOOOOO. Are you sure? I really want to go with you.

Me: I want to go with you too. I'M SORRY.

Two weeks later she wrote:

How would you feel about me going to Europe with Matt? I would OF COURSE rather go with you. Would you be upset? Be HONEST.

I felt terrible about it, but I couldn't say that since I wasn't a selfish asshole. I wrote back:

Go for it. You have my blessing.

Leela: Love you. Thanks. Now I just have to convince my parents. . . They like Matt but I'm not sure how they're going to feel about me traveling with my boyfriend.

Leela's parents had always been in favor of our plan to go to Europe since they thought a month of traveling would be good for her. They thought it would teach her to be more independent. Even though she went to school in another country, she still never had to act like a grown-up. She lived in a dorm and had a meal plan. She went to class and came back. Plus, her older sister, Vanya, was a senior at McGill, checking up on her and paving the way. Leela was lucky.

I wasn't sure if I was rooting for her parents to say yes or no.

Three days later Leela wrote:

They said yes! My mom says she likes the idea! She says she feels even safer knowing he's with me. Sexist but at least they said yes.

I didn't respond right away. She was going to Europe without me. She was going to Europe with Matt.

Leela finished her freshman year at McGill in the middle of May and came home.

At the beginning of June, she stormed into Books in Wonderland, where I work every summer, tears streaking her cheeks. "Matt kissed some girl named Ava at a bar," she said.

I took a break and led her outside. We sat on the edge of the sidewalk, our knees hiked up into our chests. "How do you know?" I asked.

"He admitted it. I asked if something was going on, and

he said yes. Claimed it was a mistake. He didn't *mean* for it to happen. He was at a party, and it was an accident. He was freaked out about how serious we were getting. He said he's still freaked about how serious we're getting. But come on, how do you accidentally kiss someone?"

I considered. "I'm not sure. I think it's physically impossible. You'd both have to have your mouths open, and you'd have to bump into each other at a very bizarre angle."

She hiccup-laughed. "Exactly. So what am I supposed to do about Europe?"

"Damn."

"No kidding."

Matt and Leela had decided to travel through Europe together for a month. Four and a half weeks, to be exact. They were flying to London on July first and flying out of Rome on August second. They were leaving in three weeks.

"Do you still want to go?" I asked.

"With him?"

"No. Not with him. You can't go to Europe with a guy who just cheated on you. Do you want to go to Europe by yourself?"

"No, I don't want to go by myself! I can't go by myself!"

"Of course you can. People travel by themselves all the time. You can go wherever you want. A bookstore in London. A beach in Italy. The Louvre! You'll eat gelato! Macarons! Stinky cheese!"

"He doesn't even like stinky cheese," she said, sniffing.

"Then he has no taste."

She turned to me. Her expression was hopeful. "Come with me."

I laughed. "I can't."

"You *can*, Sydney. Please come." She brightened. "Isn't Addison working at Sunny's this summer?"

"Yeah." She'd gotten a job at the grill by the local pool.

"So she's here. And she has her license now, right? She can help your mom."

"She *just* got it last month. I'm not sure she feels comfortable driving yet. I think she'd be really mad."

I've always tried to shield my sister from the stress of taking care of our mom. I was the one who made sure my mother left the house every day. I was the one who drove her around. In the years right after the divorce, my sister had been too young to help, and I didn't want to worry her. Besides her stammer, she also started to fall behind in math. Luckily we found tutors and speech specialists who could come to the house.

"Your mom would be mad?"

"No, Addison would be mad. *And* my mom. They both would. I can't go. I'm sorry. I wish I could but I can't."

"Can't? Or won't?" Leela asked. "Think about it. It's the trip of a lifetime. And you deserve it, Syd, you really do. You do so much for your family. You need time off. And we never get to see each other anymore. I miss you."

"I miss you too," I said. And I hadn't exactly been the

world's greatest friend this year. And Leela needed me. She really did. And she'd always, *always* been there for me.

Maybe my mom would be okay if my sister helped her? It was only four and a half weeks. I looked back at the bookstore. Eleanor, the owner of Books in Wonderland, wouldn't mind. She had enough extra staff.

I blew out a breath. "How much would the trip cost exactly?"

Leela squeezed my arm. "Not THAT much. We can do it on sixty dollars a day. That's like two thousand for the whole thing."

"Plus the flight. How much was yours?"

"Eight hundred. Flying into London and flying out of Rome. Are you going to come? Please say you're going to come!"

"And how do we get around?"

"Eurail. Seven hundred."

"So three thousand five hundred. That's a lot. But I have some Bat Mitzvah money left. And I've been working here for the last month . . . I think I have about three thousand dollars I could scrape together."

"Maybe your dad has airline points?"

My dad did have airline points. He had a shitload of airline points. He never invited us to stay at his one-bedroom apartment, but he always offered us airline points.

"Take a vacation," he'd say. "Have some fun."

"I don't even have a passport," I said.

"You can get one fast. I swear. We'll expedite it."

Could I do this? Could I go? The possibility felt like a window being cracked open. I could practically taste the fresh air. The fresh air, gelato, macarons, and stinky cheese.

"I bet we could stay with Kat for part of the time," I said. I'd met Kat at college. She was working at a gallery in Paris for the summer, and her parents had rented her an apartment. "That would save us a few euros."

"Yes!" she said. "We can do this! You're coming to Europe! Woot!"

My cheeks flushed. "Don't get too excited. I have to talk to my family."

That night I waited for Addison to get dropped off at home. When she walked into the foyer, her hair was wet and piled on top of her head. We both have our mother's curly brown hair and round face and our dad's light brown eyes. Addison's shorter than I am and more muscular since she swims almost every day and plays third base for the JV girls' softball team.

She wasn't the same helpless kid she used to be. She could drive. She had a job. She had even lost her stammer.

"Hey," I said, lowering my voice since our mom was in the kitchen. "I have a crazy question."

She dropped her knapsack on the floor. "What?"

"Matt cheated on Leela—"

She made a sour face. "Jerk!"

"I know. But the thing is, now she wants me to go to Europe with her."

She blinked. Fast. "Oh. Okay. You always wanted to go, right?"

"Yeah."

"Do you have the cash?"

"Maybe. But I would only do it if you think you can handle Mom. Could you? You can drive so I wouldn't be leaving you stranded. All you have to do is make sure she walks around the block once a day to get some exercise and drive her around if she has to go somewhere. It's only a month. Four and a half weeks. Would you be okay with that? In theory?"

She shrugged. "I guess."

"Yeah? Think about it. I don't have to go."

"No, you should go. Sounds fun."

"Yeah? And you'd get the car to yourself all summer. . . ."

She smiled. "I definitely like the sound of *that*."

"If something horrible happens I'll come back early. I'll get on the next plane. Swear."

She rolled her eyes. "What do you think is going to happen exactly?"

"Who knows with Mom? She could refuse to leave her bedroom entirely. Or stop showering. I don't know. Something. If there's an emergency I'll come back. Deal?"

"Deal," she said. She unzipped her knapsack, took out her

wet bathing suit, and uncrumpled it. She didn't seem worried at all.

Hope swelled inside of me.

"What's Mom making for dinner?" she asked.

"Chicken stir fry."

"Do you think it's ready? I'm starving." She headed into the kitchen, wet bathing suit in hand, not a care in the world.

Okay then.

My heart hammered over dinner. Could I really do this? No. Yes. Should I bring it up? No. Yes. What would my mom say?

My sister helped herself to more chicken and broccoli. "So I hear it's just us this summer, huh, Mom?"

Shit.

"What do you mean?" my mother asked, eyebrows scrunching together.

Addison made an *oops* face at me. She clearly hadn't realized I had not discussed this with Mom yet.

Now or never.

I stared at my plate and the words tumbled out of my mouth like vomit. "Matt cheated on Leela, she's miserable and needs someone to travel with, I want to go, Dad has airline points, it won't cost you anything, Addison will help you, is that okay?"

My mom put her fork down. "Can you repeat that? Slowly?"

I repeated it. Slowly. Her face got paler and paler with each sentence. Oh, no. Was she going to have a panic attack right at the table?

Instead of speaking, her shaking hands reached for her glass of water.

"Do you hate the idea?" I asked, my shoulders falling. "I don't have to go. Forget it."

She cleared her throat. "No," she said. "You should go." She took another sip of water. She seemed to notice her hands were shaking and hid them under the table.

"We'll be fine," my sister said, rolling her eyes. "It's not that big of a deal."

It was a big deal. But I wanted to go. And Leela needed me.

That night, I lay in my twin bed, the same bed I'd slept in my entire life, staring at the glow-in-the-dark stars I'd stuck to the ceiling when I was eight. Could I really do this? My mom said she'd be fine. My sister said she could handle it. I wanted—desperately—to see Europe.

I took out my phone.

Me: OK. I'm in.

It's nine p.m. East Coast time and two a.m. London time when Matt finally comes over to talk to Leela. We're very busy picking at our terrible airplane food, aka our second meal of the night. It's also the meal we're supposed to be sleeping through.

"Hi, Leela," he says. "Can we talk?"

27

I focus intently on the cold pasta and mushy tomatoes. Mmm. Stale bread.

Leela glares at him. "You should have talked to me before getting on this plane."

"I tried to find you at the airport. I didn't see you."

"*Before* the airport. You should have called."

His cheeks turn red. "I'm sorry. I shouldn't have surprised you."

"What are you doing here, anyway?" she barks. "I thought you weren't coming."

"I know. But I didn't really have anything else to do this summer, and I already had the ticket, and . . ." His voice trails off.

The plane starts to shake. The seat belt sign comes on.

". . . and I wanted to see you, I guess."

Leela stares at her hands and doesn't respond.

"Enjoy the cookies," he says, and walks back to his seat.

I *am* planning on enjoying my cookie. It's wrapped in plastic and looks delicious.

We wait until we're sure he's gone.

"He wanted to see me?" she squeals. "What does that mean? He wants to get back together?"

"Do you want to get back together?" I ask. The possibility of them getting back together hadn't really occurred to me. If they get back together, what happens to me exactly? Will I have to travel Europe with both of them? I do not want to be a third wheel on my own travel adventure.

"No!" she says. "Of course not. He cheated on me! He's a jerk!" She wraps a lock of dark hair tightly around her finger. "But do you think he came to Europe to get back together?"

I imagine being on a top bunk while the two of them have muffled make-up sex in the bunk bed below me.

Did I remember to pack earplugs?

"Please put your tray tables away and your seats into the upright position," the flight attendant announces on the loudspeaker, startling me awake. "It's now six a.m. and we will be landing shortly. The temperature in London is twenty-one degrees Celsius."

I yawn. I got about an hour of sleep, tops. But I did finish *One Day* and half of *The Paris Wife*. I'll probably be an exhausted mess, but it's okay because I have four and a half weeks—four and a half weeks!—to rest. I have no essays, no midterms, no group projects, no mother and sister to take care of. I am officially on vacation. I haven't taken an actual vacation since before my parents got divorced. And I've never, ever, gone away with Leela. Her family invites me to join them in Naples, Florida, every winter break, but I never wanted to leave my mother. This year Leela brought Matt.

I look over to see that Leela is already awake and trying to repack everything that spilled out of her purse.

"Morning," I say. "Twenty-one degrees? We're going to freeze! Just kidding. It's Celsius! How cute is that?"

"Very charming," Leela says. "That's about seventy degrees. They use Celsius in Canada too, you know."

I open my window cover as the plane descends, not really seeing much. Just clouds. But I know the Thames River and the London Eye and everything else are right below.

When the plane touches ground, half the people clap and I join in because, well, why not? We made it, didn't we? I gather my books, and make sure my passport didn't somehow slip out and end up under someone else's seat, and then rummage through Leela's discarded pillow and blanket in case she forgot anything.

"Are we walking slowly or quickly?" I ask, filing into line.

"Huh?"

"Do we want him to catch up to us or not?"

"Oh. Not. If he really came to Europe to find me, he can run after me."

When we step off the plane, there are hundreds of travelers of all ages walking in different directions, with carry-ons, wheelies, and backpacks. And there are a whole lot of stores I don't recognize. Boots, which seems like a pharmacy. And WHSmith, which has displays of bestselling books. There is even a cute dark-haired boy studying a paperback. "Leela! They have pharmaceuticals, books, and cute boys here! We're going to love it."

"Let's find a bathroom," she instructs, not looking around. "Fast." She didn't go once the whole plane ride.

30

"To the loo!" I say.

"Don't make me laugh, I'll pee in my pants." We spot a sign that says "Female Toilet," and make a run for it.

Even the bathrooms are different. The toilets are square-ish, and there aren't any visible tanks.

"How do you flush?" she asks. "There's no flusher!"

"It's on the wall!" I call out.

"Thanks!"

When I get out, she's brushing her teeth in the sink. Her hair looks combed.

"Do I have to do that too?" I ask.

She spits. "No, you're not about to face an ex-boyfriend."

I wouldn't care if I were. My last relationship was in January and only lasted two months. Theo was an economics major and a friend of Kat's. I slept with him six times and I thought he was sweet until he started speaking in an Elmo voice and saying things like, "Theo is so sad when Sydney doesn't sleep over!" and "Theo wants to see Sydney's house!" Also, while he was a good kisser, he wasn't great at the sex part. It lasted about fifteen seconds and he hummed the whole time.

Anyway. Matt was Leela's first boyfriend. First everything.

While she applies one of her seven lipsticks, I take my phone out of my backpack and debate turning it on. I guess I should. To make sure everything is okay at home.

A text message pops onto my screen. **FREE MSG: Your**

31

phone number has exceeded $15 in global data charges. Data is $2.05/1MB.

WTF? Fifteen dollars in global charges? In four seconds? Oops. I forgot to turn on an international plan, and I'm roaming.

Three texts pop onto my screen, too. All from my sister, Addison.

All OK!

Are you there yet? I can't find the car keys.

Crap. I turn my phone off in case my bill doubles in the next four seconds. I'll deal with the car keys and charges later.

"Syd . . . " Leela says.

"Yeah?" I return my phone to my bag.

"Did you know about this?" she asks.

"Huh?"

She turns to me, brown eyes wide. "Is this a surprise?"

I have no idea what she's talking about. "Is what a surprise?"

"Did he tell you he was coming? Is this whole thing a big surprise for me? Like my dad surprised my mom?"

I suddenly remember that her father surprised her mother at a tea place in London. And then he proposed. Does she think Matt hooking up with Ava was a hoax? That the whole last month was a trick to surprise her in London and propose?

"Oh, sweetie," I say. "No. I've never spoken to Matt

32

before today, except with you on FaceTime. I don't think he's showing up at the tea place with an engagement ring."

She looks down. "I didn't think he was going to *propose*. I just thought maybe he was planning on winning me back and showing up with flowers and telling me he loves me. Do you know he's never said I love you? Not once."

"I'm sorry," I say. "But I haven't talked to him. I swear."

She sighs. "Okay. Just checking." She repacks her bag and heads out the bathroom door. "Onward."

"We're in the *Queen's* Terminal. The queen's!" I exclaim, trying to cheer her up. "I love the queen. I want to meet the queen."

"We probably won't, though."

As we make our way to Passport Control, I catch Leela scanning the line for Matt.

I give her arm a squeeze.

Finally, it's our turn to step up to a booth. "Where do you reside?" the man asks. He has a British accent, and I love him immediately. I resist the urge to ask him if he knows Mary Poppins.

"Maryland," I say.

"How long are you here for?"

"We're traveling for a month," I say. "Four and a half weeks. Do you need to know all the countries we'll be visiting?"

"No," he says, and stamps our passports.

My first stamp. I know I have a dumb smile on my face,

but I can't help it. It's just a little black box that says "Immigration Officer," the date, and "Heathrow," but it's my first international stamp and it's awesome.

We follow the signs to baggage reclaim. Not claim. Reclaim. Adorable!

"Do you see him?" she asks, clearly trying very hard to not look around.

"Not yet. But he was at the back of the plane."

A few minutes later I spot him by the door. "He's here," I say. "He sees us."

She freezes but doesn't give herself away. "What's he doing?"

"Walking toward us. Should I laugh or something? Pretend we're having a great time? Pretend you've just said something incredibly witty?"

"Yes, please."

"Ha, ha, ha!" I force a massive smile. "We're having such a great time! You've just said something so incredibly witty! Now do you want me to casually leave?"

"No, please."

Matt says something to the guy beside him, and I realize that it's the cute guy I saw looking at the books, and that he must be the person traveling with Matt. They probably met up in the terminal. The guy's hair is straight and dark brown, almost black, and he's tall. Taller than Matt, anyway. Square jaw. Dark eyebrows. Perfectly smooth olive skin.

He's kind of hot. Actually, he's really hot. Why have I

never seen him in any of Leela's photos? I'd rather look at him than a plate of poutine.

"He's with a really hot guy," I say.

"Huh?" she asks. "Is it Jackson?"

"I don't know who Jackson is," I say. "But maybe?"

The guy-who-is-possibly-Jackson spots his backpack—it's a deep red—at another conveyor belt and hoists it over his shoulder in one swoop.

Leela closes her eyes. "I can't *believe* he's traveling with Jackson."

I know there's a story here, and I am looking forward to hearing it.

Out of the corner of my eye, I spot my spankin' new backpack and leap over to pick it up. It's pale blue with black stitching and lots of zippers, and it has adjustable arm straps and a band that I can snap around my waist, which will supposedly help distribute the bag's weight. Am I really going to wear this on my *back* for over four weeks? Or is that more of a figure of speech?

Also, now I have two backpacks: the small one I'm already wearing on my back and a huge one. My plan was to roll the small one up and pack it when it wasn't in use, but I can't exactly do that here. I'm going to have to wear one on my back and one on my front. That'll be super attractive. Maybe I'll wait until Hot Jackson is no longer in the vicinity.

"Hello again," Matt says as the two of them approach us.

"Fancy seeing you here," Leela replies drily. Her arms are

crossed in front of her chest. "Sydney, this is Jackson. Jackson, Sydney. Syd, I believe you already met Matt."

"We go way back," I say. "All the way to row thirty. Hi there, Jackson. We missed you on our flight."

"I flew from Vancouver," he says, turning toward me. "But I hear yours was a party."

"It was definitely wild and crazy," I say, smiling.

He smiles back, and I realize I am no longer the third wheel. Jackson and I are in this drama together.

Leela shakes her head and glares at Matt. "I can't believe you're crashing my trip."

I'm not sure how I feel about Matt, but I may not mind Jackson crashing my trip.

"I'm not crashing," Matt says. "I'm going to Europe. With Jackson. I already had the ticket. Trust me, I tried really hard to switch the ticket to leave from Toronto, but I couldn't make it happen. I'm sure our plans will be completely different, so don't worry."

"They better be. How long are you staying in London?" Leela asks, eyes narrowed.

"Four nights."

Her jaw clenches.

I spot Leela's suitcase coming our way. She's using one of those duffel bags on wheels, instead of a backpack. She had decided backpacks were dorky. I completely disagree. Backpacks are awesome.

"Leela, your bag," I say, deciding that their conversation

could use an interruption.

She twists her head toward the belt and tries to drag it off the conveyor.

"Let me help you," Matt says, and reaches toward it.

"I don't need your help," she snaps, grabbing it. "I can get along fine without you."

"Okay, then." He reaches over to the conveyor and picks up and puts on his own black backpack. Then he walks backward and away from us. "You're on your own. Have a great trip."

"Nice meeting you," Jackson says to me with a half smile.

"You too," I say, adding a little wave. Good-bye, Hot Jackson, good-bye.

"I'm going to kill him," Leela mutters, turning around. She studies the black bag. "Damn. This isn't even mine. I got a Canadian bag tag. Help me put it back?"

"You're not actually Canadian," I say, hoisting it back onto the conveyor belt. "You know that, right?"

"Europeans like Canadians better than Americans," she says. "We have to be careful here, you know. I brought one for you, too. It's in my bag."

We stand side by side watching for her suitcase.

It doesn't come.

I see Matt and Jackson disappear through customs.

"Seriously, I am going to kill him," Leela says. "Maybe the murder laws are different here. Perhaps you're allowed to kill your ex?"

"Probably not in the UK. The Brits are supposed to be uptight." I smile. "But maybe in France."

We wait for Leela's bag. And wait some more.

All the other bags come through and get picked up.

Not hers.

Leela's breathing fast and her jaw is clenched again and I can tell she is about to start crying. "Omigod. I can't deal. I can't take it. I can't handle him being here and losing my luggage. I just can't. I need my lucky black dress! And my hair dryer!"

"It's going to be fine," I say. "Let's go talk to someone."

"To who?"

"To them!" I say, pointing to the counter in the corner that says Customer Service. "They will help us! They will find your bag. If not this very moment, then soon, and then they will send it to us. You have a lot of stuff in your carry-on, right? Is it enough to keep you going for a day or so? I saw you brush your hair and teeth so I know you have those. Plus magazines. And makeup."

"Yes," she says. "I have those. And an extra pair of undies. And my pills."

"What pills? Anything fun?"

"Birth control pills. You are welcome to party with them all night long."

"You're still on birth control?"

"Of course. I'm not getting off just like that. They make my boobs ginormous."

"Do you think they would make my right boob as big as my left?" I ask.

"I can't guarantee that," she says. "But I appreciate your attempt to make me laugh and forget that I might have to walk around London in my undies."

"Knickers," I say. "They're called knickers here." I hoist the big bag on my back, and the small one on my front. "Now let's go get some customer service."

Tip: The Tube is the cheapest way to get from Heathrow into London.

We are sorry to inform you that the Tube is the London subway and not, as we had hoped, a cross-city waterslide.

Forty-five minutes later, on the other side of customs, Leela is still duffel-bag-less. Customer Service has promised that when they locate it they will have it sent to our hostel. I can only hope we are still in London by then.

I feel slightly brain-dead, so I lead us toward an Italian coffee place called Caffè Nero. We use the pounds we exchanged at home to get us started to buy two cups of Americano and take big, long sips.

"Ahhhh," I say.

"Should we just take a cab?" Leela asks.

"No, we shouldn't," I say. "A cab will be a fortune. This coffee just cost like four American dollars each and we're supposed to be budgeting. We said we would take the subway. It's called the Underground here. The Tube! Doesn't it sound like a waterslide?"

"How awesome would that be?"

We follow the signs to the Underground. There's an elevator—a lift—that takes us to floor "-1." Ha! Minus one! You're so cute, London.

When we get to the ticket machines, I feel a wave of uneasiness. I have no idea what to do.

"What station are you going to?" a man in uniform asks me.

Thank goodness. Help.

"Covent Garden," I say. "But I think we're supposed to get an Oyster card." I read that in my *Travel Europe* book.

We each put twenty pounds on our cards, which, at the exchange rate of 1.5, cost us like thirty dollars each. I hope that will last the whole time, otherwise we're never going to be able to do this on sixty dollars a day.

My mom ordered *Travel Europe* from Amazon for me, which was pretty sweet of her. Obviously she should have bought it from Books in Wonderland, especially since I get an employee discount, but it wasn't like she was going to leave the house to visit the store on her own.

"It's a trip of a lifetime," my mom said. "I wish I had done it."

She never would have. She hated traveling even when she was my age.

I had done as much planning as I could in the three weeks I'd had. Leela had been kind of a mess after the breakup, so she'd lie on my bed while I looked things up and made reservations. I'd booked the first hostel, plus loosely planned our days, and reserved our train to Paris. There, we'd stay with my friend Kat for five nights. After that, we'd save more money by taking an overnight train to Berlin instead of a day train. After Berlin, we could see what we felt like doing. Maybe Prague, which wasn't too far from Berlin, and Vienna, and then maybe another overnight to Italy? But we would play it by ear. As I'd told Leela, nothing was set in stone.

"You're the best," she'd said, tracing circles into my pillow. "Matt had wanted to just go and figure things out as we went along, but having a plan is so much smarter."

"I don't mind," I said. "I like planning."

And anyway, in a way it felt like I was paying Leela back for years of looking out for me.

Years.

After my parents' divorce, she'd cheered me up with funny pictures she'd drawn, and sleepovers and daily calls just to say hi.

On my fourteenth birthday, I insisted my mom take me and Leela and Addison out for Japanese. We never went to restaurants, but it was my birthday. My birthday! I didn't want to eat dinner at home. I wanted to do something special. After dinner, Leela would stay the night.

My mom drove. I sat in the passenger seat. Everything was fine.

She had a panic attack while we were eating our sushi.

Her hand started shaking while she held the chopsticks. Her face flushed and she was breathing hard and fast like she was running up stairs.

Every emotion hit me at once. Worry for my mom. Guilt for forcing her to go out even when I knew she didn't like to. Embarrassment that this was happening in front of Leela. But I jumped up and waved down the waiter to get water and I rubbed my mom's back. I was too ashamed to look at Leela. But when Addison started to cry, Leela put her arm around my sister and whispered to her that everything was going to be okay.

Later that night, when I turned off the lights, I told Leela the truth. I stared at the glowing stars on my ceiling and let my words just be words floating in the dark.

When I was finished, she sat up in bed and I could feel her looking at me. "You were so awesome tonight. You took care of everything."

I shrugged but felt pleased. And relieved.

"I won't tell anyone," Leela said. "Not even my mother if you don't want me to."

"You can tell your mom," I said. "But, please, no one else."

She nodded.

Afterward, Leela started coming to my house more often.

She made sure I always had a way to and from every school play, every school dance, and every birthday party. Leela always, *always* made sure I was okay.

Now I would do the same for her.

There's already a train waiting for us since this is the first stop on the Piccadilly Line. I sit. The seats are plush and fuzzy, which seems like the wrong choice. What happens if someone spills something on them? Like an Americano, perhaps? I hold my coffee tightly.

I can't believe I'm here. On a train in London. Holding a coffee. This is crazy. This is amazing. This is scary. What if I get us lost? I look down at the map in my *Travel Europe*.

"First stop, London, here we come!" I say, trying to sound brave.

"How many days are we staying here again?"

"Five nights," I say. "Then Paris."

"Is that enough time?"

"*Travel Europe* says so."

She laughs. "Well, if the guide says it, it must be true."

"Did I tell you there's a *Travel Europe* app too?"

"You did."

"Did you download it yet? It's only $2.99."

I know I'm doing most of the planning on this trip. But that doesn't mean I want to deal with *everything*.

"Haven't had a chance," she says. "An app makes more sense, though. That book looks heavy."

"I'm going to rip out the pages when we leave a place," I say. "To lighten it up."

"Smart," she says. "Speaking of leaving places, I'm glad you're not making me go to Amsterdam." She makes a face. Amsterdam had been the only must-see for Matt. Since *Travel Europe* spent a lot of pages describing how the city is famous for sex tourism and drugs, I could see why Leela had been concerned that he'd been a little too excited about the place.

"We have a packed schedule without Amsterdam," I say. I flip through all the countries. "There's so much to see and do."

"Maybe we should make up our own guide," Leela says. "*The American Girls' Guide to Traveling Around Europe While Avoiding Your Ex*."

"Maybe just the *Girls' Guide to Europe*. Snappier."

"Definitely," Leela says. "Where are we getting off again?"

"Covent Garden," I say.

She looks out the train window. "And you know where we're going?" Leela asks.

"Yes," I say, but my voice shakes. I look down at the map in my book. "Maybe. I guess we'll find out."

When we get out of the train, the line for the lift is really long—and there are no escalators.

"Let's just take the stairs," I say. "We've been sitting forever."

"But you're wearing a backpack."

"It's not that heavy," I say. The band around the waist really works. It's pretty smart engineering. "And the line is insane. Is one of the elevators broken? By the time it's our turn, our four and a half weeks will be up. How many flights of stairs can there be, anyway? How deep underground are we?"

It turns out we are very deep underground. After four flights, my heart is pounding. "I bet you're not so sad about your missing luggage now," I pant.

"You'd bet right," she says cheerfully.

"You're so not borrowing my underwear."

"If we ever get out of here alive, I will buy my own underwear. But can I use your deodorant?"

"No. That's disgusting. Also there might not be any left by the time we see sunlight. I think I'm going to have to reapply any second."

"Please let me help you with your bag," she says.

My heart is racing, and I think I might throw up. "Okay," I say.

She takes the back and I take the front. Up. Up. Up. A kid around thirteen passes us and gives me a dirty look.

"I bet Matt took a cab. You have no idea. His parents pay for everything. Bullshit he couldn't get a new flight. He better not be at our hostel. He probably won't be. I'm sure he got something fancy and not a room without its own bathroom. What do you want to do first?"

"Can't talk," I huff. "Climbing." Am I going to pass out? I'm beginning to see spots. I'm not going to faint, am I?

"How much farther do you think it is?" I ask Leela.

"No idea," she says.

Another person pushes past us. "Excuse me?" I ask. "Do you know how many flights are left?"

"You're almost halfway," he says.

My chest hurts. Suddenly the staircase starts to feel even smaller. What is wrong with me?

Oh, no.

Is this a panic attack?

No, no, no.

I am not having a panic attack. I am not. This is not a panic attack. This is just what it feels like to be out of shape and climbing a million stairs while carrying a massive back-pack.

Spots crawl across my vision. "I don't think I can do this," I admit.

"Do you want to go back down?" she asks.

"Maybe," I say. "Will you hate me?"

"I could never hate you," she says. "And this weighs a ton."

We return down the stairs and join the now even longer line for the lift.

"Sorry about that," I huff. My breaths are still coming fast. But that was not a panic attack. I've seen panic attacks and that was *not* one. That was just an insane amount of stairs.

"No worries, I was getting tired, too." She shakes her head. "I can't believe he came with Jackson."

"So what's the deal with Jackson?" I ask, picturing him in my mind and enjoying the image.

"He's not my favorite of Matt's friends."

Oh. Boo. "He was very hot, though."

"Yes. He's also a bad influence."

"What do you mean?"

She rolls her eyes. "He's kind of a man whore. We were all in the same residence, right? During Frosh I counted the number of girls that came out of his room. Are you ready? Nine. Nine! Frosh was less than a week! And they came out with their shirts on inside out or their hair all messed up, with dopey smiles on their faces. And he just got worse over the year. Plus he was with Matt when he kissed Ava. I bet he was pushing Matt toward her, telling him that she was flirting with him, that he couldn't spend the whole month depressed about me. Jackson is not a big believer in relationships. I'm sure he'll try to get Matt to sleep with every girl he meets across the continent."

"He sounds charming," I say, pushing the image of Mr. Hotness out of my mind. I do not lust after man whores, no matter how good-looking they are.

Another lift fills and closes, and we move up. Still not our turn, though. It's so dark in here. What happens in a power failure?

"Oh! One night he hooked up with two roommates!"

"Gross. Did they know?"

"Yes! Sorry, was that not clear? He hooked up with them

47

together. They didn't even like each other. But they both liked him and . . ." Her voice trails off and she shakes her head. "I can't believe that's who Matt's traveling with."

Finally, the elevator doors open, and it's our turn. We step in with about ten other people, and I end up all the way in the back.

It's feeling a little crowded in here. I still haven't gotten my breath fully back from the stairs. How long is this going to take?

"They're not even that good friends," Leela continues. "And Matt's always trying to impress him. He drinks more when Jackson's around, smokes more. And then he's a mess. It's horrible. And embarrassing."

The doors open, and I can see light. Hurrah! I readjust the backpack and step outside.

"Oh no," Leela says. "It's pouring!"

At this point, I don't care if there's a blizzard. I push my way outside and take a huge, glorious breath of wet London air.

"'Allo, London!" I cry. "It's more of a mist."

I try to take it all in at once. There are tourists looking around and businessmen and women in suits and younger men in tight jeans and women in ballet flats.

It smells like exhaust fumes and rain.

The cars are like regular cars, but fatter and shorter. Smushed. And the cabs are all black.

"Look! It's a double-decker bus!" I say, pointing ahead.

48

It really is a double-decker bus. Just like in the movies.

"And there's a red phone booth!" Leela says. "I guess they still use phone booths here?"

"Maybe they just keep them because they're so cute."

"Take a picture of me in it!" Leela cries, tossing me her phone. She squeezes inside, and picks up the pay phone. "Omigod, it stinks in here."

"Smile!"

She smiles.

Snap.

"I'm captioning it 'London's Calling,'" she says. "Clever, huh? Huh?"

"Very clever," I say.

"Do you know which way our hostel is?" Leela asks.

"Um, no," I say. "I put my book in my backpack. Can you check your phone? You have 3G over here, right? Or whatever they call it in London?"

"Oh, right! Let me use Google Maps. Thank God I didn't pack my phone in my luggage."

"Why would anyone pack their phone in their luggage?"

"I'm sure some people do. Okay, here we go. What's the name of the hostel again?"

"It's called Zuhause." It's five minutes from Covent Garden, which I read was a great location. And we have our own room. Not our own bathroom, but our own room. And they had a web special so I got it for only thirty pounds a night, which is fifteen pounds each, which is like twenty-five dollars.

"Oh. Right. Z-o-o house? Like it's a zoo?"

"No. It's German for . . . I don't remember."

"So how do you spell it?"

"I don't know. You have the phone." I try not to sound irritated.

"Don't get cranky. I'll find out." She spends a few more seconds typing on her iPhone. "It's this way," she says, pointing across the street.

"Okay, let's go," I say.

"Should we stop so I can get some stuff?"

"Can we just check in first? My back is feeling numb."

"Let's cross," Leela says. She looks left and takes a step into the street.

A black cab goes zooming by her from the other side.

"Look right!" I yell as she jumps back. "You have to look right! They drive on the other side of the street here!"

"That was crazy," she says. She points down. "Hey! It says it right there!"

Indeed, painted on the paved road it says "Look Right" in white.

"Look right," she repeats, and we do.

We walk into a bar.

"Are you sure this is it?" she asks, scanning the room. There are a few groups of travelers eating runny eggs. Flags from different countries line the wall.

I drop my backpack on the ground with an "AHHH" and

march up to the desk. "Hi," I say with extra cheer. "We're checking in."

"Check-in is at foh," the not-so-helpful, pink-haired twentysomething at the registration desk tells us.

Foh? "Four?"

She nods.

"But it's only ten," I say.

She nods again. "Right."

"What are we supposed to do for six hours?" I ask. My cheer has disappeared. I'm tired. And wet. I need a shower.

"Dunno."

"Will you text us if our room becomes available early?"

"Sure," she says.

"Give her your cell," I instruct Leela.

The woman pretends to write it down. I don't think we're going to be hearing from her.

"I'm too tired to walk around," I say. My eyes are heavy. I'm starting to get dizzy. I need sleep. My body is confused.

"I have to get stuff anyway," Leela says. "Who knows when my bag is coming."

"All right," I say. I turn back to the woman at the desk. "Can I leave my bag here?"

"You could, but it might be safest in your room."

"But I don't have a room yet."

She nods. "Right. Should be fine. Might be fine. I don't know."

"Just leave it," Leela says. "It's locked, right?"

51

"Yeah." But I don't want to lose mine, too. "I guess I can take it with me. We won't go too far."

"Can we eat?" Leela asks. She turns back to the woman at the desk. "Can you recommend a place for brunch?"

She looks at us blankly. "Brunch? No. But you can eat here."

"I don't think I want to eat here," Leela says under her breath. "Any place else? What's really good?"

"Freya's is all right, and it's just down the road," she says.

"And what about shopping? I need shampoo and stuff. My luggage got left in America."

"There's a Boots on King's Road," she says. "And an Haiche-an-em."

"What?" I ask.

"Haiche-an-em," she repeats.

"H&M?" Leela asks.

She looks at us like we're morons. "Yeah. Off you go."

Okay. I think we were dismissed. "We need to find an ATM too," I tell Leela. "I only have twenty pounds."

"Let's just eat and then figure it out. I'm starving."

At the restaurant, we both order porridge because we think it sounds British, and coffees, which arrive in super tiny cups and are so not going to do the trick.

"Can I have another one of these, please?" I ask our waiter. "Thanks."

"Should we call our parents?" Leela asks.

52

"It's like five in the morning at home," I say.

"My dad told me to call as soon as I could," she says. "I don't want him to wake up and get nervous that my plane crashed."

"Go ahead," I say. "I'm afraid to look at my phone." I'm going to have to figure out what to do about my data plan, but I'm too tired to deal with it right now. I am worried about my family, but they're asleep now anyway.

I relax into the chair as she dials.

"Dad! It's me. I'm here. No, I'm fine. But they lost my luggage. They're not sure. Really? Are you sure? How much? Yes, I have it. I'll let you know. Love you."

She hangs up the phone. She's smiling.

"What?" I ask.

"The credit card we got the ticket on has baggage insurance. I can spend five hundred bucks on new things."

"Really?"

"Yes!"

"Then let's go spend some pounds."

"Look at these!" she cries in Boots. She waves a lipstick at me. "British makeup!"

"It looks a lot like American makeup," I say.

"Omigod, they have Nails inc. And the nail polish is only seven pounds. Do you know how much it costs at Sephora? UK makeup shopping spree!" she cheers, admiring a bright red lipstick. "This is like the best thing that has ever happened to me."

"Shouldn't you buy some clothes too?" I ask. "In case you don't actually get your luggage?"

"I guess," she says. "But look at this NYX Soft Matte lipstick. I can't resist it. My lips are going to look so soft! So matte!"

"Maybe you should also buy some pajamas. And a pair of shorts and a T-shirt. And a bathing suit? Maybe some flip-flops? Or a sweatshirt? It's chilly."

"Okay, fine," she says. "But let me treat you to a lipstick. Or a nail polish? Something?"

"How about an umbrella?"

"Done," she says. "Let's go get cute matching ones."

I let her buy me a yellow umbrella since the mist outside has turned into a downpour. What if it rains the whole time? What if I've spent all my money and deserted my family and I'm miserable the entire four and a half weeks?

No. That's not going to happen. And my family is fine. Hopefully. I should check on them. No, I can't. It's five hours earlier at home so they're probably still sleeping.

"Let's take a selfie with our umbrellas," she says on the street corner.

I stand beside her, and she lifts up her phone. "Smile," she says.

I smile.

She studies the pic. "You're smiling with your lips, but not with your eyes."

"My eyes are tired," I whine. "So very tired."

"One more," she says, and puts us back in position. Snap. Snap. Snap, snap, snap. "Oh! Look! So cute! So London! I got the umbrellas and the rain and everything. I'm adding the London geofilter. You look adorable."

"Yay," I say, although I suspect my voice lacks conviction. "Any texts from the hostel?"

"Nope," she says. She doesn't seem so bothered. The shopping spree has reenergized her.

At three that afternoon, still roomless, I decide I can finally call home. "Can I borrow your phone?"

"Sure," she says, and hands it to me. "Just dial regularly."

I type 1 and then my home phone number.

It rings. Once.

"Hello?" my sister barks.

"Hi! It's me."

"Thanks for answering all my texts," my sister says.

"I'm sorry, I couldn't. I'm roaming. I'm using Leela's phone. How's Mom?"

"Upstairs. Working."

"But is she . . . okay?"

"She's fine."

I let out a breath I didn't know I was holding. "Good. Is it your day off?"

"Yes."

"Great. Did you find the car keys?"

"No."

"Did you check the right drawer in the kitchen?"

Pause. "Oh. Yeah. Here they are."

"Good. Did you take Mom out yesterday?"

"Yes, I took her out."

"Great," I say. "Can I talk to her?"

"I don't want to go upstairs," she says. "Can you call later?"

"Okay," I say.

"Are you having fun?"

"Yeah! Well, I just got here, right?"

"Where are you?"

"In London. Our room isn't ready yet," I say. "But Leela lost her luggage and got a credit from AmEx so she gets to spend five hundred bucks."

"Ask her if she wants anything," Leela says.

"Do you want anything?" I ask, my voice suddenly hoarse.

"A snow globe?" Addison asks.

I laugh. She used to be obsessed with snow globes. Our dad brought them home for us when he traveled around the country for business. "I'll get you a London snow globe," I say. "No, I will get you a snow globe from every city we visit."

"That's a lot of snow globes," she says.

"I love you *that* much," I say. "And I feel incredibly guilty for leaving you with Mom."

"It's fine! We'll be fine!"

I bite my lip. "Okay. Good. Love you."

She ends the call.

I stare at the phone before giving it back, feeling lost. I can't believe I really left them. My sister is only sixteen! What happens if there's an emergency? And instead of being there, I'm cold and wet and on the other side of the ocean? What am I doing here?

I need to lie down. "Let's go check in," I say.

"You think our room is ready?"

"It better be."

By the time we get back to the hostel, I am wiped. Wiped and wet. My bag is wet too. Which means all my clothes are wet.

Also our room is on the third floor. I no longer have feeling in my shoulders or back.

The clerk types our key code—649—into the lock and motions us in.

The room is tiny. There is a single bed against each yellow wall, and a green dresser, a wooden chair, and a tall white fan beside a window. At least the white sheets and pillowcases look clean and bleached. A white towel is folded neatly on the bed. I brought two of my own, one shower and one beach, but I guess it makes sense to use the ones they provide when they provide them. Less laundry. Where are we doing our laundry anyway? I don't know how to do my own laundry. One advantage to having a mother who doesn't like to go out is that she spends a lot of time doing laundry.

The wooden window frame has blue curtains and over-looks an alleyway.

"Enjoy," the woman says, and closes the door behind her.

"I need to nap," I say.

"Aren't we supposed to stay up as late as possible tonight? To get adjusted?"

"I don't think I'll make it," I say. "Quick nap. Set your phone alarm for five p.m. London time."

Leela lets out a big yawn. "'Kay."

I pull the curtains closed and plop down on the bed and everything goes dark.

"Syd, wake up!" Leela says. "It's eight-fifteen. We have to eat dinner."

"Mmmmmn," I murmur, my head stuffed with cotton. I sit up, my head pounding. Where am I? Who am I? What day is it?

She opens the curtains to darkness. I hear laughter from the room next to us. A group of girls, I think. I try to make out some words. "*Ristorante . . . birra . . . sesso . . .*" Italian, maybe?

"I'm going to shower," Leela says. "Then you're getting up for reals."

I pull the sheet over my head and fall back asleep.

"Your turn," she says twenty-five minutes later.

"Mmm," I say.

58

"Come on, come on," she says. "I'm starving. Let's go get some fish and chips."

"How's the shower?" I ask.

"Not my best shower. Also, I may have used all the hot water. Sorry."

"Great."

"I'm kidding. There wasn't any hot water to begin with. Come on. Wear your flip-flops. It's slimy in there."

"Going, going," I say. I get out of bed, even though my limbs feel numb.

I unzip my bag and find my toiletries, and my flip-flops, and wrap my towel around my body.

The shower is three doors down and small. It takes me a few seconds to figure out how to get the water to work, but then it does and it's effing freezing.

Tip: When in London you must have the fish and chips.

Chips are french fries, by the way. And please, for the love of Prince Harry, don't be a tourist and ask for ketchup.

"To us," Leela says, lifting a glass of chardonnay. She only drinks white wine. Red wine stains her teeth, beer burns her mouth, and other drinks, she claims, are gross.

"To the drinking age being eighteen!" I say back. I'm drinking a cocktail called a Pimm's. It's orangey-brown and tastes fruity and sweet. *Travel Europe* recommended it.

Travel Europe also recommended this pub, The Royal Swan, for fish and chips, so here we are. We're sitting at one of the outside tables. The one-page menu is sticky and covered in plastic, but the food is supposed to be good. We order a plate of fish and chips to share. The fries are pretty amazing. The fish . . . well, they are not frozen fish sticks. More like huge slabs of whitefish fried and then fried some more, and then even more, and one more time for good luck.

"So what are we doing tomorrow?" Leela asks.

"I don't know. What do you want to do?"

"Everything," she says.

"Let's see. We definitely want to go to Buckingham Palace."

"And we have to go for tea," Leela says. "At the place my parents got engaged."

I hesitate. "Are you sure?"

"Yes. Absolutely."

"But . . . well, you're not expecting Matt to show up, right?"

"I'm not. Well, a teeny little part of me is, but the rational part of me isn't. I swear."

"Maybe we should skip tea?"

"No. I want to go. It's part of my story. Screw Matt."

"Okay, then. We're going to Selfridges," I say.

"What's Selfridges?"

"Isn't that the tea place where your parents got engaged?" I take another bite of the over-fried fish.

"No. I think that's a department store. They got engaged at Claridge's."

"Oh. Sorry. Never mind. Got them confused. To Claridge's! And maybe tomorrow we should start with the Red Bus tour, so we'll get the lay of the land."

"Sounds good. We'll wake up early and hit the road," she says. She picks up a chip, aka a french fry. "I really need ketchup."

"Don't be a tourist," I say. "You're supposed to eat them with salt and vinegar."

She waves around her. "We're surrounded by tourists. This restaurant is for tourists. This whole area is for tourists."

"Fair point," I say.

She waves the waitress over. "Can I have some ketchup, please?"

I sprinkle the vinegar over the fries and take another bite. "It's really not bad. Not good. But not terrible."

Back at the hostel, I spend an hour on hold trying to get through to my phone company. Eventually, I discover that my options are ten bucks per day for unlimited everything or forty bucks per month for a hundred texts and hardly any data. Ten bucks per day is over three hundred dollars. And I'm guessing I would blow through the one hundred texts in about five minutes. They suggest I put it in airplane mode and rely on finding free Wi-Fi, so I can still FaceTime, send iMessages and emails, and use my apps. Luckily the hostel has Wi-Fi. Unluckily, I am once again flooded with messages from Addison:

Are you really gone for five weeks?

Where's the AAA card?

Never mind I found it.

Mom said she's not feeling well and doesn't want to go out.

I write back:

Four and a half weeks!

Great.

Fine today but insist tomorrow, k?

I log in to Gmail.

Nothing from my mom, but a short email from my dad.

All OK? How was your flight? I'm so proud of you. Have a great trip. Love, Dad.

I write him back, telling him I'm fine and thanking him again for the points. Then I type a quick note to my mom telling her I love her and that I hope she feels better tomorrow.

I hope I feel better tomorrow, too. Right now my body feels like I've gotten off a seven-hour ride on a Tilt-A-Whirl.

"Come with me to get ready for bed?" Leela asks.

I turn off my phone and follow her to the bathroom.

"Oops," I say when I finally open my eyes. It's two p.m.

It took us forever to fall asleep. Partly because of our massive nap, partly because I was worrying about my mom and sister, partly because of the time difference, and partly because the people in the next room were up all night partying. Part of me wanted to knock on their door and tell them to be quiet; part of me wanted to knock on their door and ask if we could join. They were clearly having a much better time than we were.

"We have to get up," I say, stepping onto the cold, hard floor. "Red Bus tour, here we come."

"I think we're too late," she says. "We need a full day on it, no?"

"So what should we do?" I ask.

"Eat something?"

I smile. "Fish and chips?"

She groans. "Please no."

We take turns showering and head downstairs.

I see a group of girls sitting in the corner, and hear some Italian.

"That's them," I say. "The girls from 3B."

"I hate them," Leela says. "They kept me up all night."

"Do we hate them?" I ask. "Or do we want to be friends with them? I can't decide."

"It's a tough call," Leela agrees.

"I'm going to say hello," I say.

"You are?" she says, shocked.

"Yes."

"That's so unlike you," she says.

"It's the new me," I say. Leela and I stayed pretty much to ourselves growing up. We had other friends, but were never exactly outgoing. "I had to talk to strangers when you left for school, you know."

I stand up and walk over to their table. "Hi there," I say. "Where are you guys from?"

They look up and stare.

"*Roma*," one of them says.

"Oh, cool," I say. "We're going to Rome. We can't wait. How long are you in London for?"

"A week," one says. Then she turns back to her friend and starts speaking in Italian again.

I stand there for a few minutes waiting to be included or spoken to. But it doesn't happen. My face burns. All right. At least I tried.

I turn around and head back to Leela.

Leela pats my shoulder. "Bitches," she mutters. "Who needs them? Let's get out of here and get some goddamn tea."

"This place looks fancy," I say. "I thought going for tea was like going for Starbucks?"

"Guess not," Leela says nervously.

"I hope we're dressed okay." I'm wearing my jeans and a white T-shirt. Leela is wearing a black sundress and pair of sandals she bought at Haiche-an-em.

It's our turn at the hostess's table.

"Hi," I say. "Can we have a table for two, please?"

"Do you have a reservation?" the woman asks. She looks over my jeans and running shoes.

"No," I say. "Do I need one?"

"Yes," she says. "We're booked for today. Perhaps next week?"

"We'll be gone by next week," Leela says. "Please? Is there any way you could squeeze us in? Please?"

"I don't think so."

"We're leaving in a few days, and my parents got engaged here. I didn't know we had to make a reservation. Maybe if someone cancels? Don't you ever have no-shows?"

"Well . . . There was a cancellation . . ." She looks down at her list, then looks up at us and winks. "I believe I can squeeze you in."

Forty-five minutes later we have a table.

"This is fantastic," Leela says, admiring the crystal chandeliers, high ceilings, and white tablecloths. "Is this not the most beautiful place you've ever seen? Let's take a picture."

The dishes are all striped white and green. My mother would love them.

Leela takes a selfie of us looking at the menus.

Omigod, I think, the prices registering. This is nothing like Starbucks. "Leela. This place is a fortune. This is like my whole sixty bucks in one day."

"I guess we're not getting the champagne?"

"No! Although I kind of want the champagne. You drink champagne?"

"Of course. It's white wine, isn't it? So we are getting the champagne?"

"No. We're not. Don't be crazy."

"At least it's already four. This is like our breakfast, lunch, and dinner."

"It has to be, for this price," I grumble. "There better be a lot of food. I love you, but we can't spend fifty-nine pounds on tea. That's like ninety bucks. That's insane. Is the tea made of gold?"

"It's not just tea. It's tea sandwiches too. And look! Scones!"

The scones do look delicious. But come on. Fifty-nine pounds?

"Leela, I'll stay if you want me to, but . . ."

She sighs and looks around. "He's really not coming?"

"No," I say.

She sinks into her chair, defeated.

"Screw it," I say. "Let's do it. What's fifty-nine pounds in the grand scheme of things?"

She smiles, and I can see her dimples.

We order the traditional afternoon tea.

It comes in stages.

First come the mini-sandwiches. Omigod. So yummy looking. There are ten of them, spread out on a green-and-white striped plate. Two smoked salmon, two ham, two chicken, two egg, and two cucumber. All are crustless and cut into tiny rectangles.

"Let's take a picture," Leela says, taking out her phone. "Smile!"

Snap, snap.

"Posting it," she says.

We eat them all. I leave the ham ones for Leela since I don't eat ham. I'm not kosher or anything, but there are certain rules I follow. Bacon yes, ham no. Cheeseburgers yes, burgers with a glass of milk, no. I didn't go to Hebrew school every Sunday for nothing.

Next come the scones.

"Smile!"

Snap, snap.

I spread clotted cream and strawberry jam onto a hot scone. Mmm. I spoon more jam on my bread and take a bite.

A blob of jam drops on my thigh.

I take out my napkin and try to rub at the spot, making it worse.

"It'll come out in the wash," Leela says.

"But it's only day two. And I only packed one pair of jeans. And I'm not sure where we even do our wash."

"I'm sure your friend Kat has a washing machine," Leela says.

"She probably does," I say.

Leela takes a long sip of tea. "How nice is this apartment going to be?"

"Nice," I say.

On the first day of my History of Western Civilization class at the University of Maryland, Katherine Malone sat down next to me and said, "Hey! You're in my Intro to Sociology class too, right?"

I nodded. Kat had stick-straight light brown hair with

blond highlights, pale skin, and light blue eyes. She wore ripped, expensive jeans, diamond stud earrings, and chunky necklaces. She grew up on the Upper East Side in New York City and went to the all-girls school Chapin. All her friends went to UPenn. She hadn't gotten in. Kat bought expensive Jacques Torres chocolates and liked to share.

Kat took terrible notes and talked to everybody. She was in three of my classes and pretty much adopted me.

I hung out in her dorm between classes and went to parties with her at night.

I'd even crash at her place once in a while, but I always went home as soon as I could to make sure everyone was okay. I never told Kat why I was going home. I liked keeping College Me separate from Home Me.

"So what are you doing this summer?" she'd asked as we lay on her dorm bed eating Jacques Torres and studying for finals.

"Working at Books in Wonderland," I said. Since it was only three blocks from my house, I had spent a lot of time there as a kid and had started working whenever they were short staffed—partly for the extra money and partly for the 40 percent employee discount.

"No vacation?"

"Not this year," I said, popping another chocolate into my mouth. Mmm. Orange cream. "You?"

"I'm interning at some gallery in Paris."

"Really?" I asked, almost dropping the chocolate.

"Yup. A friend of my mom's friend owns it, so off I go!"

Kat's mom is a fancy interior designer. Her dad runs a hedge fund. According to a mutual friend, their apartment is an entire floor of a doorman building on Park Avenue.

"Lucky," I said. A pit of jealousy grew in my stomach.

"You should come visit. I have an apartment right near the Latin Quarter—for June, July, and half of August. You can totally stay with me."

"Maybe," I said, the pit getting bigger. I knew I wouldn't. But now I actually would.

"She's so *nice* for letting us stay at her place," Leela says now, but her tone is weird. Her tone is always weird when she mentions Kat. Fake pleasant. "How's your friend, Kat?" she asks, like my mom asking about one of my dad's new girlfriends. But what did she expect? That she'd go away to school, and I would hole myself up in my house for four years? And anyway, I liked who I was when I was with Kat. I met new people. I went to parties. I broke out of my shell.

By the time we are on our second pot of tea, I am stuffed and wired.

"Where to next?" Leela asks.

"Why don't we walk around? I need to find an ATM to take out more pounds. Then we can head to Soho for a drink?"

"Let's do it," she says, and I try not to cringe as we pay the bill.

★ ★ ★

I stand at the machine, debating how much money to take out. My bank charges a fee for me to withdraw money, so in theory I should take out a lot. But I don't want to have that much cash on me in case something happens, since hostels aren't the safest places. Also, I don't want to get left with too many pounds when we go to Paris, since they use the euro. Hmm.

"You okay?" Leela asks.

"Yup. One sec." I decide to take out two hundred pounds. I'm left with only eighteen hundred dollars in my account. That was fast.

We spend the next few hours walking around Soho. Leela buys another lipstick, another sundress, shorts, two tank tops, and a sleep shirt that has the London Underground logo on it. She is clearly warming up to the idea of buying new clothes.

We walk into shops, try on necklaces, and take more pictures outside of red phone booths.

"Look at the two of us," I say. "Women of the world! Travelers! We're going to have adventures!"

She checks her phone. "One hundred and seventy-five likes for the scones. Pretty much everyone I know except Matt. He hasn't posted a single picture. Where do you think he is?"

"I don't know. Maybe he's at Selfridges." I smile.

"Ha! He's probably at a pub."

I picture Jackson sitting on a stool, nursing his beer,

70

looking around the room for a cute girl. Seeing me. Smiling.

Leela sighs. "Did I ever tell you that he's missing one of his pectoral muscles?"

"Huh? Jackson?"

"No, Matt. He's missing his left pectoral muscle. He was born without it."

"Does it look weird?"

"Not at all," she says. "You can barely notice. But he's so self-conscious about it. He never works out because he thinks if the other one gets big it will be more obvious. But you know what? It's my favorite part of him. It fits my head perfectly. He's the best cuddler." She sighs again. "I miss him."

"I know, sweetie." I put my arm around her.

We pass a small restaurant called Meredith's Tea Shoppe. The menu says they have high tea for twelve pounds.

"Next time we eat there," I say.

"Deal."

I feel a drop of water on my forehead.

"Oh no," she says. "I forgot my umbrella!"

"I have mine," I say, and pull it out.

"I have a great idea for a picture. Open the umbrella and stand like Mary Poppins."

"No," I say.

"Fine, then I'll do it," she says.

Snap. Post.

She looks. "I need to reapply my lipstick."

71

I have five new messages from Addison when I get back to the hostel.

OMG I had to take her to the post office today and stand with her the entire time.

It was ridiculous.

You do that?

For someone who doesn't drive she is the worst back seat driver ever. She freaked out when I went through a yellow light.

She's making me crazy.

I write back to Addison:

Yes, I take her to the post office and I stand with her.

She's not a back seat driver with me.

But you just got your license.

Only four weeks and one day left!

I resist pointing out that I handled Mom's issues for the last seven years, and she never heard *me* complain.

I also get an email from my mom telling me that I should have fun and that everything is fine. I don't believe her. I keep seeing her ghostly face as I left the house. I hope she's not going to get worse. I'm not sure she can get worse.

I reply to my mom's email and send some of the photos I took during the day. I wish I could message her, but my mom doesn't even have a cell anymore. What's the point since she hardly ever leaves the house?

★ ★ ★

The next day, amazingly, we make it to the Red Bus tour by nine a.m. The bus is two levels, red, and filled with backpackers and grumpy children with overeager parents. We start off on the roofless top level. It's cloudy but warm. You can get off at any of the stops, walk around, and then get back on when you're ready and the next one pulls up. Kind of like a real bus, except these have live guides. Ours is a blond British lady named Bryony, who sounds like she reads a lot of *Us Weekly* magazines. Or whatever they call it in England. *UK Weekly?*

"This is where Duchess Catherine had her hen party!" she tells us.

"Ooooh," everyone swoons.

"Thomas Crapper lived here! He invented the loo!"

"I think that's a myth," Leela says.

"But it would explain why the toilets in London are so cool. Who needs to see the tank? Not us."

"This is where the Queen buys her knickers!" Bryony tells us a few stops later.

"Can you imagine?" I say. "Now the bus is passing Target, where Sydney Rothstein buys her days of the week undies."

"You do not wear days of the week undies," Leela says.

"No," I say. "But I bought them for my sister as a joke. Mondays are blue."

"Obviously."

"I do have polka-dot undies, though. I brought them. They're super cute."

A raindrop falls on my guidebook.

"Bloody hell," I say.

We hop off at 11:20, ten minutes before the Changing of the Guard is supposed to begin.

Luckily the rain has stopped.

We make our way down the road and toward the crowds and the palace. "Do you think the boys are here?" Leela asks.

We look around. There are a million people here. "I doubt we'd find them even if they were." I wouldn't mind seeing Jackson, to be honest. I wouldn't sleep with him, but I wouldn't mind flirting a little.

"Oh, I can find Matt anywhere. I have perfect Matt-dar. I used to be able to spot him across campus in a group of a thousand. I'm like Edward sniffing out Bella. I'm a vampire. I can smell him in any room."

"Maybe that's what the guards change into," I say. "Vampires. Get it? The changing of the guards?"

"Come on, Sydney. It's daylight! Don't be ridiculous. Maybe if the changing of the guards were at night, you'd be on to something."

"It's actually just the guards changing shifts. If you're wondering. Thank you, *Travel Europe*."

She pauses. "I wish Matt was posting pictures. Why isn't he posting? It's annoying. Wait! I hear something, I hear something!"

Off to the left we see men on black horses. They are wearing red uniforms and strange-looking red helmets.

Then from the other side men in red are marching toward us playing instruments. They're wearing tall black furry hats and remind me of the witch's guards from *The Wizard of Oz*.

We cross the street and try to get as near as possible to the black iron gates. It seems like something is happening inside. But there are too many people in front of us to see anything. We are all very pressed together.

"If I were a pickpocket," I say, "this is where I would come."

Everyone around us has selfie sticks.

"Should I get one of those?" Leela asks.

"Please don't." I pull out my phone to take pictures and hate that I'm not getting messages. Is my mother okay? What if something horrible really does happen? Would I actually go home? Yes. I promised I would.

"Do you think the guards have changed yet?"

We get up on our tiptoes to try to see. I spot a sleeve of red. I lift my phone, snap a picture, and hope for the best.

We hop back on the bus and get off again at Mayfair, right by Green Park, to find an emergency bathroom.

"The bus bumping along is not helping," Leela says. "My bladder is going to explode. Should we just go into a café?"

"Let's go into a hotel," I say. "Look, there's the Ritz!"

"You want to just walk into the Ritz to use the bathroom? They're not going to let us."

"Yes, they will," I say.

"We look like tourists."

"Who do you think stays at the Ritz? Locals? It's not like I have my backpack on me. Just walk in like you have a room. Let's go."

"When did you get this brave?" she asks, and follows me in.

"Hello," I say to the doorman.

"G'day," he says back.

We giggle as we follow the sign to the restroom, pardon me, to the *loo*, down a floor.

We giggle more as we open the door. It's all pink. Pink wallpaper, pink sinks, pink floors. Pink everything.

"This is amazing," she says. "It's like the Barbie dream house bathroom. Why doesn't my bathroom look like this?"

Twenty minutes later—we take our sweet time—we get back on the bus.

"From now on, we only use the bathroom at the Ritz," she says.

"Deal. I wonder if they have a shower?"

After a full day of hopping on and hopping off, we end up at an Indian restaurant called Dishoom. The design is retro—checkered floors, posters from the fifties on the wall, marble tables. It reminds me of an über-hip diner. We order chili cheese toast to start, crunchy *far far* to snack on, and lamb chops to share as our main. Everything is amazing. Leela's family cooks Indian food sometimes, but mostly rice, daal, and chana masala.

"Mmm," Leela says, savoring each bite. "Tomorrow we can go for bagels."

"Deal," I say.

"What else are we doing tomorrow?" she asks.

"Tate Modern, then the Harry Potter platform, then *Romeo and Juliet* at the Globe, then the Eye."

"*Romeo and Juliet?*" She wrinkles her nose. "I don't trust that Romeo."

"Who does?" I ask, eating another bite of lamb.

"Okay, fine," she says. "I'll see it."

"Good. Cause I already bought the tickets."

"You are *so* organized."

"Someone has to be." She hasn't exactly offered to help with any of the planning yet.

Leela looks embarrassed. "So is the Eye the Ferris wheel?"

"More of a cable car. But yes. *Travel Europe* says it has the best view in London and that we should go at night. It closes at 9:30, though, so we need to get there before then."

"Sounds like a plan," she says. "Dishoom selfie?"

After, we go to a pub in Soho called the Mad Dog and the Drunken Chicken.

Since the stools that line the bar and the booths on the other side of the pub are taken, I squeeze beside a girl and order myself a Pimm's and a glass of chardonnay for Leela.

Once our drinks arrive, we stand together and watch people talk to each other.

"I'd jump in," I say, "but I'm scarred from my attempted convo with the Italians."

There's a television in the corner blasting a soccer game. Red versus blue. A group of guys cheer as someone in blue makes a goal. They look around our age, but they're wearing suits and white shirts. One has a goatee.

"Matt likes soccer," Leela says. "I used to watch games with him."

I nod as she continues to talk about Matt and his love of Toronto FC. I want to be sensitive. I really do. But if she's going to spend the next four weeks mourning her relationship, I may have to put the earplugs in.

". . . I just can't believe he's in the same city as I am, and I don't know where he is. I hate that. It's driving me crazy. Maybe you should friend Jackson to see where they are? His account is private."

"If you want me to," I say lightly. Then I could look at pictures of him and see if he really is as good-looking as I remember. I take another sip. My head is starting to buzz.

"Never mind," she says. "Too obvious." She looks back at her phone. "Hey! It's the fourth of July today! Everyone is posting barbecue pictures! How did we miss that?"

"No one is celebrating America's independence *here*," I say. "Since, you know, these are the people we became independent from."

"Excellent point," she says.

The boys in suits cheer again. Then there's a commercial, and then one of them turns around and I see his eye stop on Leela.

My head is starting to feel a bit lighter. "Smile," I say. "You're being checked out."

"I am?" She stands up straighter.

"Yup. And do you know what will help you stop thinking about Matt?" I ask over the sound of the crowd.

"What?"

"A snog!"

She laughs. "You want me to kiss a random person?"

"Yes. I want you to kiss someone. Specifically, the *bloke* checking you out. Come on. Smile!"

She smiles. The guy raises his beer and jumps off his bar stool.

"Oh no," she says, panicked. "He's coming over. What do I do?"

I push her toward him. "You snog him."

"Oh God," she mumbles as he approaches us.

"You ladies fancy another round?" he asks in an adorable British accent.

"Yes," I say, finishing off the last of mine. That was *good*. "Thank you. I'm Sydney and this is Leela."

"I'm Charlie," he says. He's light-skinned, freckled, and on the short side. "Are you from America?"

"Guilty as charged," Leela says, batting her eyes. "Don't hold it against us."

"Not at all," he tells her. "I like Americans. You're so confident and obsessed with our accents. What's not to like?"

"We *are* obsessed with your accents," Leela admits. "Now say something else."

I'm so proud of her—she's talking to him! She's flirting!

"What can I get you to drink?" he asks, overemphasizing his consonants.

"Ohhh," she says.

"Are you visiting London for the summer?" he asks.

"No," I say. "Just traveling around Europe for a month. London is our first stop."

"Lucky us," he says.

"What about you?" I ask.

"I just finished uni and started working in the city," he says. "So let me spend my first paycheck and buy you ladies a drink. What can I get you?"

"I'll have another glass of chardonnay," Leela says. "Thank you."

"And I'll have another Pimm's," I tell him.

"Done," he says, but just then the game returns to the screen, and he snaps his head back to the television.

"Who's playing?" I ask him.

He doesn't answer. He just stares at the TV.

"Hello?" I say.

Leela taps me on the shoulder. "I think he's forgotten about us."

"He can't forget about us," I say. "He needs to snog you."

"I'm not sure I want to snog him," Leela whispers. "He's not even that cute."

"Leela," I say dramatically. "We are in Europe. We've been here for *three* days. We need an adventure. It's July fourth. We have to celebrate our independence!"

"We snuck into a bathroom today. Doesn't that count?" She yawns. "I'm actually getting tired. Can we go?"

"No," I say. "First snog, then go."

She shakes her head. "If you want a snog so badly, you do it."

"Fine," I say. "I will." I let the liquid courage rise up inside me and tap Charlie on the shoulder.

"Hmm?" he says, not even looking at us.

"Charlie, I need a favor," I say sweetly.

"What's that?" he asks distractedly.

"I need to snog you."

He finally tears his eyes away from the television. "Pardon me?"

"I need to have an adventure. And you are it. Would you mind?"

Leela's jaw is practically on the sticky floor.

Charlie's cheeks turn bright red. "I suppose not."

"Terrific. I'm leaning in." I can't believe I'm doing this. Am I really doing this? Yes. I am. I am going to have an adventure. My mother could have a meltdown at any moment and I might need to fly home. I need to have an adventure right *now*. I have to celebrate my independence! I lean toward him, close my eyes, and plant a huge *snog* right on his mouth.

His lips are kind of wet. And cold. And squishy. Suddenly he opens his mouth and slides his thin and sour-tasting tongue into my mouth, like a lizard.

Omigod, what am I doing? Who is this random guy with his gross tongue in my mouth?

I pull back and choke-laugh. "I think that's enough, thanks."

Charlie looks dazed. "You Yanks really are confident," he says. "How long did you say you were in London for? Can I see you again?"

"No," I say. "But it was nice to meet you. Take care."

Leela laughs as I pull her out of the pub. "Who *are* you?"

"I'm the mad dog," I say, my cheeks on fire. "Which makes you, my friend, the drunken *chicken*."

At two in the morning, we hear the Italians next door.

"What are they doing in there?" Leela asks. Then she laughs. "Did you really kiss that random guy at the pub?"

"Oh, go back to sleep," I say. I shove in my earplugs, and laugh into my pillow.

The first part of our day goes as planned. Better than planned. Leela's duffel arrives with all her things intact. It's sunny. We can't find bagels, but we do find buttery toast and jam and American coffees for cheap down the street. Then we take the Tube to the King's Cross station and find about a hundred people of all different ages and countries, waiting in line for Platform 9¾. After about ninety minutes, it's finally our turn.

"Admit you're excited," I say to Leela.

"I'm excited," she says.

"Choose your scarf," a woman in black pants, a red Harry Potter vest, and a black tie tells me. "What house do you belong to?"

"Ravenclaw," I say. The clever one.

The woman hands me the blue Ravenclaw scarf.

"You're also kind of a Hufflepuff, don't you think?" Leela asks. "Hardworking, loyal . . . Although last night you were a total Gryffindor. So brave."

"Maybe I'm Divergent," I say. I pose under the Platform 9¾ sign, point my wand, and smile for Leela's photo. This one I'm going to post.

Next we go to the Tate Modern, where many of the paintings look like my sister made them in elementary school, including one large canvas by the bathroom, which is blue. All blue.

"Seriously?" I say.

"You have no appreciation for abstract art," Leela says. She is mesmerized.

Afterward, it's time for the Globe Theater.

"Shakespeare and Harry Potter in one day?" I exclaim. "Best. Day. Ever."

"You're adorable," Leela says. She still reads books I

recommend once in a while, but she's not the bookworm she used to be.

I reserved us the groundling tickets because they're only five pounds each and right in front under the open roof. The only problem is that we have to stand the whole time and pray it doesn't rain. But still. Five pounds each!

After the play, which we both ended up loving, although we wished we had splurged on seats, we search for a nearby pub.

"Don't you want to go back to the Mad Dog and the Drunken Chicken to see your boyfriend?" Leela asks gleefully.

"No," I say. "I do not. But tonight it's your turn to snog, got it?"

"We'll see," she says.

We find a place called The Lion's Thorny Rose and sit down at a booth. We order two chicken pot pies, a side of chips (aka french fries), plus a Pimm's for me and a glass of wine for Leela.

"Why do British pubs all have animals in their names?" Leela asks.

"I don't know."

"Okay, last selfie," Leela says, reapplying her lipstick. "If he wants to see me again he'll come here. It's his last chance. He's leaving tomorrow."

I roll my eyes. "Are you kidding? Is that why you've been posting all these selfies? So he'll see where we are and come find you?"

"No." She cringes. "Maybe."

"But we're not waiting here all night, are we? I want to go to the Eye. And it closes at nine thirty. It's supposed to rain tomorrow so it's better to go today."

"I know you want to go on the Eye. But we have time, don't we? It's still light out. We want to see it in the dark, right?"

"Yes. And for the record, you're hopeless."

"Tell me something I don't know," she says and lets out an exaggerated sigh. "Now hand me the salt and vinegar. My chips aren't going to sprinkle themselves."

Thirty minutes later, the unthinkable happens.

Matt and Jackson walk through the door of the pub.

I see Jackson first, and all I think as my heart speeds up is, *Oh! It's him! Hot Jackson!*

Then I see Matt. Damn. Matt.

"Don't freak out," I say. "But it's him. Matt's here."

She looks simultaneously thrilled and panicked. "He is? Seriously? You're not taking the piss?"

"Great Briticism," I say. "But no, he's really here. He's looking around the bar."

She sits up straight. "Don't look. Be subtle. How's my lipstick?"

"So soft. So matte."

"Great. Is he with Jackson?"

"Yes." *Hellooooo, Jackson.* I try to remind myself that he might be hot but he's also a man whore. Those two should cancel each other out.

Her eyes are wide. "What do I do? Should I act surprised to see him?"

"Are you surprised to see him?"

"Yes. No. Yes. He's in London, why wouldn't he come to see me? He misses me. He knows he messed up. He's leaving tomorrow. He wasn't going to just leave the country without seeing me, was he? Without saying good-bye? Where are they now? Look quickly but don't give us away."

I glance sideways out of the corner of my eye.

"They're sitting at the bar."

"Seriously? That's how he's going to play it? Like he just happened to come to this random pub?"

"*Travel Europe* did recommend it."

"Does he look like he's carrying *Travel Europe*?"

"No. Although he might have the app. An app that you still haven't downloaded, have you?"

"I tried to," she says, wincing. "But I forgot my iTunes password."

Very, very casually, Matt spins on his bar stool and faces us.

At this point, we're both looking at him.

His mouth makes an O, and his eyes feign surprise.

Leela gives a little wave.

He waves back, still feigning surprise, and he jumps off his stool.

They're staring at each other. I can feel the pull between them.

Omigod. They're totally going to have sex.

86

I look at Jackson, who's looking at me.

He's still hot. Now he's wearing a thin gray shirt, faded jeans, and Pumas. He takes a sip of his beer.

My heart skips a beat.

Man whore. Man whore. Man whore.

They both get up and head over to our table.

"They're coming," Leela mutters.

"I see," I say.

"What do we do?" She lifts up a french fry but then puts it back down.

"What do you want to do?"

"Kill him," she says.

"I think you want to have sex with him," I say.

"That too."

"Ladies," Matt says, smiling. "Fancy running into you here."

"Oh, please," Leela says. She looks up at him. "You totally saw my post."

"Post? What's a post?"

Leela rolls her eyes. "Ha, ha."

"It's a famous pub," Matt says. "I wanted to check it out."

"I call bullshit." She takes a sip of her wine, her eyes not leaving his.

"Can we join you?" Matt asks.

She scoots over on her side. Okay, then. We're doing this. I scoot over on mine.

"So," I say to Jackson. "How's your trip?"

"Pretty good," he says. "Yours?"

"Fantastic," I say. "Although it's kind of a bummer none of my ex-boyfriends showed up here too."

"Why not? Don't they follow Leela's social feeds?"

"Aha! So that *is* why you're here!" Leela calls out, turning toward us. "I knew it."

Matt puts his hands up in mock defeat. "You caught me. I wanted to see you."

She crosses her arms in front of her chest. "You could have spent the whole trip with me."

"You're the one who told me not to come."

"You're the one who kissed some girl at a bar."

"It was just a stupid kiss. It didn't mean anything. I was freaked out. We're only nineteen, and you were practically picking out our wedding invitations!"

"I was not!"

"You kept telling me about how your dad proposed!"

"That's because we were going to London!"

"You look at wedding magazines!"

"I like the pictures!" she yells. "Don't make me out to be the messed-up one. We were together all year and you never even said I love you! Why is saying I love you so hard? It's just three words!"

I poke Jackson's leg under the table, and motion toward the bar. "Drink?"

"Yes," he says, and the two of us stand up. "We'll be back."

"So," I say, balancing myself on a stool. "Are they always like this?"

"Loud? Yes."

I laugh. "Argumentative."

"Yes."

"You live on the same floor at school?"

"Yup."

"Where are you from again?"

"Vancouver. It's near Seattle."

"I know where Vancouver is," I say.

"Ever been to Canada?"

"Nope."

"You came all the way to Europe before visiting your closest neighboring country? Do you have something against Canadians?"

"You're too polite," I say.

"I'm not that polite," he says. "So did you Americans do anything special to celebrate July fourth yesterday?"

"Nope," I say. "We practically forgot it was happening. It's easy to get lost in the days here. Did you guys do anything fun?"

"I got on a plane for Canada Day. It was July first."

"You guys have your own day?" I ask, faking shock. "Adorable. Oh no." I spot Leela and Matt back at the booth. "They're making out."

He spins his chair. "That didn't take long."

"But I wanted to go to the Eye," I pout. "And it's going

89

to rain tomorrow. It won't be as good."

"Do you want me to interrupt them?"

I sigh. "No. You're leaving tomorrow, right?"

"Yeah. We're going to Amsterdam."

"So tonight is their last night," I say, nodding to myself. "Yeah, they're definitely having sex."

"Definitely. Those two are like bunnies." He stands up. "I'll go with you."

Huh? "Where?"

"To the Eye. Didn't you say you want to go?"

My heart races. "You will?"

"Yeah."

"And we just leave them?"

He laughs. "I'm sure they'll come up with another activity."

"You don't mind?"

"Do I mind spending my evening going on a Ferris wheel with a hot semi-stranger? No, I don't."

I blush at the hot part. "I'm not sure if it's a Ferris wheel exactly. I think it's more of a cable car."

"Works either way."

"All right, then." I jump off my stool. "Let's do it."

Leela and Matt could not care less that we're leaving them to go to the Eye. I'm not entirely sure they even notice. They're too busy PDAing.

"Let's walk," he says. "I've heard the Queen's Walk is nice."

It is. The paved promenade is lined with trees and metal benches on one side, and beautifully carved lampposts and the winding Thames River on the other.

"So," he says.

"So," I repeat.

"What's your story?"

"What does that mean?" I ask with a laugh.

He smiles. "Boyfriend? Girlfriend?"

"No and no. You? Girlfriend? Boyfriend?"

"No and no."

"I already got the scoop on you from Leela," I admit.

He winces. "That's not good. She's not my biggest fan."

"She doesn't dislike you," I say. "She just blames you for Matt's kissing indiscretion. And for convincing Matt that he shouldn't have a girlfriend. And for all the rain these last few days."

"That last one was totally my fault. I have magical weather powers."

"You do? Amazing! Can you keep it at seventy-five and sunny for the next four weeks? I would so appreciate it."

"Your wish is my command." He looks at me sideways. "So what else have you heard?"

"That you've slept with the entire freshman class. And possibly the sophomores, too."

He laughs.

"True?"

"I don't kiss and tell."

I snort. "So it *is* true."

"I like girls," he says. "But I'm a gentleman. I swear. Scout's honor."

"Were you a Boy Scout?" I imagine a smaller, younger version of him with short boyish hair and a rounder face.

"No. Were you a Girl Guide?"

"A what?"

"Girl Scout. Sorry. It's called Girl Guides in Canada."

"Weird. And for one year. Brownie."

"What happened? Couldn't light a fire without a match?"

"I wasn't great at the cookie selling," I say, which is only a partial lie. Girl Scouts require a lot of maternal involvement. A lot. A lot of social maternal involvement. "Although I was really good at eating them. Mmm. Tagalongs."

"I would totally buy your cookies," he says.

"Oh, you would, would you?"

"If your cookies are for sale," he says.

I stop and turn to him. "For sale? No, my cookies are not *for sale.*"

He turns bright red. "I didn't mean it like that. Not for sale! I was just getting caught up in the cookie joke and . . ." He shakes his head.

I laugh. "So you don't think I'm a prostitute?"

"I absolutely do not. I am not interested in buying your cookies. Any type of cookies. Even Tagalongs. Or Thin Mints. Especially not the Rah-Rah Raisins."

The sun is now setting against the river. It's red and orange and extremely beautiful. I turn back to Jackson.

"Want to know a secret?" I say. "*Nobody* likes the Rah-Rah Raisins."

By the time we get to the Eye and step inside, the sky is dark and the city is lit up.

It really is a cross between a Ferris wheel and a cable car. It's extremely slow. Like you can't even tell it's moving. Most people stand against the glass windows, but there are a few seats.

"I feel like I'm in the *Millennium Falcon*," I say. "Doesn't this look like a spaceship?"

"It does," he says.

There are six other people in our car. A family speaking German and a couple speaking Japanese. As we climb into the sky, the dark river surrounds us. In the distance, I see a lit-up Big Ben.

"So Leela told you all about me," he says, looking over at me. "But all I know about you is that you were a Girl Scout for one year, you like Tagalongs, and you're not a prostitute. That hardly seems fair. I need more info."

"What do you want to know?"

He leans closer to me. "Tell me another secret."

A shiver runs down my back. "What kind of secret?"

"Tell me something most people don't know about you."

"Hmm," I say, trying to think of something sexy yet

entertaining. "When I was in seventh grade, I practiced French kissing on balloons."

He laughs. He has a nice laugh. Low and deep. "Really? Why balloons? Latex turns you on?"

"No," I say. "They were just squishy. Your turn. Tell *me* a secret."

"I get turned on by women in latex. Also women in lace. And flannel nightgowns. And—"

"Okay, I get the picture," I say. This is not helping with his man-whore reputation.

"That was three secrets."

"More like one," I say. As we get higher and higher, the building lights and headlights and streetlights get smaller and smaller until they're spread out in front of us like glittering stars.

"Still. Your turn again," he says.

"I sent Leela a secret admirer note in the sixth grade. She was sad that I had gotten one and she hadn't, so I sent one to her and never told her it was from me."

"Really?"

"Don't get excited, I didn't actually have a crush on her, I just didn't want her to be sad."

"I got that," he says. "That's sweet. Does she know it was you?"

"No. You can never tell her. We spent hours dissecting who could have sent it. Hours. Your turn."

"I killed my brother's frog," he says.

I gasp and tear my eyes away from the shimmering darkness outside. "What?"

"By accident. I promised I would feed it when he went to hockey camp, but I completely forgot about it and it died. My dad checked on it and its eyes were all bugged out and my dad tried to resuscitate it—he's a doctor—but it did not work. I felt terrible."

"That's so sad. I'm sorry."

"It was fifteen years ago. I'm over it. Mostly. Your turn again. Tell me something really important. Something that makes you *you*." He looks right at me.

I'm not sure why I say it. Maybe because he already turned the conversation sad with his frog comment. Or because at four hundred feet above a foreign city, nothing seems real. Or because even though we're not alone, no one else in the car seems to speak English. "My mother's agoraphobic."

He blinks but doesn't look away. "She won't leave the house?"

"Right."

He shakes his head. "Is she afraid of germs or of something happening? Like a terrorist attack? Is that why she's afraid to go out?"

"No. That's not it. She's more afraid of what *she'll* do. She's afraid she'll have a panic attack and somehow lose control. And embarrass herself. Or me. She used to be afraid of driving off a cliff by accident, but I think now she just doesn't want to put herself in any situation where she thinks she might panic."

"Oh. Wow."

"Yeah. She'll do *some* stuff if she's with me. Like she'll sit in the car if I drive. But even with me, she won't go to a grocery store or a school event or any place that's packed with people."

"That sounds hard," he says, our eyes locked. "For her and for you."

"It is," I say, and take a deep breath.

"So she's fine with you leaving the house? She's not worried about you being so far away?"

"No. Yes." I shake my head and try to explain. "She's not afraid of *me* having panic attacks. But I think she is afraid of me not being there to help her."

"Is your dad around?"

"Nope. They're divorced. Hopefully my sister, Addison, is taking care of her, but she's only sixteen. I told her I'd come home if there was a disaster." I laugh nervously. "So there you go. Now you know what makes me, me. Sorry you asked?"

"Not at all," he says. "Just sorry you have to go through it."

I can't believe I just told him all that. Leela knows my whole story, but I've never even told Kat.

Our eyes are still locked. Are we having a moment?

I clear my throat. "Your turn. Spill it. What makes you *you*?"

He leans in close. "You're going to be the only one who

knows this about me. Are you ready?"

I smile. "Oh, I'm ready." I have no idea what he's going to say, but I'm kind of excited to know what makes him tick.

"You have to promise to keep it a secret."

I make an X across my chest. "Girl Scout's honor."

He takes a deep breath. "I have never seen any of the *Star Wars* movies. Not one."

Now it's my turn to blink. I thought we were being serious. But I don't want to show him I'm disappointed. "No way," I say. "How is that even possible?"

I step forward and press my face against the glass.

"It was actually pretty difficult. Both my brothers are obsessed with them so I had to make a real effort." Now he's standing behind me.

"But why?"

We're not touching or anything, but I can feel him.

"My dad thought I was too young. My brothers saw it and then they bugged me about it, so I started saying I didn't want to see them anyway. Then it became a matter of principle."

"So you just pretended to get my *Star Wars* reference before, huh?" I ask.

"I did. I'm trying to impress you."

He steps beside me, so we're standing side by side against the window, holding on to the railing. His hand brushes against mine and my whole body tingles.

Neither of us says anything. But he doesn't move his hand

and neither do I. We just stare straight ahead, watching the city rise and fall beneath us.

"Do you mind stopping at the gift shop?" I ask as we step off.

"Sure," he says.

I pick up a snow globe that has a teeny tiny London Eye inside. The base is blue, and it says "London" in block letters over a red bus.

"Cute," he says. "Who's it for?"

"My sister," I say. "I promised her a snow globe from every stop."

"That's going to be a lot of snow globes."

"I know. That's why I'm getting the small ones."

"How old did you say she was again?"

"Sixteen, almost seventeen. Her birthday is on July nineteenth. I gotta do it. It's part of the bribe."

"Aren't you nervous they'll break?"

I cock my head to the side. "I wasn't before. But it does seem like a fairly likely possibility now that you point it out."

"Yeah. I would make sure to wrap them in bubble wrap. Like twelve layers."

After it's packed up into a much larger package than I have room for, we walk across the Golden Jubilee Bridge.

"I'm glad we did that," he says, smiling at me.

"Me too," I say.

"Where to now? Should we go to your place or mine?"

I stop. "Excuse me?"

He turns bright red. "I didn't mean that the way it sounded."

I laugh. "How did you mean it exactly?"

"I meant that Matt and Leela are probably using one of our rooms."

"Aha," I say. "But which one? She can't text me. I can only see iMessages when there's Wi-Fi."

He pulls out his phone. "They're in my room."

"You're getting messages?"

"Canadian plans are better, what can I say?"

I look over his shoulder to get a peek at the text. It says:

With L. Crash somewhere else.

"Subtle," I say. "Where exactly is he expecting you to sleep?"

"Who knows? I'll find someplace."

My cheeks heat up.

Am I just supposed to invite this not totally random, but somewhat totally random guy to sleep in my hostel room? That does not seem like a good plan. Unless I want to hook up with him. Do I? Sleeping with Jackson would definitely qualify as an adventure. On the other hand, what happens if Leela and Matt get back together and I have to travel with Jackson for the rest of the summer?

Shit. Are they getting back together?

What if they want to travel just the two of them for the

rest of the summer? And Jackson wants nothing to do with me, and I have to travel alone?

Maybe Jackson should interrupt them. No. She'd kill me.

Do I even have a choice in this situation?

"You can come to my hostel," I say. "We'll hang out in the bar and see if she comes back."

I don't look at him when I say it. Does he think I mean he can come to my room? I'm not sure. Do I want to hook up with him? I'm not sure. Does he even want to hook up with me?

Back at the bar, I spot the Italians at the corner table. They eye Jackson and then whisper to one another.

Ha. I would have introduced you ladies if you hadn't been such bitches.

We sit down at a red vinyl booth.

"Oooh," he says. "They have ketchup crisps. I'm going to get a bowl. And whatever they have on tap. What about you?"

"Pimm's. It's my London drink."

When the crisps—which I'm pleased to see are actually American chips—come, we both dig in.

"These are good," I say.

"You've never had ketchup crisps?" he asks.

"No. We don't have them in America. Do you have them in Canada?"

"Yup."

I take a sip of my drink. But only a sip, because I don't

want to get drunk and do something stupid like have wild and passionate sex with him.

Not that I'm thinking about having wild and passionate sex with him.

Or thinking about licking that bit of ketchup powder off his lip. Or off his fingers.

Okay, I totally am.

He's hot. He's really hot. And he's mine.

Not mine, exactly, but sitting at a table with me. The Italians are looking at him. Everyone's looking at him. He's tall and has good shoulders and a good laugh and is leaning back in his seat like he owns the place, and I could just crawl onto his lap and wrap my legs around him and—

Yeah. No more drinks. I can't hook up with him.

Not counting Charlie, I have never kissed, never mind seriously hooked up with, a guy I barely knew.

And the only reason I kissed Charlie was because I knew I would never see him again.

If Leela and Matt get back together, I could be seeing *a lot* of Jackson. I could be traveling with him for the rest of the trip. Hooking up with him seems like a very risky move. A dumb move.

Never mind that he's a man whore. And I've only had sex with two people. Theo and Adam, my good friend from high school. I didn't like him like *that*, but I knew he had always had a thing for me. I decided to just do it already over winter break our senior year. I trusted him, and we'd had fun. It was nice to feel like I was making someone's dream come true, even though I'm pretty sure he only got it three quarters of the way in.

I am pretty sure Jackson knows how to get it *all* the way in.

Is it getting hot in here?

I stuff another crisp into my mouth. Mmm. Good. Ketchupy.

"Last call," the barman says.

I glance up at the clock. It's already two a.m.? How did that happen?

"Don't worry about me," Jackson says. "Go to sleep. I'll just crash here."

"In the booth."

"Yes."

"I'm not sure they'll let you do that," I say.

"Then I'll go back to my hostel. I have to pack soon anyway. We're leaving in the morning."

"Okay," I say, leaning in. "If I let you crash in Leela's bed, you're going to be a perfect gentleman, right?"

"Of course," he says. "Scout's honor."

"Any chance you have an extra toothbrush?" he asks, looking around our room. It's a mess. Leela's clothes and magazines are strewn everywhere.

"No," I say. "I figured I could buy an extra one here if I needed. Not so much room in the backpack."

"A toothbrush is pretty small. Smaller than ten snow globes."

"Yes, but when you're trying to accommodate ten snow globes, something's gotta give."

"Fair point."

"I'll be back," I say. "I'm going to brush my teeth. Don't steal my stuff."

"I don't know. Your flip-flops look pretty comfortable."

"Oh, I'm wearing those to the bathroom," I say, and slip them on. The bathroom is, thankfully, empty. I pee, wash my hands, brush my teeth, wash my face. I am going for the I-don't-care-what-I-look-like, I-just-happen-to-be-really-cute look. I hope it's a good look for me, but I have no idea.

I want to make it clear to this guy that I am not putting out. I am not going to be one of his girls. In fact, I am still wearing my bra.

I open the door.

He's lying on Leela's bed, the white sheet pulled up to his waist. He is not wearing a shirt.

I look away. Fast. But oh. Those shoulders. Smooth skin. And abs.

"It's hot in here," he says.

"You can open the window," I say. "But it gets really loud."

I climb into my bed and pull the sheet up to my neck.

He is still shirtless. He is still hot.

I am still wearing my bra. Do I take it off? I want to take it off because it is not comfortable to sleep in a bra and also I only brought four bras with me and can't really afford to waste one for sleeping. But I can't just take it off and toss it on a chair, now can I? That would definitely be an invitation. Or at least a waving of a white flag. Beige, in this case.

I can't let him see my beige bra. It is not cute at all. I turn over on my side so I am staring at the wall. I am never going to be able to fall asleep with a hot shirtless guy a foot away from me. Also I am not going to be able to fall asleep while wearing a bra. Unless I can slip it off and keep it under the covers? I can try. I move very, very slowly.

Twist. Creeeeeak.

My hand is stuck. What is wrong with me? It's really not that hard. Now a bra strap is wrapped around my neck.

CREEEEEEEEAAAAK.

There. Did it. I'm sweating. Look at me all braless! I'm wild and crazy! Maybe I should hook up with him. Why wouldn't I? The opportunity has presented itself. There is a super-hot guy in my room. He is a friend of a friend, so he is not a complete stranger. I am in Europe. Isn't that why I'm here? To have flings with hot guys who happen to be shirtless in my room?

Yes. Clearly this is an opportunity I should jump on. I should face him. If I face him and he's looking at me, I'll give him a sign. I'll say something frisky like, hey, is it too hot for me to join you?

Okay. Here we go. I flip onto my back. The bed creaks. I wait.

I look over at him.

He's flat on his back. Still shirtless. His left arm is flung over the bed, almost touching the floor.

I think his eyes are closed. Is he really sleeping? How can he sleep at a time like this?

Then I hear: "SHHHHHHHLLLLMPH."

Omigod. Is he snoring? I guess he didn't have as much trouble falling asleep as I did.

"SHLLLLMPHhhhh."

Hilarious. I wonder if he stays the night with all the other girls? Have they heard this?

I hear laughter from the Italians.

"SHLLLLMPHhhhhSHHHHHH."

They better not be laughing at my man. Bitches.

I hear a key turn in the door. I wake up and see light spilling through the cheap curtains and I twist to look at the door.

It's Leela. She's wearing the same clothes as last night and smiling.

I need coffee. A lot. I think I only fell asleep about fourteen minutes ago.

She looks back and forth between Jackson and me. He's still asleep. "Did something happen?" she mouths.

I shake my head.

She mouths something else, but I have no idea what. It

looks like *leather shoe.*

"Huh?"

She waves me to come with her.

I slip my flip-flops back on and follow her into the hall.

"He wants me to come to Amsterdam!" she says gleefully.

"Okay," I say, my heart sinking. It's happening. Is she
going to ditch me? I guess it's not the end of the world.
Maybe she just doesn't want to stay at Kat's. I guess I could
do Paris by myself and she could go to Amsterdam and we
can meet up in Berlin. "Are you going to go?" I ask.

"I don't know," she says. "Do you want to?"

"Oh. Me too?"

Her eyes widen. "Yes. Both of us. I'm not just going to
ditch you. I would never ditch you."

I feel a flood of relief. "But we're supposed to go to Paris.
Tomorrow."

"It's pouring rain. Didn't you say it's supposed to rain all
day? Let's just switch. Let's go to Amsterdam today. You said
nothing was set in stone."

"But I thought you didn't want to go to Amsterdam. Isn't
he going to be high the whole time?"

"Hopefully not. But even if so, I'd rather be there with
him than not. I don't want my boyfriend getting high and
going to prostitutes."

"Prostitutes? Really?" I've already spent way too much
time on this trip talking about prostitutes. "Wait. Boyfriend?"

She throws her hands up. "I don't know what's going on!"

I eye her warily. "I'm going to guess you slept together last night."

"Of course we slept together. But now what?"

"He invited you to go to Amsterdam," I say.

"Yes. He said we should both come. Jackson thinks you're hot."

I flush. "He does? For real?"

"Yes. Matt texted Jackson to make sure it was cool to invite us and he said yes. You don't hate him, do you?"

"No," I say. "Not at all. We had a good time."

"Perfect. So can we go? Please? Pretty please?"

"But what about Paris? What about Berlin?"

"We'll just go a few days later. Kat won't mind, will she?"

"Probably not," I say.

"Isn't the whole point of traveling through Europe to be spontaneous?"

"I thought it was to eat stinky cheeses and gelato and see the *Mona Lisa* at the Louvre."

"Pleeeeeeeease?" she begs.

I think of the hot half-naked man in my room. "Okay, okay," I say. "Let me text Kat."

AMSTERDAM, NETHERLANDS

The Basics: Amsterdam is the capital of the Netherlands, which is north of Belgium and west of Germany. The native language is Dutch, and the currency is the euro. Prostitution and marijuana are both legal here.

If you are looking for a caffeine fix, do not wander into a coffee shop looking for different kinds of lattes. Coffee shops in Amsterdam sell pot. Different kinds of pot.

After I say a somewhat awkward, I-might-see-you-later-I-might-not good-bye to Jackson, Leela goes to shower and I message Kat that we're thinking of going to Amsterdam, and would she mind if we came to Paris a few days later.

It takes her about thirty minutes, but she writes back: **No worries!** 😃 **Try the Lemon Haze!** 🌬️ 💨

"Is that a dessert?" Leela yells over the sound of her newly delivered hair dryer.

"No idea," I lie. I have *some* idea. It's not a dessert. But I don't want her thinking Kat is a pothead, because she totally isn't. We've smoked a joint or two at parties, something I've never mentioned to Leela, who I'm pretty sure has never smoked anything in her life. Leela and I used to roll our eyes at the potheads at school who fell asleep during class and played way too much hacky sack. Matt's enjoyment of pot was one of the things that drove her crazy about him.

"But your friend is okay with the new plan?" she asks, still upside down.

"Seems so," I say.

"Fantastic. I really think—" Suddenly her hair dryer sparks bright red and turns off. "Shit. What happened? It's dead. She just came back to me and now she's dead!"

"Oh, no! Did you use my converter?"

"Yes! I did!" She unplugs it from the wall. "See? Oh shit."

"What?"

"I think this is the wrong thing."

"What do you mean?"

"I think it's a converter but we need an adapter. Or maybe it's an adapter when we need a converter. Because the electricity is stronger."

My cheeks heat up. "Shit. Sorry. I didn't realize."

"Oh well," she says with a sigh. She drops the hair dryer in the garbage with a thump. "She was old, anyway. One less thing to carry to Amsterdam, right?"

That doesn't make me feel better. Knowing I let her down gives me a pit in my stomach.

"Time to pack," she says. "How am I going to fit all my new things in my duffel, anyway?"

I take in the mass of stuff. "I don't think you are. I can take the extra." All I had acquired so far was a snow globe, a mini-umbrella, and a paperback Carole Matthews romance from Waterstones. "I ripped out almost thirty pages of my *Travel Europe* guide. That gives me, like, twenty free pounds."

She laughs. "Thanks, but I'll just stuff it all in a Boots bag. I don't want you breaking your back in week one."

Luckily, we're able to switch our train tickets, although not to the one the boys are on. But at least the hostel the boys are staying at has an available room with two single beds. I reserve it with my bank card.

It's unclear to me who will be sleeping where.

Leela pokes me awake.

I open my eyes and blink. I'm on a train.

"We're almost there. Wake up."

That was fast. I slept the whole time. And here we are. Amsterdam.

We pull out all of our bags from the storage overhead as the train slowly grinds to a halt.

"They should already be at the hostel," Leela says. "This is going to be so fun."

We step onto the platform and look for the exit signs.

"Let me text and see if they can meet us here and help us with our bags," Leela says.

"I don't need help," I say. "It's all on my back, baby. And some on my front."

"Matt's not going to want us getting lost. This way they can show us where the hostel is. Why should we wander through the streets?"

I check my phone before we leave the station and I lose Wi-Fi. There are so many messages from my sister.

She is crazy. Totally crazy.

Why aren't you answering me?

She's having a spell.

Why don't we live with Dad?

You better be having the best trip ever.

Why won't she see a shrink? I don't get it.

I'm thinking of slipping a sedative into her coffee.

And more. I pop my shoulder in annoyance. Really? She's freaking out after five days? I deal with our mother *all the time.* She's lucky that I've never forced her to do all this stuff before. I probably should have. But she'd only been in fifth grade when my parents divorced, and she'd had all those tutors. And then she had her swimming and her softball and I just had Leela and my books and a driver's license so it made sense for me to do more—all—of the mom shepherding.

So, yeah, I guess it's not Addison's fault she's freaked out. I basically shielded her for years and then dumped all of my mother's craziness in her lap. You can't just deflate someone's raft and expect them to know how to swim.

I write back:

Sorry! Time zones!

By all means if you can get her to see someone, great.

Don't give her drugs without her knowing please.

She tried pills. They made her groggy.

Hope you had a good 4th!

My sister will be fine. My mother will be fine. My mother won't have a total breakdown and need me to come home early. She won't.

Has she only left the house that one time to go to the post office? Are they mad at me? Do they hate me? Am I a horrible person for abandoning them?

It's only four weeks, I remind myself. *Then I'll take over again.*

I try to stop thinking about home as we head outside to the busy courtyard. Leela drags her duffel behind her and checks her phone again.

The sun is out, but the air is breezy. The courtyard is busy. There are lots of tourists and tons of backpacks.

Leela is tapping on her phone. "He didn't write back," she says. "Oh, wait. He says—they just sat down at a coffee shop and to meet them there. Good. I could use some coffee."

"Um, Lee? I don't think coffee shops here serve coffee."

She drags her suitcase behind her. "What do you mean? What do they serve?"

"Pot."

"No way."

"Yes way."

She shakes her head. "That can't be right. Why wouldn't they call them pot shops, then?"

"Maybe they're trying to be subtle?"

"He says it's on the way to the hostel. I guess we'll pass by and see."

We start walking down Prins Hendrikkade. There are tourists everywhere. In the windows, all the shops seem to sell is blue-and-white pottery and drug paraphernalia. Bongs. Hemp blankets. T-shirts with marijuana leaves.

As we keep walking, the street gets a little nicer. To the right of us is a row of thin and high town houses. To the left of us is a road with traffic going in the same direction as us. Some cars, but a lot of bikes. So many bikes. Men on bikes. Women on bikes. Kids in bike baskets. And no one's wearing a helmet! Then farther over, there's a murky canal with small red-and-blue boats passing us by. Then there's another road of traffic going the other way, then another line of town houses.

The air smells like french fries and weed.

"I love this," Leela says, gesturing around her.

Clearly she doesn't notice the weed smell.

"Look at the canals. And the fact that we're double dating in Amsterdam. I've always wanted to go on a double date with you."

"I thought you didn't approve of Jackson?" I ask.

"I wouldn't normally. But he seems like the perfect guy for you to have a summer fling with, don't you think? At least we know he's not a serial killer."

"Glad we're setting the bar so high for me."

"And who knows? Maybe you two will fall in love."

I snort-laugh. "Don't hold your breath."

"Omigod, imagine you really did fall in love and then you decided to transfer to McGill to be with both of us? That would be amazing."

Now she's really getting delusional. "I am not transferring to McGill."

"Oh come on, we could be roommates."

"We could be roommates after you graduate. In Maryland. Or DC." My shoulders tighten. It doesn't help that I'm carrying a hundred pounds on my back.

"You have to leave eventually, don't you? You're not going to live with your mother forever. This trip is a test. You'll see how she does. Maybe she'll surprise you. Maybe when you get back she'll be driving herself to DC and jogging in the park."

"Once again, don't hold your breath," I say. "Let's just enjoy the rest of our trip."

"McGill! McGill! McGill!" she chants.

Heat creeps up my neck. "Can you stop? I'm not transferring schools. I like my school. And why are we even discussing me moving to Montreal for a boyfriend I don't actually have?"

"You'd be moving for me too!"

"Leela. Stop," I snap.

She steps back in surprise. "Sorry. Ignore me. This whole Matt thing is making me wonky. And I just miss you." She pauses. "Do you know where we're going?"

"I think we turn right soon. Just a few blocks up."

It's getting really pretty. The outside of the town houses here all look like they've been recently refurbished. They're clean-lined and modern. There are tulips in the windows.

A few blocks more and we spot the coffee shop.

"There they are," she says.

Jackson looks up and smiles. His eyes are bright red.

Matt's too.

They are clearly very high. And very happy to see us.

"Ladies!" Matt calls out, jumping out of his chair. "You made it. Excellent." He wraps his arms around Leela, and kisses her sloppily on the lips.

Jackson and I raise our eyebrows at each other.

"Long time no see," he says.

"Miss me?"

"I did, actually."

He smiles. I smile back.

"Sit down," Matt calls out. "Order something."

The sidewalk is crowded, and our bags are big.

"Maybe we should drop off our stuff first?" I say. "So it's not in the middle of the street?"

"'Kay," Leela says, still smiling from Matt's kiss.

"See you soon."

Leela looks like she's about to say something else but just nods.

"Do you guys need help?" Jackson asks.

"No," I say. "We're fine. Thanks."

We walk down another block until we see the sign: "The Apartment." I buzz once. No one answers. I buzz again.

"*Reservatie?*" a voice in the intercom asks.

"Yes," I say.

The buzzer goes, and I pop open the door.

There's a steep flight of stairs. No elevator.

We march to the top. I heave my bag on my back, and Leela bumps hers up the stairs.

Once we're at the top, there's another door that leads into what looks like a big living room in a frat house. There are ratty couches around a coffee table, and an old-looking TV. A bunch of touristy flyers for bus tours are piled on a side table. There's a small kitchen on one side, a pool table, and a short blond guy sitting behind a desk, scrolling through Twitter.

"*Hallo,*" he says. "*Inchecken?*"

"Do you speak English?" I say.

"Checking in?" he asks without missing a beat.

"Yes."

"Passport and credit card." He rolls his *R*s. He sounds Irish.

We hand over our stuff and wait.

"Dorm room?"

"No, we're supposed to get a private room."

"You just booked today, right? That's all we 'ave. Sorry. Coed room."

"But—"

Leela shakes her head. "That's not going to work."

"It's. All. We. Have. You can go somewhere else?"

I am not lugging this bag back down the stairs and then prowling the streets looking for somewhere to sleep. And anyway, dorms are cheaper. And I'm already about a hundred and fifty dollars over budget.

"It's fine," I say.

Leela turns to me. "But what if I end up in Matt's room again?"

"I don't care."

"But what if you want to be with Jackson? You know? *Be* with him?"

My back hurts. "Let's just settle in and worry about that later. Maybe another room will open up tomorrow?"

"Nope," the guy says.

He's not exactly Mr. Positive. "It's fine," I say to Leela. "We were planning on staying in some dorms. We need to cut costs."

"Here are your keys. You're on the fourth floor."

Awesome.

Up we go. We open our room, to see that there are six bunk beds total, three against one wall, and three against another. Three have stuff on them and the others are empty. Each bed has a pillow and a hopefully bleached white sheet and brown blanket. Locked backpacks are in the corner. Travel books are piled on the tables. I think they're in Russian.

"This place is gross," Leela says. "We better not get bedbugs."

I shudder. "Please don't even joke about bedbugs."

"Bottom or top?"

"Top," I say. I love bunk beds, actually. I always wanted one as a kid.

"Should we go back to the coffee shop?" Leela asks, dropping her bag on the bottom bunk.

"I just need to pee," I say. "And let's get to an ATM. We need euros."

"They'll probably still be there, right?"

"They did not seem like they were in much of a hurry."

The bathroom is down the hallway. The toilet seems to have two flushers. I use the small one and it works. I wash my hands and return to the room.

"My turn," Leela says.

"There are two flushers," I tell her. "I'm not sure why."

"Thanks for the heads-up."

"Anytime," I tell her.

Tip: Like everywhere else in Europe (except the UK and Switzerland), the Netherlands uses the euro.

What is up with you, UK and Switzerland? Euros are super cute! The bills look just like Monopoly money, plus they have coins instead of one- and two-dollar bills that accumulate in your pocket and can be used to buy a pair of wooden clogs. Kidding! Don't buy a pair of wooden clogs. You'll never wear them, and they are way too heavy to carry around in your bag.

"Hi, boys," Leela says, and takes an empty chair. "Is the plan to just sit here all day?"

Matt nods. "Yes. I think it is. But we're going to need more pot."

"I'll get it," Jackson says, standing up.

"I want to see how this works," I say. "You just go in and order?"

"Yup," Jackson says. "Just like McDonald's."

"But not as classy?" Leela asks.

"Classier. Seriously." He laughs. He really does have a great laugh. "Come on."

I follow him inside.

It basically looks like a sandwich shop. Except instead of selling sandwiches they are selling weed.

"The menu is on the wall," Jackson tells me, pointing.

I look up. The choices are written in white chalk.

Under the headline WEED it lists about fifteen different choices, including Strawberry Haze, Super Silver Haze, Super Lemon Haze, and Blueberry Cheese. Aha! Lemon Haze!

Then it also lists Space Cakes, which includes muffins,

brownies, special cakes, and organic special cakes. Organic special cake? Really? There is also a section of hash and a list of pre-rolled joints.

"You really don't sell coffee, huh?" I say to the barman.

"We do," the barman says. "But the tea is better."

His English has a heavy Dutch accent.

"Is it *special* tea?" I ask.

"No," he says. "Regular green tea."

"I'll have one of those," Jackson says. "I saw one outside. Looks good."

"Me too," I say.

"What else can I get you?" he asks us.

Jackson looks at me. "Let's let the lady choose."

"Um . . . I have no idea."

"Is it your first time smoking pot?" Jackson asks.

"No," I say. It would be my third, but I don't go into details. "But I've never bought it myself. Usually it's more like—hey, do you want to smoke a joint? And I say, Oh, okay. This is definitely my first pot menu." I look back at the barman. "Any suggestions?"

"Do you want something relaxing or uplifting?"

"Uplifting, I guess? It's the middle of the day."

He nods. "Why don't you try the Purple Haze."

I look up at Jackson and shrug.

"We haven't had that yet," Jackson says. "Sounds good."

"How much?" the barman asks.

"I don't think Leela is going to have any," I say.

"I figured," Jackson says. "One gram of Purple Haze. And four teas, please. My treat," he says, reaching for his wallet.

"So this isn't your first time buying pot?"

He smiles. "It's not."

The guy hands us a small container of what looks like basil and we head to the table. "We'll bring out the teas," he calls after us.

We sit back down.

Jackson starts to mash the weed in some sort of small grinder, and then drops some into rolling papers.

"You seem to know what you're doing," I say. I can't decide if I'm impressed or concerned.

"He definitely does," Leela says, her eyes narrowed. I can tell she's annoyed. But it *is* Amsterdam. What did she expect? Don't you *have* to smoke pot in Amsterdam? Isn't that the law or something?

"I've rolled a joint or two," he says. He licks the paper and hands it to me. "Spark it up."

"Me? What do I do?"

"Lick the end, and I'll light it."

I can feel Leela's eyes burning into my head. I contemplate saying no just to appease her, but I decide against it. I'm in Amsterdam. I want to smoke a joint in Amsterdam. That does not make me a bad person. "Okay," I say.

I look at Jackson and lick the end of the paper. I put the other side in my mouth. "Light me up," I say with the joint in my mouth. I know I'm flirting.

He leans in closer without losing eye contact. He uses his lighter and the flame flickers in front of me.

I inhale.

I cough.

Leela laughs.

I inhale again.

The joint is lit.

"Nicely done," Jackson says.

I inhale again. A warmth passes over me. I inhale once more and look at Leela. "Want?"

"No," she says.

I shrug and pass it to Jackson.

Our fingers touch in the exchange; his are hot.

"Here are your teas," the waiter says, putting them in front of us.

He hands over four tall glasses stuffed with thick green leaves.

"Teas?" Matt asks.

"They came highly recommended," I say.

"I bet these teas don't come with cucumber sandwiches," Leela says.

"Mmm. I could go for a cucumber sandwich," Matt says.

"You had your chance," Leela grumbles.

I pick mine up. "They don't even look like teas. They look like waters with leaves."

"They taste delicious," Jackson says, taking a long sip.

Leela sniffs hers suspiciously. "Is there something in it?"

"Yes," I say. "Tea." I take a drink. "Omigod, this is good. This is, like, the best tea I've ever had."

"It is really good tea," Jackson says, leaning back in his seat.

"Mmmmmm," Matt says.

"I've never seen you have tea in your entire life," Leela says to him.

"You've only known me for ten months," he says.

"Have you ever had tea before?"

"No," he admits. "But I will again if it tastes like this. Why don't they have green tea at home?"

"They do," she says.

"I've never seen it."

Leela rolls her eyes.

The sun kisses my face. I smile and take another sip. "This really is amazing," I say.

"You guys are all high," Leela says.

The three of us start to laugh.

"Yes," I agree. Matt passes the joint back to me. "I believe we are."

"I *need* to have this," I say.

"You do not," Leela says.

We stayed at the coffee shop for a long time. We watched the sun set. Now we are walking around and wandering into different stores.

"I really do," I say. I am holding a travel hairbrush. It is the most amazing hairbrush I have ever seen. It's a compact but when you open it, bristles pop out. Pop go the bristles! It's so cute. It's blue with pink flowers. I love it. I need to have it. And it's only eight euros.

"You are on a budget," Leela tells me. "You do not need it."

"But I didn't bring a brush."

"But your hair is curly. You don't brush your hair. You have strict rules about curly girls brushing their hair."

It's true. I do. And the main rule is: NEVER USE A BRUSH. But maybe because I've never seen a brush this adorable before?

"Jackson?" I ask. "What do you think? Is this not the most adorable brush you've ever seen?"

He nods. "It is."

"See?" I say. "Do you want one too?"

"It's a little flowery for me."

"I'll get one for my sister," Matt says. "And for you, Leela. Do you want a brush, babes? My treat."

"I think we should get matching brushes," I say. "To remember Amsterdam."

"But they don't say Amsterdam on them," Leela says.

"True," I say. "But we'll always remember Amsterdam when we brush our hair."

"You're stoned," Leela says. "You realize that, right?"

I nod. "Yes. So you keep reminding me. But I haven't bought anything for myself yet. And this seems like a good

124

idea. Cute but also functional. And only eight euros. It's a steal."

I march up to the cash register and pay for mine with coins. I love the coins. The banknotes are adorable, too. They barely feel like money.

And now I have a souvenir. Yay!

Matt pays for his two and hands one to Leela. "Enjoy."

"Thanks," she says. "Can we go now?"

We step outside and make it halfway down the block, when I see an entire window display of strangely shaped shoes in bright colors. Yellow. Red. Green. I point. "What are those?"

"Wooden clogs," Jackson says. "They're everywhere."

"Do we want them?" I ask.

"No!" Leela yells. "Absolutely not. There is no way those are comfortable. They are made of wood!"

"There," Matt says. "Let's go there. Magnum."

The name makes me think it is a condom shop, but the place he is pointing at across the street has ice cream bars in the window.

Yes. Yes. Yesssssssssssss.

"I one hundred percent agree," Jackson says.

"I love ice cream bars," I say dreamily.

"You're still hungry?" Leela asks. "How is that even possible?"

The line is long. But we will wait! We will wait.

La, la, la.

It is my turn! It is my turn. The turn it is mine.

"*Mevrouw?* Toppings?"

"Sydney!" Leela says. "The guy is talking to you. It's your turn. Go."

"Oh. Hello! Um, what do I do?"

"Haven't you been listening?" Leela asks. "First you pick three mix-ins. Then you pick your ice cream flavor. Then you pick your toppings. They dip your ice cream bar in the toppings."

Yes, yes, yes. I pick meringue bits, cookie crumbles, and fudge bites. Then I choose a chocolate ice cream bar and white chocolate coating. They pour the coating over the ice cream bar, then cover it in toppings.

Omigod. I want that in my mouth right now.

"You want the chocolate drizzle?" the guy asks.

"Yes," I say, nodding. "I want the chocolate drizzle."

He puts it all on a magic paper plate of deliciousness and hands me a fork. I savor my first bite. "Omigod," I say. "This is heaven. Right here."

"Can I try some?" Jackson asks. Even though he already has his own.

"Yes," I say.

He dips his fork into my plate and takes a large chunk off the corner of my bar.

"Hey! That was a lot. I want some of yours."

"Go ahead," he says, and holds his plate toward me. I take a forkful of dark chocolate. Then I lick my lips. Slowly.

Obviously. I don't know why I do it. But I do.

He raises an eyebrow.

This is getting interesting. Although I am very aware that I am no way in a position to make any sexual decisions.

This is a really good ice cream bar. Do they have these in America? I might need one every day.

"You guys look ridiculous, you know," Leela says. "You're, like, French kissing those things."

"I think I'm in love with it," Matt says.

Leela gives him a dirty look. "Oh, so *that* you have no problem using the L-word on."

"I love it too," I say.

"I think I want to marry it," Jackson says.

The three of us start laughing.

"You guys are ridiculous," Leela says, but then Matt gives her a chocolate ice cream kiss and she starts to laugh too. "It *is* pretty good," she says.

"Where to next?" Matt asks, stepping back outside onto the sidewalk.

"Sex show?" Jackson asks. He raises his eyebrows at me again.

Leela stops walking. "You're not serious."

"We're in Amsterdam," Jackson says. "That's what Amsterdam is known for."

"I thought it was known for the pot," I say.

"I thought it was known for its tulips," Leela says.

"Maybe they use tulips in the sex show," Matt says.

"That's disgusting," Leela says.

"I was imagining sex on a bed of tulips. But interesting to see where your mind went."

She elbows him in the side. "I'm not sure I want to go to any type of sex show," Leela says. "Tulips or no tulips. And I don't think I'll ever be able to look at a tulip in the same way again."

"So I shouldn't get you tulips for your birthday this year?" he asks.

"No. We're not really going to a sex show, are we?" she asks.

"It'll be fun," Matt says. "Sydney, what do you think?"

"This may sound naive," I say, "but what is a sex show *exactly*?"

"People having sex!" Matt cries. "On stage!"

"But is it like porn?" I wonder. "Are there bad story lines? Is there going to be a pizza delivery man and two sisters who don't have any money to pay?"

"I'm impressed by your knowledge of porn tropes," Jackson says.

"I wrote a paper on women in porn for my Intro to Feminist Theory class," I say.

He gives an exaggerated sigh. "That's a much less fun answer than what I was imagining."

"I'm sure," I say.

"So does that mean you want to go? At least you'll have a topic for Feminist Theory 201."

I laugh. "Sure. Why not? When in Amsterdam . . ."

"Let me Google what the best one is," Matt says.

"I don't know how I feel about this," Leela mutters to me.

"You said you didn't want him doing this stuff without you," I say. "Isn't it better to do this with him?"

"I guess," she says. "But a sex show? You really want to see a sex show?"

"I have to admit I'm kind of curious."

"We found one!" Jackson shouts. "It's called Pink Dolphin."

"Let me check my book," I say. I look up Pink Dolphin in the index. "Oh! It likes it. 'If you're going to go to a sex show, this is the one.' Perfect. I'm in. It's in the red-light district."

"Obviously," Leela says. "It wasn't going to be in the museum district."

"There's a sex museum, too," Matt says. "Should we do that later?"

Leela snorts. "Let's save that for tomorrow."

"I was hoping to check out the Heineken factory tomorrow," Jackson says.

"I want to see Anne Frank's house," I say. "Although out of the three choices, mine does sound the least fun."

"What about the tulips?" Leela asks. "Aren't there tulips we're supposed to see?"

"Follow me, people," Matt says. "To the red-light district we go."

★ ★ ★

There are women in the windows.

Seriously. Each window features a scantily clad woman posing provocatively.

"What does it mean when the drapes are closed?" Leela asks.

"It means they're in use," Jackson says. "Sydney will explain it. She's an expert in the sex trade."

"Prostitution is legal here," I say.

"This is gross," Leela says.

"I agree," I say.

"I know I'm going to get yelled at for this, but what's wrong with buying sex?" Matt asks. "Why is that worse than buying any type of other client services? Like a haircut? Or a back massage? And what's wrong with getting paid to do something people like to do?"

"It's just wrong," Leela says.

"But what if these women want to be prostitutes? What if they like sex and see it as a good way to earn money?"

"I think the problem is that a lot of these women have no other options. They have no education and no other way to eat," Jackson says.

"And what about STDs and underage prostitutes and the objectification of women and sex trafficking?!" Leela shakes her head.

"All are a lot easier to regulate when prostitution is legal," I say.

She gives me a look. "I'm going to need a glass of wine."

Matt puts his arm around her. "Okay. Got it. I'll shut up

now. Oh! There it is! The Pink Dolphin!" A pink neon dolphin floats above a building in the distance.

There is a line around the block.

"What time is the show?" Leela asks.

"It's rolling admission," Matt says.

"What does that mean?" Leela asks. "People just have sex the whole time?"

"As people leave, they let new people in," Jackson says. "It's open twenty-four hours."

Leela laughs. "People come to this during the day?"

"Will there be costumes?" I ask.

"Probably," Jackson says.

"I'm really going to need some wine," Leela says as we get in line on the sidewalk. The street is packed with people. Americans. Europeans. Children. Bachelor parties. Bachelorette parties. Sports teams.

"Good," Matt says. "'Cause the ticket price includes three drink tokens."

"How much are tickets?" I ask.

"I'm not sure," Matt says.

The line moves fast.

"Look—those people are waiting to see the sex show," an American woman says as she walks by, pointing at us.

"Omigod, this is embarrassing," Leela says. "No one take a photo of this. I do not want this online. I want to get a job after college."

Hurrah! We're finally at the front of the line.

Tickets are fifty euros each. Crap, crap, crap. "That is a

131

lot of euros," I whine. "I'm trying to only spend sixty dollars a day. I'm going to run out of money by next week."

"You can always stay here and work it off," Leela says. She points to a window across the canal. "You'd look good in black spandex."

"I'm more of a latex girl," I say, and smile at Jackson. "But maybe I'll just try to spend less money on sex clubs tomorrow."

I pony up the fifty euros to enter and get a dolphin stamp on my hand. It glows in the dark. Perfect. Marked for life. I head down the dark hall to a theater.

There is a large sign that says no cameras or phones.

"Good," Leela says. "I won't accidentally be in someone's selfie."

As we walk in, it feels like we're late because it's in the middle of an, um, act.

There is a fully naked man sitting on a chair while a woman in green stilettos, and only green stilettos, is straddling him and having sex with him.

"Omigod," I say.

Leela has a shell-shocked expression on her face. I'm sure I do too.

"I guess we missed the foreplay," Jackson says.

We file into four empty red velvet couch-like seats. They are surprisingly comfortable.

A waitress—in what I can only describe as a sexy dolphin costume—comes over to take our drink order.

"A glass of chardonnay," Leela says over the thump of the electronic music. "Please."

"*Nee*," the waitress says. "*Wodka? Bier?*"

"No wine?" Leela asks.

The sexy dolphin shakes her head. "*Wodka? Bier?*"

"Vodka and cranberry juice?" I ask. "Juice?"

"*Oranje?*" she asks.

Leela and I both nod.

Jackson and Matt both order vodka straight up.

I look back at the stage. "Wait a minute. Is the floor spinning? Or did I smoke too much today?"

"It's spinning," Leela says.

"Wow," I say. "We can see them having sex from every angle."

The guy onstage is just kind of sitting there, smiling. He has a buzz cut and looks around our age. He's smiling smugly as the woman on top of him jumps up and down.

"Is it weird that I like her shoes?" Leela asks.

"They are a great color," I say.

"They'd be *amazing* in a flat."

Our drinks arrive in plastic glasses and we slurp them down. The couple onstage abruptly stops, stands up, waves to the audience, and exits.

A woman dressed as a nurse comes on stage.

"I bet she's not really a nurse," I tell Leela.

Matt chugs the rest of his drink. "Another round?"

★ ★ ★

Mouth-to-mouth does not resuscitate an injured man on a hospital bed, and the nurse is forced to remove her uniform and screw him back to health.

"He's cured!" I cry. "Hallelujah." Next up is a firefighter who removes all of his clothes and then jerks off into a pretend fire, putting it out.

"Omigod," Leela says, covering her eyes. "I can't watch this."

"You should," I say. "I'm studying his technique." Also, he has the largest penis I have ever seen in my entire life, and that includes all the movies I had to watch for my porn paper.

Once the fake fire has been properly extinguished, a ballerina in a sparkly silver tutu, a red leotard, and black toe shoes slides onstage. She points to the audience. *"Kan ik een vrijwilliger?"*

A bunch of hands shoot up.

"I think she's looking for a volunteer," Jackson says.

Matt throws up his hand.

Jackson starts laughing.

"Matt, no," Leela begs.

"Why not?"

"Because you're plastered."

"Am not," he says.

He totally is. He used all of his drink tokens and one of Leela's.

"Come on," he says, his face flushed. "It'll be fun."

The ballerina points to him, and he whoops with joy. He

squeezes his way past us and skips up to the stage.

"Jackson," Leela pleads. "Stop him."

Jackson shakes his head. He's laughing too hard.

Leela slumps into her seat and covers her face with her hands.

Meanwhile, on stage, the woman shimmies and twirls.

Suddenly, she pulls her tutu down and tosses it into the audience. Then she snaps off her leotard and stands tall in her black satin thong and matching bra. She points to Matt and then to her bra and makes an unhooking motion.

He turns bright red and tries to unclip it. And tries again.

"Oh my God, he's the worst at this—you have no idea," Leela says.

Now I can't help but laugh.

Matt is still trying to take off the woman's bra. The audience begins to hoot until finally, finally, it comes off. Matt holds it up and waves it like a flag.

The ballerina proceeds to shake her boobs in Matt's face.

He looks shocked, but also delighted.

"If he has sex with her, I'm never speaking to him again," Leela says.

"He's not going to have sex with her," I say. I lean over to Jackson. "He's not, right?"

"No," Jackson says. Then he shrugs. "That would probably cost extra."

The ballerina slips off her panties and plants them on Matt's head.

The crowd cheers.

"This is too much," Leela says. She stands up. Her hands are shaking. "I'm leaving."

"You can't just leave him up there," I say.

"Yes," she says, "I can. This is disgusting. Stay if you want." She glares at the stage and storms out of the room.

I turn to Jackson. "I think I should go."

"We'll follow you as soon as this is over," he says.

"'Kay," I say, and hurry up the aisle and out of the theater.

Leela is standing outside beside the canal, arms crossed, face stormy. "That was ridiculous."

"They'll be out in a second."

"I should leave him here," she barks.

"It didn't mean anything," I say. "He was just . . ."

"He was just showing off," Leela says.

"For you?"

"Me? No. For *Jackson*. He's always showing off for *Jackson*."

Jackson and Matt step through the door. Matt's face is still flushed and Jackson is still laughing. "What's wrong?" Matt asks.

"Seriously?" Leela yells. "You want me to watch you make out with some other person?"

"It was just a joke," he says. "Come on. Calm down. I love you. You know that."

She looks shocked. "You do? You've never said it."

"Of course I do. I love Leela Veer!" he yells into the

canal. "I'm crazy about Leela Veer!" He turns back to her and hugs her. "You're my tulip."

"You're so wasted," she says, but now she's smiling.

"Yes," he says. "But I still love you!"

"Come on," Leela says, tugging his hand. "Let's go back to the hostel."

Part of me wishes she weren't so easily won over. On the other hand, I *was* laughing, so maybe it wasn't that big of a deal. And he is totally high.

"Did you see me on stage?" he asks. "What was wrong with her bra?"

"At least it wasn't a front snap," I say.

"Those are tricky," Jackson agrees.

"Did you guys get any pictures?" Matt asks. He's holding Leela's hand.

"No pictures allowed," Leela reminds us. "Thank goodness. I'm hoping to forget this ever happened."

Matt points to a coffee shop. "Can we go get more pot?"

"I think you've had enough, buddy," Jackson says.

"Nooooooo. We're in Amsterdam. The night's not over until the fat lady gets high and—"

He barfs all over the street.

Tip: If you do visit a coffee shop, make sure you know your limit.

Vodka + weed + more vodka = bad idea.

We take him back to his room at the hostel.

He runs to the common bathroom and barfs again.

"He can never hold his booze," Jackson tells me as we hear more heaving.

"I can stay with him tonight," Leela says. "If you want my bed."

"You sure?" Jackson asks. "I don't mind taking care of him. Wouldn't be my first time."

"You've done more than enough," she snaps, and turns her back to us.

"Okay, then," he says, looking at me. "I guess I'm bunking with you."

"Me and six Russians," I say. "I think."

"Perfect," he says. "Do I get top or bottom? I enjoy both positions."

"I'm sure you do," I say, my heart speeding up. "You get the bottom."

"We're becoming excellent bunkmates," he says as we climb up the remaining stairs.

"We are," I agree. "You're not going to snore again, are you?"

"I don't snore!"

"You absolutely do."

"My dad snores," he says. "And my grandfather snored. So I'm not entirely surprised. Horrifically embarrassed, but not surprised." He stops. "You know what? I think I'm going to take a shower. I'm covered in barf."

"Yeah, that's probably a good idea. You're a little smelly."

"I'm just going to get my stuff. Keep mc company?"

Did he really ask that? "In the shower?"

He laughs. "I meant going back downstairs. But I like how you think. And yes, I would love it if you would join me in the shower." He takes a small step closer to me. "Is that on the table?"

"I don't think the showers are coed," I say, my mouth dry.

"Yeah," he says, taking a step back. "See you soon."

He walks downstairs and I go into my room.

My heart is thumping. So he does like me. Good to know. I can't believe I said that. I can't believe he thought I might do it. I've never showered with anyone. Not true. My sister and I used to shower together when we were little. Showering with Jackson would definitely be different.

I would like to see him naked.

But I am very drunk. And stoned. And tired. And it's two a.m.

Maybe I'll take a nap and then wake up. Then I can hook up with him. If I still feel like it. If the room is still empty and the Russians are still gone. Where are they, anyway? It's the middle of the night! Maybe they're on Russian time?

Since the room is empty, I strip off my clothes and slip on a sleep shirt. I climb into my white sheets and put my head down.

I forgot to brush my teeth. And wash my face. Must wash my face. Don't want to break out. Don't want bad breath.

Need to floss. Need to sleep. Very tired. Left lights on. Just need to close my eyes.

Ah. Better.

I wake up with a start.

The bed shakes slightly.

He's back. And on the bottom bunk.

My mouth feels dry and rank. No. I will not ask him to join me. I'm too gross. My hands are sticky.

I probably should have joined him in the shower. Or at least taken a shower.

Tomorrow will be our night. I'll shower. And shave my legs. And downtown.

I listen as he gets comfortable. "Hey," I say.

"You're up?" he asks.

"Barely. Fun night, though, huh?"

"Yeah," he says. "Although my head is spinning."

"Mine too."

"Good night, Syd."

I like that he called me Syd.

A few minutes later I hear it: "Snooooort!"

I fall back asleep, smiling.

"Wake up, sleepyhead," a voice says.

I open my eyes and see Jackson on the bunk bed ladder. At first I think—oh! He's climbing into bed with me! He's going to try and get it on! But then I realize it's morning and he's dressed in black shorts and a T-shirt.

"What time is it?" I ask.

"Don't you still want to see Anne Frank's house?" he asks.

I sit up. "Oh! Yeah. You want to come?"

"Yeah," he says.

"Gimme five," I say, and get out of bed. He looks at my bare legs and raises an eyebrow.

I wrap a towel around me. Then I grab my shower bag, some clothes to change into, and my brand-new kickass travel hairbrush. I slip on my flip-flops, walk out the door, and blow him a kiss.

The line is around the block.

"Wow. I was not expecting it to be this busy at nine a.m.," I say.

"At least it's longer than the line at the Pink Dolphin," he says. "That gives me faith in humanity."

"Have you read *The Fault in Our Stars?*" I ask, remembering that Hazel and Augustus had kissed in the attic.

"Yeah. In high school. I'm guessing you read Anne Frank's actual diary too?" he asks me.

"Of course. In fifth grade. It's required reading for Jewish kids."

Now that I'm here, I kind of wish I hadn't left my Star of David necklace in Maryland. I had left it partly because *Travel Europe* told me to be careful bringing jewelry, and partly because I was worried about advertising my Jewishness. You never know these days. "You're not Jewish, are you?" I ask.

"No," he says, running his hands through his hair. "Anglican slash Protestant slash nothing."

The line moves, and we step up. I ask Jackson to text Matt to tell them where we are in case they want to come. They don't respond.

The line continues to crawl until finally we're inside. We read the plaques on the walls that explain how Anne Frank wrote her diary while her family was in hiding during the Holocaust.

We follow the tour through the front office and the secret bookcase and up into the annex. The stairs are small and creaky. The room is small and dark.

"I can't believe she lived in here for two years," he says.

It's unbelievable. There is barely room to move. Anne would have done anything to get out of here. My breaths are coming faster and faster.

I think about my house.

My mother stays in our house on purpose. On *purpose*. Why would anyone trap themselves in a house on purpose? What's wrong with her? Suddenly I feel dizzy, like the room is spinning. I start to see spots. My heart beats even faster and I feel nauseated. I have to get out of here.

"I need to leave," I say.

He looks surprised. "Really?"

I nod. "I'm sorry." My voice sounds foreign to me. Like it's coming from outside of me instead of inside of me.

"Don't be. Let's go. Hold on to me."

I hold his hand and we hurry through the rest of the house and around the back and down the stairs.

"Excuse me, excuse me," he says.

We push through the bookshop and back outside.

It's muggy and hot but it still feels better than being inside. We walk toward a bridge and lean against the railing.

"I'm sorry," I say. "So sorry. I don't know what happened."

He's still holding my hand. "That house happened. It's horrifying."

"Yeah, but I can't believe I panicked like that." My heart is still racing. Everything's okay, I tell myself. I'm fine. I take more deep breaths until I feel better. "I'm not a panicker. At least not usually. Although this is the second time this has happened on the trip." I sigh. "I better not be turning into my mom."

His eyes are full of concern. "That place is intense. I'm sure you're not the first person who needed to get out of there."

"Yeah," I say. I try to shake it off. "Well, don't worry about me. You can go back. I'll be okay out here. I can just hang out and get a coffee or something."

"It's okay," he says. "I've already been."

"You've already been to the Anne Frank house?"

He nods.

I'm so confused. "When? Yesterday?"

"No. When I was a kid. My dad had a medical confer-
ence here and he took us."

"Oh. Wow. Lucky."

"Yeah," he says. He lets go of my hand. "Syd? I want to
tell you something." His voice is suddenly serious.

"Yeah," I say. I have no idea what he's going to say. That
he has a girlfriend? That I'm freaking him out?

"It's just . . . My mom's dead."

"Oh," I say. I wasn't expecting that. I realize he's mentioned his dad twice but never his mom. "I'm so sorry."

"Yeah. It's just that you told me about your mom in London, and then when you asked about me I should have told
you, but I said that stupid *Star Wars* thing instead." He puffs
out a breath. "So I wanted to tell you. That my mom died.
In a car accident. A truck hit her car. And she died when I
was five so I don't really remember any of it. Or her. My
brothers do, but I don't. They're older." He stops talking.
"I'm sorry I didn't tell you then."

"Don't be sorry," I say quickly. I put my hand on his arm.
"I'm sorry I keep complaining about my mother when yours
isn't around."

"Oh, no, I didn't mean it like that at all. You're just so
open with all your stuff and who you are, and it didn't seem
fair. So I want you to know."

"Okay," I say, feeling warm all over. "Thank you for telling me."

He nods. He looks out at the water.

"Do you want to go back to the gift shop at least?" I ask.

"Nah, that's okay," he says.

"But I was going to get an Anne Frank snow globe."

"Please tell me you didn't see any Anne Frank snow globes."

"I'm kidding, totally kidding. But I do need to get my sister a snow globe at some point."

"We have a few days."

"There you are," we hear, and look up.

Matt and Leela are standing on the corner, holding hands. I guess they kissed and fully made up. Hopefully he brushed his teeth.

"You're done?" Leela asks.

"Yeah," I say. I try to forget about my meltdown upstairs. "Time to see the tulips? You wanted to see the tulips, right?"

"Yes," she says. "But it's apparently the wrong season for tulips."

"Heineken factory?" Matt asks hopefully.

Really? He vomited all night and now wants to go drinking? "It's 10:30 a.m.," I say. "Do you really want beer?"

I look at Leela.

She shrugs.

"Lunch first," she says. "Then Heineken. It's a tour, right? I like tours. I don't like beer, but I like tours."

The tour, otherwise known as the "Heineken Experience," basically walks us through the process of beer making. We see barrels, taste the stages, and play games. Then we go into a bar area, where we are each entitled to two beers.

"No wine?" Leela asks the bartender.

He shakes his head no. "*Bier.* Heineken. Only."

"I guess I'll try it," she says. She takes a sip, and makes a face. "Beer is disgusting."

I catch the bartender rolling his eyes.

The floor is gummy, but we stand by a bar table and hang out.

"This is delicious," Matt says.

"I don't think I've ever had a Heineken before," I say, taking a sip. "It's sweet."

"You're sweet," Jackson says, eyes shining.

My cheeks heat up. But maybe it's the beer.

"I think he likes you," Leela says as she reapplies her lipstick in the bathroom mirror. "Are you into him?"

"Maybe," I say. "I don't know. He's hot, but I can't get the man-whore thing out of my head."

"You don't really have to fall in love with him, but he's not a terrible option for a fling. As long as you use a condom. Two condoms, even."

"I'm pretty sure that doesn't work."

"Did you hear Matt say I love you last night?" Leela asks.

"I did," I say.

"I know he was wasted, but it still kind of counts, right?"

"Kind of."

"What do you think it means? Do you think he thinks we're back together?" She makes sure she doesn't have any lipstick on her teeth.

"I don't know. Do you want to be back together?" I ask the question carefully, not wanting her to think I don't approve in case they end up back together.

"I miss him," she says. "I know he acted like an idiot with Ava and then again last night. But I think he's terrified of relationships. His parents totally messed him up."

Whose haven't? I think but don't say. Leela's not exactly the most independent person and I'm sure being babied by her parents and sister has something to do with that.

And I don't even want to think about the damage my parents have done to me.

"Well," Leela says, "if you're into Jackson, and Matt and I are back together, how would you feel about traveling with them for a little longer?"

"I'm not opposed to the idea," I say. "How much longer?"

She smiles sheepishly. "The whole trip?"

Oh! "Seriously?"

She studies my face in the reflection. "No? Obviously not if you're not into him."

"A month is just a long time to travel with a guy I barely know."

"Never mind. We don't have to. Maybe we could split up with them now but then meet up somewhere later? Like we could go to Paris like we're supposed to but then meet them in Berlin. That's what we were planning on doing anyway, right?"

"Right," I say. We could meet them in Berlin. That could be fun. And if we're still all hitting it off, maybe they could come with us to Prague. . . .

"Although Paris is the city of romance," she says, and pauses.

That sounds like a hint. "Leela, do you want to go to Paris with Matt?"

"Kind of," she admits, biting her lip. "I don't hate the idea. You're going to be with your friend Kat anyway, and she won't care if I don't stay at her place, right? Maybe it makes sense for Matt and me to take a few days together to figure stuff out since everything has been so messed up."

"But what about Jackson?"

"I'm sure he'll find a bed to sleep in." She laughs. "He's good like that, no?"

"I guess," I say. It's not the end of the world if I stay with Kat on my own. Although I had wanted Kat and Leela to get to know each other. I was excited for Leela to see a sliver of my college life. "If that's what you want to do, I'm fine with it. We can meet up at the end of the five days."

"Okay," she says. "It sounds like a possibility. I'll discuss with Matt tonight. Thanks."

We meet the boys outside.

"Do you ladies want to go on a cruise?" Matt asks.

"Right now?" I ask.

"Yes! There's a boat that tours around the canal. It leaves in four minutes."

"How much?" I ask.

"Fourteen euros," Jackson says.

"Okay," I say, and try not to worry about it even though I just spent eighteen euros on the Heineken tour. My feet are tired and it's a beautiful day and I wouldn't mind sitting down. And I'll just have to figure out the money stuff later.

There's a bar and gift shop on the dock, right by the boat.

"Maybe they have a more appropriate snow globe here?" Jackson asks.

"Good thinking," I say. "Which one do you like?"

We look at the various options. Every single one has a windmill.

"I haven't even seen a windmill," I say.

"Yeah, they didn't have any in the red-light district or Heineken factory."

"Maybe tomorrow we should broaden our horizons slightly," I say. "What happened to the tulips again?"

"Out of season."

"Oh, right."

I purchase the smallest snow globe they have.

He buys a windmill postcard and hands it to me. "A gift," he says. "For you. In case we never actually see a windmill."

"Thanks," I say. "I like it. And it can double as a bookmark."

"I'm thoughtful like that."

We're handed earphones as we step onto the boat. We find four seats near the back.

I sit next to Jackson, and Matt sits beside Leela, facing us. The seats look a bit like a booth. They're orange leather, and the table between us is a map of Amsterdam. Look at us. An adorable little foursome.

The boat starts moving almost immediately.

Ah. The wind feels great. And the streets look different from this angle. From the canal, we can see all the people standing on their balconies.

"Is it the beer or are all the houses tilted forward?" Matt asks.

We all stare at the houses.

"I think you're right," Leela says. "They are tilted. And I only had a sip, so it's not the beer."

"See those hooks on the top floor?" I say. "It's to help lift furniture and stuff from the canals. The houses were built to lean so that the furniture doesn't smash into the houses."

"Interesting," Jackson says. "How do you know that?"

"*Travel Europe*," I say.

"My stepmom bought me a copy of that too," Matt says.

"Matt's parents are divorced, too," Leela tells me, then turns back to him. "So are Sydney's."

"Did your mom remarry as well?" I ask. "Or just your dad?"

"Both did," he says. "My mom remarried twice. She's on husband number three. The guys keep getting older and richer."

"Matt keeps in touch with stepfather number two though," Leela says, putting her hand on his knee. "It's sweet."

"We both like soccer," he says. "He takes me to games." Right. The Toronto FC.

"Did your parents remarry?" Matt asks me.

"No," I say. "My dad has had a few girlfriends, but nothing works. And my mom doesn't go out much." I laugh at my choice of words. I turn to Jackson. "Does your dad date?"

"Not much," he says. "I wish he would."

"You should fix up your parents and call it a day," Matt says.

"Now that would be weird," Leela says.

Jackson leans back and stretches his arms behind him. "Is this a guided tour?"

I wave the earphones in the air. "We should listen." I open the plastic, put the earphones in, and flip through the channels. One is French. Two is Dutch. Three is German and four is English.

I sink into my seat and listen to the clipped voice of the guide explain everything as we pass. There are no mentions of the Queen's underpants or who invented the toilet.

What a pretty day. What a pretty view.

What a pretty breeze. My eyes start to feel heavy and I let them close.

"Good morning, sleeping beauty," Jackson says.

I open my eyes. The sun is setting over the water. I must have passed out on the boat. I guess the leftover jet lag and light breeze got the best of me. But I feel great. Like I slept for a hundred years.

"I fell asleep too," Matt says.

"We all did," Leela says. She stretches her arms above her head.

"So where to now?" I ask.

"Coffee shop?" Matt asks.

"Again?"

"I'm starving, actually," Jackson says.

My stomach growls. "Me too."

"Do you want to get food?" he asks me.

"Sure," I say. "What do you all want?"

Jackson lowers his voice. "Actually, I thought maybe we could go somewhere on our own? And give them a chance to talk?"

"Sure," I say. I'm not sure if this is a date or if he's doing his friend a favor. "I wouldn't mind changing first."

"Why don't we all go back to the hostel together and then we'll split up," Leela says.

"Then we can paint the town red?" Matt asks.

I laugh. "It's pretty red already."

★ ★ ★

"How do I look?" Leela asks me, twirling.

"Gorgeous."

She's wearing her sister's lucky short black dress, flats, and a high ponytail. She looks a little like she's going to a formal.

"Why don't you wear your hair down?" I tell her.

"He likes my neck. It's his favorite of my body parts."

"Your neck is his favorite body part? I doubt that."

"Second favorite. No, third. Fourth if you count each boob. Five if you count my —"

"Okay, then," I say. "Let's show off that neck."

"What about you?" she asks. "Are you wearing that?"

That does not sound approving. I am wearing my jeans with a low-cut black tank top. "What's wrong with this? It's my sexy top!"

"You always look gorgeous. But those are the jeans with the jam stain!"

Oh. Right. Is that still there? "I only brought one pair! And I haven't had a chance to wash them yet. And they make my butt look good."

"They do make your butt look good. You have a great butt. Forget what I just said, you look amazing."

"I'm not even sure what this dinner is. Is it a date? Or is it a 'we should keep ourselves busy so Leela and Matt can have more make-up sex'? On the other hand, he's been pretty sweet with me. I don't know."

"What do you want it to be? He's definitely a player.

153

And you were right—you're probably not getting married or anything. But if you are going to hook up with someone, it might as well be him. I hear he's a great kisser."

"Really?" I raise an eyebrow. "From who?"

"Word on the street. I want a full report if this goes down."

"Deal."

"But use a condom."

I'm glad we're alone in our room. "I always do. But that was a quick jump from kissing to condoms. He's that good?"

"That's what I hear."

"Well, of course I would use a condom," I say. "Not that I have any."

"I'm sure he has one. No, I'm sure he has tons."

"You're making him sound less appealing."

She laughs.

"Have fun," I say, and give her a hug. She hurries out of the room, leaving her stuff in a huge mess on her bed.

I change into a red sundress and put on my nicer-looking sandals and my lip gloss and a bit of mascara.

When I meet Jackson in the living room area, he whistles. "Hi there," he says. I feel his eyes on me. "You look nice."

"Thank you," I say. "So do you."

He's wearing jeans and a button-down instead of a T-shirt. His hair still looks wet.

This feels a lot like a date.

"I heard about a place in the red-light district," he says,

clearing his throat. "A restaurant."

I raise an eyebrow. "In the red-light district? Really? It doesn't involve naked people, does it? I'd prefer not to eat my dinner off someone's cleavage."

"No naked women. No masturbating men either. It's called Anna. Modern Dutch food, I think. It's supposed to be really good. It got a high rating on TripAdvisor. But is there anything you don't eat? I should have checked with you first. I was going to text you but I didn't have your number." Is he nervous?

"Sounds great," I say. "I eat everything. Well, most things." No need to go into my "kosher" laws right here.

"What about barbecue pumpkin seeds? They're on the menu. Have you ever had those?"

"I have not," I say. "I'm willing to try, though." But I'm thinking: He checked the menu? He put that much effort into finding us a place to eat? Barbecue pumpkin seeds? Is that a thing? Are we a thing?

"After you," he says.

We climb down the stairs, slowly. Downstairs, he takes my hand, setting my fingers on fire.

Yes. This is definitely a date.

Our table is at the back of the restaurant, near the windows, overlooking the medieval church square at the edge of the red-light district. It's still light out, but there are already drunken bachelor and bachelorette parties spilling past us.

The restaurant itself is very sleek. Each row of tables is on its own level, descending toward the windows, so that walking toward our table feels like we were going down steps. Round brass light fixtures hang from the ceiling, the chairs are cube-shaped, and the floors are shiny wood.

We order two glasses of sauvignon blanc from the wine menu, but I laugh when the waiter brings them.

"What's so funny?" Jackson asks.

"I've never ordered wine at a fancy restaurant before," I admit.

"Really?"

"Yes!"

"You're not a drinker?" He leans toward me and lowers his voice. "Just a pot smoker?"

"I'm not a pot—"

"I'm kidding," he says. "I could tell you're not a pot smoker."

"Well, the drinking age *is* twenty-one in America."

"No fake ID?"

"No," I say.

"I can't imagine college with no legal booze. Molson beer sponsors everything at McGill. I live in Molson Hall. The gym is the Molson Stadium. Molson practically comes out of the drinking fountains. And the showers."

I smile. "Crazy. I'm sure you guys get lots of work done."

"You'd be surprised," he says, smiling and picking up his wine glass.

"What are you studying?" I ask, putting my napkin on my lap.

"I'm doing a humanities degree," he says, taking a sip. "It's basically liberal arts. You?"

"English lit, probably."

A woman wearing a penis-shaped hat runs by our window.

"Only in Amsterdam," I say, lifting my glass. "Cheers?"

"*Proost*," he says, smiling at me. "That's cheers in Dutch."

"*Proost*," I repeat, smiling back. Our eyes lock, we clink glasses.

To start, we order the barbecue pumpkin seeds, or the *pompoen soorten can de bbq*, to share.

"What do you think?" he asks, reaching for one from the plate between us.

"Interesting," I say. "I'll have to remember to make this on Halloween."

"Do you dress up?" he asks.

"I did this year," I say, my cheeks burning.

"As what? You look embarrassed."

"I am. My friend Kat convinced me to dress up as an emoji with her. You know the dancing girls who are holding hands? We wore black leotards and cat ears. And we—"

"Held hands?" He laughs.

"Yeah. Don't tell Leela. She would totally make fun of me. What did you dress up as?"

"Myself," he says.

"Oh, you're *that* guy. Too cool for school?"

"That's me."

"Maybe you can get one of those penis hats for next year. You'd kill it."

"I'll look into it," he says, as the waiter takes our empty plate and puts down Jackson's burger and my cod and couscous.

"So that's the second time you've told me not to tell Leela something," he says, picking up his burger, which looks delicious on its brioche bun.

"Is it?" I ask, swallowing a piece of cod and couscous. Mmm. Crispy. "I just know she'd make fun of me. She has a thing about emojis."

"And pot," he says.

"Yes." I take another bite. "She's not a fan of either. She is a big fan of Matt, though."

"Oh, I know," he says. "She never leaves his side."

I take a sip of wine. "You make her sound like a stalker."

"No, I didn't mean it like that. I like Leela. She's funny. And he was—is—really into her. He just also needed some time on his own, you know?"

"Ava, you mean?" I ask.

"Ava," he repeats. "Which, for the record, I did not encourage."

"Did you discourage?" I ask.

He hesitates. "No."

I don't love his answer, but I appreciate the honesty. "Shouldn't you have?"

"Maybe. But I'm glad I didn't."

I take another bite of food. "Why's that?"

He raises his eyebrows. "If I had, then you would be home for the summer, wouldn't you?"

"Nice save," I say, pointing at him with my fork. "So what do you think is going to happen now? Do you think they're back together?"

"Looks like it, doesn't it?" He smiles. "I hope you're not sick of me yet."

I smile back. My skin starts to tingle. "Not yet."

We walk slowly back to the hostel, hand in hand.

Men chanting a Spanish song walk by us. They're all wearing red undershirts. I suspect it is soccer-related but can't be sure.

We stand on one of the bridges. For a minute, we're the only ones here.

"I had a great time tonight," he says.

"Me too."

He leans closer toward me.

"I like you," he says.

I smile. "Good."

"Do you like me?" he asks.

"Are we in kindergarten?" I take a step closer toward him.

"No. We're in Amsterdam. It's very grown-up here."

"I'd say."

We're only a few inches apart now. His eyes are liquid brown.

He steps even closer.

Am I going to do this? Yes. I'm pretty sure I am.

I take the final step toward him and his arms are around me and mine are around him and his lips are soft and then harder and stronger.

Sparks burn through me. I want this. I want him.

"Whoa," he says, pulling back. "I wasn't expecting that."

I'm out of breath. "Seriously? I feel like that was totally expected."

He laughs. "No, I guess I was expecting *that*. I just wasn't expecting it to be so . . . whoa. Can we do that again?"

"Yes."

He pulls me back toward him.

We walk, making out as we go. We can't keep our hands off each other.

"Where are we going?" I ask.

"Hostel?"

"I'm in a bunk room."

"I'm not."

"But what if Leela and Matt are using it?"

"We have to get there first," he says.

"Let's go!" I grab his hand and we run fast, laughing, together.

We reach the hostel and buzz. When we're let in, we hurry up the steps. Halfway up, I push him against the wall and nibble on his neck.

"You're killing me," he says.

"I know," I say.

His hand trails down my back and leg.

Oh God. My whole body is burning. "Third floor?" I ask.

"Mm-hm. Here," he says, fumbling for his key.

And then we hear voices inside.

"I hate you! You know that? I hate you!" It's Leela.

Crap.

"You're being crazy!" Matt yells.

"You always say I'm being crazy. Women aren't crazy just because they have feelings!"

"You always have feelings!"

"Well, I have to have enough for both of us since you don't seem to have any!"

I look at Jackson. "This is not good."

He shakes his head.

"What do you want from me?" we hear Matt yell.

"I want you to say you're sorry for being an idiot! I want you to put me first! I want you to care about what I want!"

"Then will you stop talking?"

"Go to hell, Matt. This is so over."

The door flies open and she sees us standing there, dumbstruck. "Sydney!"

"Are you okay?" I ask.

She wipes tears from her eyes. "No. He hasn't changed at

all. He's a drunk idiot who doesn't give a shit about me, and I want to leave right now. I hate this place. This whole city smells disgusting."

I look at Jackson. He looks at me. I look back at Leela. "Come on," I say, and put my arm around her.

"Sorry," I mouth to Jackson.

He nods but makes a sad face.

Leela's fists are clenched as she stomps up the stairs.

I unlock the door. Two men and two women are inside, chatting in Russian in the corner. They turn to look at us when we walk in. "*Privyet*," the woman says.

"They can't tell us to leave," Leela exclaims. "It's our room too."

"I think that means hello," I whisper to Leela. "It just *sounds* like private." I gently pull her toward her bed. "Sit down. Do you want to tell me what happened?"

"He's just . . . he's impossible," she says. "I don't know what I was thinking. What's the definition of insanity again? Doing the same thing again and again and expecting a different outcome?"

"Yes," I say.

"Well, then I'm insane. I keep thinking he's going to be a good boyfriend, but he's not. He's a joke."

"I'm sorry," I say.

She looks up at me. "Hold on. What's happening with you and Jackson? How was your night?"

"Don't worry about me and Jackson," I say, not wanting

her to feel worse. "Tell me what Matt said."

"That he doesn't want to go to Paris with me. That he wants to go to Berlin with Jackson. He'd rather drink beer than have a romantic few days with his girlfriend. He said maybe we could meet up later. *Maybe?* I can't believe I followed him here. What's wrong with me? Why am I so pathetic?"

"You are not," I say, hugging her. "Matt is a jerk." And I guess we will not be traveling as a foursome after all. Goodbye, Jackson. I think of the way he kissed me earlier, and can't help but feel sad.

"Can we leave in the morning?" she asks.

"So soon?"

She nods. "I need to get out of here."

"Sure. Of course. I'll just text Kat and let her know that we're coming."

"No," Leela says. "I don't think I can face Paris yet. Too much romance. Can we go somewhere else? For a bit? Please?"

I want to be understanding, but how many times are we going to change our plans? "Where do you want to go?"

"Not Berlin."

I sigh. "Okay. We're in Europe—there are a million other places to go. Let me check the book. We'll go somewhere that's on the way to Paris. Okay?"

"Mmmph."

"I'll find somewhere we can go. Promise."

"Tomorrow morning?"

"Yes."

"Thank you. You're the best. You really are." She turns onto her stomach and closes her eyes. "I need to go to sleep. I feel sick."

"Don't worry," I say soothingly. "I'll figure it out."

"I love you, Syd."

"I love you, too."

"I'm so glad you're here."

"I know." I kiss the top of her head. "I'm going to ask the lobby guy for suggestions."

I take my phone and my travel book and slip back outside the dorm. I take a few steps down the stairs and stop in front of their room.

I knock on the door, lightly.

No answer.

I guess I'm not saying good-bye?

I take the next flight down to the common room.

Jackson is sitting on one of the couches. I feel lighter already. "Hey," I say.

He stands up. "Hey."

"Well, that was a hot mess," I say.

"Yeah. If only we'd gotten to the room faster," he says.

I sit down beside him.

He puts his arm around me and pulls me into him. "So this is it?"

"I think this is it," I say softly. "We're off in the morning."

"To where?"

"Unclear. I'm thinking I'm in the mood for waffles."

"Bruges?"

"Yup."

"I hear it's nice," he says. He stares at me. "I'm glad I met you."

"I'm glad I met you, too," I say.

He sighs and leans back. "I'm guessing our paths are not going to cross again this trip?"

"Probably not," I say. I look around the room. No one is here but the Irish lobby attendant, and he's facing the other way.

I lean in and kiss him.

It goes on. And on. Until I pull back.

"Can I get your number?" he breathes. "For the next time I'm in Maryland?"

"You've been to Maryland?"

"No," he says. "Do you ever come to Montreal? Or Vancouver? No, you said you've never been to Canada."

I shake my head. I don't want to give him my number. What's the point? So he can not text and then I can feel bad and imagine him hooking up with someone in Berlin? We didn't even sleep together. We'll never see each other again. "Maybe we should leave us here."

He blinks. "Just like this?"

"Yes."

"Okay," he says hoarsely.

"We'll always have Amsterdam," I say, and give him another kiss.

"And London." He kisses me.

"And London," I repeat. "Good night," I say. I kiss him once more and then get up. I walk up the stairs. I don't look back.

BRUGES, BELGIUM

The Basics: The kingdom of Belgium is a smallish country south of the Netherlands, north of France, and west of Germany. The people speak Dutch, French, and German.

Go have a waffle. Immediately. Do not stop at go. Don't stop to use the bathroom. Run!

"Maybe he'll stay in Berlin," Leela says as we streak through the countryside on the train. "He'll decide it's his favorite city, that he loves Volkswagens and sauerkraut too much to ever go home. And then I'll never have to see him again."

"Anything is possible," I say. "I've never had sauerkraut."

"Did I totally mess up your itinerary?"

"Well . . . not really. We're off by two days. We can still take the overnight train to Berlin from Paris."

"No way," she says. "I don't want to go to Berlin anymore. At all. What if they're still there? Forget it."

"Okay," I say, trying not to get annoyed. "So no Berlin. And then probably no Prague since it's close to Berlin and kind of out of the way otherwise. Maybe we could go to Barcelona? What do you think about Barcelona?"

"I like the sound of Barcelona," she says. "And we speak some Spanish. Remember Señora Poncé and that days of the week song?" she asks, before breaking into song. "*Los días de la semana son . . .*"

"*Siete, siete,*" I finish. "I do. Except they mostly speak Catalán in Barcelona. But still. Paris and then Barcelona. Perfect."

"Great." She heaves a sigh of relief. "But I am sorry I messed up the plan. I'm the pathetic girl who follows her boyfriend from place to place and messes up her life. I'm a stalker."

I stretch my legs out in front of me, thinking about my conversation with Jackson last night. "You're not a stalker. He was your first love. You wanted to believe in him."

"But is he not the worst boyfriend ever? He doesn't take anything seriously! He vomited on me! He hooked up with a stripper in front of me! He volunteered for it! Even Jackson didn't raise his hand!"

I could not imagine Jackson ever raising his hand for something like that. He would never be such a try-hard.

"Tell me more about what Matt said last night," I say. "He wanted to travel with Jackson?"

"Yeah. He said maybe we could meet up at the end of the

trip. But he also said he thought we should be able to hook up with other people."

"What? Together? Like an orgy?"

She looks horrified. "No! You've spent too much time in Amsterdam. He thought we should go our separate ways after Amsterdam, and that if something happened, no big deal, we'd get back together later."

"He wanted to have an open relationship?"

"Is that what it's called?"

"I think so," I say.

"Then yes. He wants to sleep with other girls and then sleep with me again. You know, pick up HPV and gonorrhea and then pass it over to me. How nasty is that?"

"Pretty nasty," I agree.

"He wants to be open to experiences." She puts experiences in air quotes. "He doesn't want to have any regrets." Regrets goes in air quotes, too. "I blame Jackson."

I flush. "Seriously?"

"Yes! Seriously! Jackson has probably slept with ten girls since . . ." Her jaw drops. "You didn't sleep with him last night, right? You barely told me about your night! First I force you to go out with him and then I ruin your night. I really am the worst."

"Don't worry about it," I say.

"But what happened?"

"Nothing," I say. My cheeks heat up.

She laughs. "Liar."

"Fine. Yes. But not much. We kissed a little."

"You did? Shut up! Is he as good a kisser as everyone says?"

"He is a pretty good kisser," I admit.

"Practice makes perfect, I suppose," she says. "I hope you don't have gonorrhea."

"You can't get gonorrhea from kissing!"

"I know. I'm kidding."

I can still feel the kiss. It was a good kiss. A *really* good kiss.

She leans closer to me. "So do you think you would have slept with him if I hadn't freaked out and ruined your hot night?"

I think about his hands. "I definitely think we were heading in that direction."

"Then it's probably a good thing I stopped it. You don't want to be just another notch in his belt, do you?"

I roll my eyes. "Did you *really* just use the expression 'notch in belt'?"

"I totally did."

"What does that even mean? Why would anyone make a notch in someone's belt?"

"In cowboy days they used to make a notch in your belt if you killed someone," she says.

"Why do you even know that?" I ask.

She shrugs.

"What about my belt? He would have made a nice notch

in that. I only have two notches. And they aren't even good notches. I'm not absolutely sure the Adam notch counts since it didn't go all the way in." I sigh. "I definitely wanted to sleep with Jackson last night."

I can't stop thinking about him. I can still feel his lips. I'm sure in a few days that won't be the case. A feeling is like a bruise. After a day or two it'll be gone.

"And anyway," I say, "yesterday you were throwing me at him. Today you think I'm lucky I escaped?"

"I've come to my senses. Not that it matters now." She yawns. "I barely slept at all last night."

"I heard you tossing," I say. I don't mention that the dark circles under her eyes are a giveaway.

"Did you find a hostel for tonight?" she asks.

"Not yet," I say, looking back at my *Travel Europe*. "The two places they list are already booked. Since it's kind of last minute."

She shrugs. "We'll find something."

"And by *we*, you mean *me*."

"I can do it," she says, taking her phone out of her blue bag. "I don't mind."

"Okay, great. Can you look up Huiswaarts?"

She stares at her phone vacantly. "Hise warts?"

"No. H–U–I–S–W . . ."

She blinks repeatedly.

"Never mind," I say. "I got it. I have Wi-Fi here anyway. Why don't you take a nap?"

171

"I look like crap, huh?"

"A nap would be good for you," I say. "I'll find us some-thing. Don't worry."

We get off the train at eleven. I hike my backpack onto my back, and Leela drags her duffel behind her.

"There's a hostel we can walk to from here," I say. "It's in the town. I got us two beds in the dorm."

"You're the best."

"At least we'll save some money."

"Okay. That's good. I've spent way too much cash on sex shows in the last few days."

I laugh. "That's not a sentence I ever thought I'd hear you say."

"Me neither."

Our hostel looks like a giant dorm.

After checking in, we climb the staircase and use our key cards to enter.

There are five bunk beds. Four of them look like they're in use.

Leela drops her bag. "What now? Nap?"

"You just napped! It's time to go out."

"And do what?"

"Explore. We're in Bruges, the most fun city in Belgium! Come on," I say, my voice extra bouncy. "You need to cheer up."

"But I feel like shit." She ties her hair back in a ponytail.

"I know. You just broke up with your boyfriend. But! Are you ready for the but? It's a pretty good but."

"What's the but?"

"The but is that we're in the land of chocolate. Belgian chocolate! That's like the best kind of chocolate! You just broke up with your boyfriend, and we're in the land of chocolate! Come on. Put your shoes back on and let's go get some."

Bruges reminds me of Amsterdam with its canals, but the houses and architecture are a lot more medieval. The roads are cobblestoned and all the houses and buildings have excessively pointy roofs and are a golden color. But we're quickly sidetracked from enjoying the scenery by a waffle stand.

"That," Leela says, pointing. "I want that."

"Who wouldn't?"

There's not even a line.

We order one waffle each with ice cream and strawberries and something called pearl sugar.

We sit down beside a green-bronzish statue of a Flemish painter named Jan van Eyck.

I lift my plastic fork and dig in.

"Omigod." I swoon. "This is it. This is what I've been searching for my whole life." Pearl sugar is like chunks of melty sweetness.

"Do waffles always taste like this?" Leela asks, talking

with her mouth full. "I should be ordering these every day. Why am I not ordering these every day? For breakfast, lunch, and dinner?"

"I don't think they taste like this in Maryland. Maybe in Montreal, but definitely not in Maryland. Clearly I should marry a Belgian, bring him to America, and start a waffle shop with him." I savor the last bite. "I think I want another one."

"Me, too," she says.

We order another one. This time we mix it up with jam and Chantilly cream. Mmm.

A family with small Belgian children passes us. They're super cute and wearing brightly patterned outfits and holding hands. I look for a single Belgian man I could marry and import. We'd be very happy with our waffles and adorably patterned children.

"A third?" I ask when we're done.

"Don't be crazy," she says.

"Okay, fine," I say. "But can we come back for dinner?"

"Yes," she says. "Where to now?"

"Um . . ." I flip through the book. "I don't know what you want to do. Why don't you have a look and choose something?"

"Can we just walk around?" she asks, ignoring the book.

It's starting to seem like she's never going to look at this book. I'm going to have to organize and plan the entire trip. Isn't this why her parents wanted her to travel in the first place? So she could learn to do stuff on her own? How did she survive the year at college? Did her sister and Matt do everything for her? How will she become more independent if I do everything for her? Should I say something?

Maybe today isn't the day for that.

I take a deep breath instead. I feel the sun on my face. It's warm, but not too hot. Like the perfect waffle. I inhale the sweet smell of sugar.

"Okay," I say, and stand up. Oh wow, I'm full. "Let's go that way. I'm going to need to pee really soon."

We pass by a beer shop and a chocolatier and a touristy store.

"Let me get a snow globe," I say. I think about Jackson. He helped me pick the last two. But no more. Now I'll have to rely on Leela.

"This one?" I ask, pointing to one with some sort of bell tower in it. It says Belfort of Bruges on it.

"This one's cuter," she says, picking up one that's three times the size and has little buildings in it.

"They need to be small," I say, and buy the first one.

We keep walking until we end up in what my book says is the Markt, a pedestrian-only square. In the center is another green-bronzish statue of two guys. Around us are flags, as well as restaurants and stores, and the actual Belfort of Bruges. It's a tall medieval tower overlooking everything.

"Want to take a picture of me in front of the Belfort while holding the Belfort?" I ask. "It'll be very meta."

"If you want," she says.

I hand her my phone and smile. "Waffle!" I say.

Three cute guys walk by us. They look like college students. I try to listen to hear where they're from. Two are wearing sleeveless shirts that show off their nicely sculpted arm muscles.

I recognize the language from Hebrew class.

"Israelis," I say, motioning with my chin. "You like Israelis. Let's follow them! Let's have an adventure!"

She shrugs. "I'm still pretty tired. Can we go back to the hostel?"

The taller one is looking at us. "Are you sure?" I ask. "We're being ogled."

"I'm not in the mood to be ogled."

"Even by a super-hot Israeli?"

"Even by."

Wet blanket. I feel bad as soon as I think it. She just broke up with a guy she loves. She's sad. But still . . .

"Want to take a horse-drawn carriage home?" I ask, pointing to one.

"No."

I sling my arm through hers. "Okay," I say. I give up. "Let's go back. Oh! Oh!"

"What?"

"I know just what will cheer you up!"

She raises an eyebrow. "What?"

"A waffle!"

She laughs. "I think you're right."

We eat one more waffle and call it a day.

Back in the hostel, there's a beer tasting at the bar.

"Want to go?" I ask.

She shakes her head.

Okay, then. We return to our room and get ready for bed.

"I'm not really feeling Bruges," she says, stretching out on her bed.

"Why?" I ask as I climb up my ladder. "It's beautiful. It's the land of waffles and chocolate. And we haven't even tried the french fries yet."

"I don't know. It's depressing."

"How could this possibly be depressing?"

"We're in the middle of nowhere," she says. "We don't know anyone here. We could get killed and no one would have any idea. We're in this town that time forgot in a dirty hostel that hasn't been cleaned in months. And I've been wearing the same T-shirt for three days."

"Yeah. We should get on that," I say. "We should try to find a laundromat tomorrow. Also, the Israelis. They could be staying at this hostel."

"No. I'm too tired to make conversation with strange men."

"They probably don't speak English. You won't have to make conversation. You can just smooch them."

"Not interested," she says. The bed creaks as she tries to get comfortable.

If she's going to want to just lie around for the next three and a half weeks, I'm going to start getting really upset. I didn't come all this way and abandon my family for that. I sigh. "What exactly do you want to do, then? We have to do something. And it better be *fun*." I can hear the irritation creeping into my voice.

"Eat stinky cheese and macarons," she says.

My heart lifts. "Yeah?"

She nods. "Yeah. I think it's time for Paris."

PARIS, FRANCE

The Basics: Paris is the city of love. French is the language of love. Euros are the currency of love.

You probably don't want to go with your best friend if she just broke up with her boyfriend.

"Where do we get off?" Leela asks. After an almost-three-hour train ride, we're now on the subway. Excuse me. *Le Métro*.

"Next stop," I say. "Cluny – La Sorbonne."

Leela is watching a couple make out on the seat beside her. "And you're sure your friend Kat doesn't mind us staying with her?"

"I'm sure," I say. "I can't wait for you guys to meet."

It's incredibly strange to me that Kat and Leela have never met. When Leela came home for school breaks, Kat was always back in NYC.

179

My friendships with them couldn't be more different. Growing up, Leela and I lived in a friendship bubble. We had other friends, but they were always secondary. Backups. No one had ever competed.

Kat brought me out into the world. She talks to everyone. She loves everyone.

As soon as we get off the train, we're in a park that Kat said had Wi-Fi. *Travel Europe* says it's called the Cluny Medieval Gardens. We walk through the metal gate and see a beautiful passageway blanketed in flowers and trees, leading to a castlelike museum. People are sitting on benches eating baguette sandwiches.

I message her. **Here!**

Paris! We're in Paris! *The* Paris! The sun is shining and the air is hot and smells like sweat and croissants and perfume. Swarming around us are men, women, children, teenagers, and tourists on the move.

I look down at my phone for the three dots. There are none.

I check to make sure that my Wi-Fi is working. It seems to be.

"She's not answering?" Leela asks.

"No."

"Do you know her address?"

"No. She said she would meet us here."

"It's hot," Leela says.

It *is* hot. Really hot. My bra is sticking to my skin. My

T-shirt is sticking to my bra.

Yet on the other side of the gate, the men and women are still wearing scarves. Scarves! In this heat! Tied around their necks. Thin, gauzy scarves, but still. They're also wearing big sunglasses and dresses and tight suits and sandals and heels.

Inside the garden it smells sweet, like flowers. I spot rose bushes closer to the museum.

Coming to meet you! she writes back. **Gime 5!** 🖤 🖤 🖤 🖤

Leela looks over my shoulder at the message. "She uses a lot of emojis."

"She does."

Leela leans on her upright duffel bag. "And she spelled gimme wrong."

"Is there a right way to spell gimme? It's not really a word."

Leela shrugs. "It's in the dictionary."

I have a moment of dread. Is Leela going to be difficult the whole trip? Is she going to be a bitch to Kat?

I try to calm myself down. Even if she is a bitch to Kat, Kat won't be a bitch to her. Kat makes friends with everyone. Everyone likes Kat.

It's going to be fine.

"Aren't your shoulders killing you?" Leela asks. "How long is she going to be?"

"I'll just take off my pack," I say.

"The ground has bird poop on it," she says. "Put it on my bag. At least I have wheels."

"No, it's fine," I say.

"I smell," Leela says. "I need a shower. Why is she home now anyway? It's two o'clock. Shouldn't she be at work? What does she do again?"

"She interns at a gallery. She doesn't work on Thursdays," I say.

Just then we hear a screeching, "SYDNEY!"

The next thing I know, Kat's arms are wrapped around me. Her thin brown hair is wet and in a bun on top of her head, and smells sweet, like lavender shampoo.

"You're here! You're here!" She screams, not caring that people turn to look at us. "I can't believe you're here! This is spectacular! I'm so excited! I love you!"

"Yay! Hi! I missed you!" I say. My body relaxes. It's Kat! She makes everything fun. Everyone in her orbit gets sucked in. That's just the way it is. She's like a big black hole, except she's made of light. She's a sun.

She hugs me again, tighter.

Then she pulls back and throws her arms around Leela. "Hi! You must be Leela! I am so excited to meet you! I've heard so much about you!"

"I've heard a lot about you too," Leela says. She sounds like she's talking to a kid she doesn't want to babysit.

"You look just like your pictures," Kat says. "I've been following your trip online. How was Bruges? Did you go to Chez Vincent? They have the best fries. Like, amazing."

"No," Leela says. "We didn't make it there."

"Did you go to the Tara in Amsterdam? I love that place."

"No," I say.

"I wasn't a fan of Amsterdam," Leela says.

"Oh," Kat says, nodding. "That's too bad. It's definitely not for everyone."

"No," Leela says tightly, "it's not."

"But we are so excited for Paris," I say quickly. I don't want Kat to think the edge in Leela's voice has anything to do with her. I want them to love each other.

"Okay, follow me, guys—my apartment is just two blocks that way. Do you need help with your bags?"

"No," Leela says for the both of us. "We're fine."

I watch her studying Kat.

Kat is five foot three, thin, and flat-chested. Clothes always look good on her. Right now she's wearing an orange sundress, diamond studs I know are real, and gold sandals. She manages to look totally comfortable, rich, and trendy all at once.

"I can't wait to show you Paris!" Kat says. "You're going to love it. Have you been here before, Leela?"

"No," she says.

"Fun! First timers!" She links her arms through both of ours.

"Have you been here before?" Leela asks Kat.

"Yup. Twice. When I was a kid. My mom loves Paris. It's

183

her favorite European city. So I guess you want to do all the tourist stuff? Eiffel Tower? Champs-Élysées? Louvre?"

"Yes," I say. "Definitely."

"And how long do I get you for? A week?"

"No," Leela says. "We're only here for a few days. Then we're going to Barcelona. Right, Syd?"

"That's the current plan. We fly out of Rome," I say.

Kat squeezes my hand. "I was just in Rome a few weeks ago for the weekend. I ate pasta three times a day and gained a hundred pounds."

That's unlikely considering Kat only weighs about a hundred pounds total.

"But it was so worth it," Kat continues. "You're not going to believe how good the food is. Here too. I am going to take you for macarons. They are the best things you will ever eat. Should we go now?"

My shoulders are about to collapse. "Can we stop at your place first? I wouldn't mind a shower. And to put our stuff down."

"Oh! Of course! Definitely. We'll do that first. And then we'll get macarons. I need to find a great place for dinner—something you'll love. What are you in the mood for? Something really French?"

"I wouldn't mind pizza, actually," Leela says.

"Pizza. Let me think."

"I can look in my guidebook," I offer.

"Sure," says Kat. "Let's play tourists!"

"We *are* tourists," Leela says.

Okay, then.

We follow Kat down the road and then turn left on a street called the Quai de Montebello. It's a big street, filled with buses and cars and motorcycles and people walking. To the right are shops and restaurants and to the left are artists painting on easels and postcard stands. Behind them is the Seine and behind the river is the Notre Dame Cathedral.

"It's majestic," I say. The cathedral looks like it should be in a fairy tale.

"We'll go by later," Kat says.

We turn onto a street called Rue de Bièvre.

"Almost there," Kat says.

This street is narrow, yet there are restaurants and small shops lining the ground floors and apartments on top. They all have adorable little Juliet balconies. I love Juliet balconies. When I grow up I will live in a house with a Juliet balcony. No. With two Juliet balconies.

"Here we are!" she cries. "Home sweet home!"

She types in a code and when it buzzes, pushes the door open.

The stairs are thin and creaky and wooden. "Let me take the bottom of your suitcase," she says to Leela. "We'll carry it together."

"It's okay," Leela says, but Kat helps her anyway.

"It's the first floor. Which in France really means the second floor."

I'm almost surprised that *this* is where she lives. The building looks decrepit. Knowing Kat, I expected her to be in something grander.

"Here we are!" she says, putting my bag down in front of a door. It's the only one on this floor. She takes out a giant brass key from her pocket and turns the lock. "Welcome!"

The apartment we walk into is not decrepit at all.

It's gorgeous.

A beautiful crystal chandelier hangs in the entranceway. There's a small kitchen on the left, and then we step into a living room with sky-high beamed ceilings. Three open windows look over the cobbled street. They all have Juliet balconies. Yay! The linen curtains are pulled back and sway in the breeze.

"The two bedrooms are over there," she says, pointing to her right. "And this couch turns into a bed so one of you can sleep here. It gets kind of bright in here in the morning, though, I should warn you."

Leela's eyes are as big as mine are.

This place is amazing.

"Sorry there's no air-conditioning," Kat adds. "It was, like, impossible to find a rental with air in this area. I don't know what's wrong with Parisians. But at least there are fans. And bidets! Have you ever used a bidet?"

"No," we both say.

"You have to, it's hysterical. Let me show you the bathroom. There's only one, so we all have to share. Sorry, that's gonna suck. But two baths were hard to find, too."

We follow her to the bathroom, and she throws the door open. "See! That thing that looks like a short water fountain? It's a bidet! I totally wanna get one in my bathroom at home. I swear, it's changed my life."

The bathroom is entirely white marble. There's a chandelier in here too. The bathtub is small and deep, but more of a shower. There's a handheld spray and a square rain shower attached to the ceiling and a glass door.

Hair products line the counter.

Leela doesn't say anything, but her eyes are the size of saucers. She looks impressed. Is she impressed? How could she not be impressed? This place is amazing. And free.

"Hey, Kat," I say, "what's the deal with the double flushers? They're all over Europe."

"The big one's for poop," she says. "They have different water pressure."

"Aha," I say. "Mystery solved."

"They're becoming a thing in America, too. Let me show you the extra bedroom," Kat says, and motions us to follow her down the hall. Black-and-white photographs line the walls.

"Whose place is this anyway?" I ask.

"No idea. My mom found it on Onefinestay. It's like Airbnb but all the places are checked out beforehand and cleaned regularly so you don't end up in some dump. When Avery checked us in—she's the Onefinestay woman, she's

American, just graduated from Duke—she brought me this adorable basket of chocolates. It was the sweetest thing. Want?"

"Want what?" Leela asks.

"One of the chocolates," she says.

"You still have them?"

"Yes! Somewhere. Are you hungry?"

"I am kind of hungry," I say. "But the shower is the priority."

"No problem. You guys shower and change and then we'll go out."

"For dinner?" I ask.

"They eat at like nine here, but we'll have a coffee and a snack and meet Alain later."

"Your boyfriend?" Leela wonders. She's running her hand against the velvety white duvet cover.

"What? No! He's my boss. I have a boyfriend back home."

"Gavin," I say. "He's a sweetheart."

"He really is," she says dreamily. "We've been Face-Timing when he can get a signal. He's a counselor at a camp called Blue Springs this summer and their Wi-Fi sucks."

"How long have you been together?" Leela asks.

"Ten months. I met him in the dorm cafeteria like a week before I met Syd. Hey, Syd, did you find a place you want to go for dinner? Oh, you know what? I know where we should go. Chez Michelle. Pizza. You're going to love it. But go shower first. I can't wait to show you Paris."

★ ★ ★

"This is Saint Germain," Kat tells us. "It's pretty much the center of everything. There are, like, a million cafés and bookstores and museums and everything." She sips from her teeny tiny Parisian coffee cup.

We're all crunched together at an outdoor café. The tables are metal and small and round, as are the chairs. It's packed. Everyone is drinking coffee and smoking and watching the passersby.

I take a sip of coffee and try not to finish it all in one gulp. The cup reminds me of the tea set I had when I was six.

"It's so bitter," Leela says, taking a sip.

"You need to add sugar," Kat says.

"Is this the sugar?" she asks, picking up a long white tube.

"Yup."

Leela dumps the sugar in, mixes, takes a sip, and makes a face.

"What?" I ask.

"Now it's too sweet," she says.

The person at the table behind us blows a puff of smoke over our table.

Leela makes another face.

It's her fifth in the last hour.

Kat either doesn't notice or is pretending she doesn't notice. I remind myself that Leela's being difficult because she's sad and jealous. She is a *good* friend. She's always been a *good* friend.

"Everyone here smokes," Kat says. "Everyone. I bet their cigarette cartons don't have warnings about emphysema and death on them."

"So do you like it here?" I ask.

Kat nods. "I love it."

"You're not nervous?" Leela asks. "About"—she lowers her voice—"terrorists?"

"I'm from New York," Kat says. "I feel just as safe here as I do there."

"So not safe at all?" Leela asks.

Kat shrugs. "What are you going to do? You gotta live your life, you know? And anyway, I want to support Paris."

"Good points," I say. "So can we go walk around now? I want to see stuff! Paris!"

"Let's do it," Kat says. "Let's go shopping in the Marais. *L'addition, s'il vous plaît*," she says to the waiter. She pretends to sign in the air, the international gesture for 'bring me the check.'

He grunts and comes back a few minutes later.

"Let's go!"

We spend the next two hours walking. We weave our way through the cobblestoned streets and look at the old houses with shutters outside. Leela steers us to a makeup store called Mademoiselle bio, and we stop at a vintage boutique and buy almost matching clutches for only fifteen euros each. I get red, Leela gets black, and Kat gets bright blue. On the way home, I steer us to Shakespeare and Company, the famous English bookstore, to browse the books. I buy one called *Girls on Fire*, which is kind of how I feel in an excited, sparking, nervous way.

Then we go into a *patisserie* and taste a real macaron. Mine is pink and tastes like sugar and almonds and raspberries that dissolve in my mouth. We pass by a tourist shop and look at Eiffel Tower key chains. There are snow globes, too. I wish Jackson were here to help me choose.

I pick an Eiffel Tower one.

"Let's stop at the apartment and freshen up before dinner," Kat says.

"Is that a euphemism for using the bidet?" I ask.

Kat laughs. "If you'd like. I was going to wash my face and put on heels. But you can wash whatever you'd like to wash."

"I'm a bit afraid of bidets," I say.

"Oh, now you *have* to use it," Leela says. "It's a must. I don't think we can leave Paris without you using the bidet."

"Challenge accepted," I say. "Let's go use the bidet."

Tip: A bidet is not a water fountain.

I can't actually figure out the bidet. I turn it on, and the water sprays out in an arc but I can't tell how to sit on it. Or are you supposed to squat? I end up soaking the bottom of my dress and having to change.

"Is your dodo refreshed?" Leela asks on her way into the bathroom. She's known me long enough to know as a kid I referred to my vagina as my dodo. Because saying the word

191

vagina made me laugh. Also *vulva*. And I'm not sure I totally know which is which.

"Very refreshed," I say. "My dress is also very refreshed. Kat, did you say you're wearing heels?"

"Yes!" she calls out from her room.

"Does that mean that we're not walking?"

"I was going to call an Uber!"

"You guys have Uber here?" I ask.

"Of course we have Uber here. It's Paris! Uber is everywhere!" She pops into the hallway. "Omigod, I bought the cutest navy tube dress that would look amazing on you, Syd. You have to wear it tonight."

"I'll try it," I say.

She dives back into her room, grabs it, and hands it to me. Ooh. It's clean. And non-wrinkled. It has lived on a hanger. How I miss hangers. And clean-smelling clothes. And clothes that require dry cleaning.

I go into my room and slip it on over my head. It does look good. It makes me look French. Glam.

Something scrapes my neck and I realize it still has a tag. "Kat!" I go back into the hallway. "You've never even worn this! Are you sure you want me to wear it?"

"Totally sure," she says, studying me. "You look gorgeous in it. Just put on a pair of heels and you're ready."

"I don't have heels," I say. "I'm backpacking."

"No worries, I have," she says. "Yellow sandals would look perfect. You're a six, right?"

"Yeah," I say.

She comes back a second later with a pair of shiny yellow high-heeled sandals. "Do they fit?"

"A little big, but they'll be fine for tonight. Thank you!"

"I'm getting dressed. Back in a sec, gorgeous."

I step into the living room.

Leela is sitting on the couch. Staring sadly out the window.

"Hey," I say.

Startled, she looks me over. "You look . . . different."

"Good different?"

"I guess. You're like her Barbie," she says, crossing her arms. "You never let *me* help you get you ready."

"You never want to dress me," I say, sitting on the couch that is going to be her pullout bed.

"I can do your makeup," she says.

"Okay," I say, wanting her to cheer up. "Pick out a lipstick."

She studies my face, rummages through her bag, and pulls out one of her new purchases. "This will look good. Try it."

I apply it in the mirror. "What do you think?"

"Um . . . too dark for you. Let me see if I have something else. . . ." She rummages through her duffel bag. "Everything's such a mess I can't find anything. . . ."

I remove it with a tissue. "Don't worry about it. I don't need lipstick! I have my lip gloss."

"I want you to wear one," she insists. "I just need to find something that goes with your coloring. Something a little pinker . . ."

"Are you guys ready?" Kat asks, stepping into the living room. She's wearing an off-the-shoulder white minidress and green stilettos.

"Are those the same shoes the, um, dancer was wearing in Amsterdam?" Leela asks.

"Was she wearing Christian Louboutin?" Kat asks.

"Probably not," I say.

"Can I get the Uber?" Kat asks. "*On y va?*"

"Go for it," I say.

"I'm buying you a good lipstick color tomorrow," Leela tells me as we grab our new clutches.

"Okay," I say. If buying me a lipstick is going to make her happy, then I'm all for it.

Tip: Make sure to try escargots.

Escargots are snails. SNAILS.

Chez Michelle is in some hipster area called Canal Saint-Martin. There are a ton of students sitting by the canal drinking beer and smoking. Our table is outside, on a slant, overlooking the water. We order *le pizza margherita* and *vin rosé*.

"You drink rosé?" I ask Leela.

"Yes," she says. "It's practically white."

The crowd is buzzing, the breeze is blowing, and I am feeling great. I'm in Paris! Drinking wine!

I have already had a glass and a half. I am a little bit drunk.

Leela is laughing a bit more with a glass of wine in her, and she's telling the story of Matt and the sex club and making it sound kind of hilarious. She is sitting across from me and next to Kat. I think Kat could sense Leela's tenseness and organized the seating arrangement like that on purpose.

"What a jerk," Kat says, nodding. She is working hard to get Leela to warm up to her.

"Such a jerk," Leela repeats. "I'm lucky it's over."

"You so are," Kat says. "But here comes a new man. A great one. I hope he hits it off with one of you! Alain!" she hollers. "We're here!"

"I am not looking to deal with another guy's issues," Leela says to me. "You can have him."

I am not sure I am ready to meet a new man either, when I just almost slept with someone two nights ago.

But, hello. This man is *gorgeous*. Leela and I turn to see Kat waving at a tall, light-skinned, blond-haired, broad-shouldered Adonis. He's wearing a shiny slim-fitting gray suit and a shiny gray shirt, no tie. He looks like he's about twenty-one, maybe twenty-two.

"Alain!" she calls. "Come join us. Meet my friends Sydney and Leela."

"*Bonjour, mes chéries*," he says. Since the chair next to me is empty, he takes it. Excellent.

"*Bonjour!*" I say. I'm feeling flirty. Also tipsy.

"This is where you chose to come for dinner?" he asks.

"You come all the way to Paris to have pizza?"

"The pizza here is amazing," Kat says.

"Perhaps. I order you the escargots," he says. "It's delicious. Do you like escargots?"

"I've never had escargots," I admit. "But I am willing to try. I'm willing to try almost anything."

"Are you?" he asks, lifting an eyebrow.

I feel myself blush.

Kat laughs and raises both her eyebrows at me. She pulls out her phone and texts something. She gives me a look and motions to my purse.

She obviously just texted me, not realizing that I'm not on Wi-Fi. I shake my head.

She passes me her phone so I can see what she wrote.

Alain totally likes you! 😍 😉 He keeps staring at you! 👀

"*Peut-on avoir les escargots, s'il vous plaît?*" Alain asks the waiter.

"So," he says, turning to me. "Did your parents conceive you in Sydney?"

"They did not," I say with a laugh. "I'm named after a dead uncle."

"Uh, that is less romantic."

"It is," I agree. "Although I've heard he was a bit of a ladies' man."

Leela snorts and takes another sip of wine.

"I was in Sydney a few years ago, and it was *fantastique*," Alain says.

"Do you travel a lot?" I ask.

"Yes," he says. "When I can."

"Alain works at his parents' gallery, too," Kat says. "I report to him."

A few minutes later, the plate of escargots arrives. It looks completely disgusting. But! I will try it! Because I'm adventurous like that!

"Am I supposed to squeeze lemon on it?" I ask him.

"I'd need a bucket of lemon to eat that," Leela says, nose wrinkling.

"Oh, stop," Kat says. "I tried it last time I was here. We'll do it on the count of three. 'Kay?"

"'Kay," I say.

Alain stabs his fork into one of the snails and lifts it to my lips. "*Un. Deux. Trois,*" he says.

I hold his gaze and bite it off his fork.

I chew. And try not to gag.

"That is not good," I say.

Kat spits it into her napkin. "Yeah, I don't think I liked it last time either."

Leela laughs.

"You sure you don't want to try?" I ask her. "Didn't we make it look fantastic?"

"I'm sure," she says with a small smile.

We spend the next two hours continuing to eat and drink. When we ask for the check, Alain insists on paying.

"We should have ordered the champagne," Leela says

under her breath.

Yeah, if I'd known, I would have made a push for the champagne too. It can't get more French than that.

After dinner, the four of us walk along the water.

Somehow, Leela and Kat are up ahead, and Alain and I are behind.

"How long are you in Paris?" he asks. He pronounces it *Par-ee*.

"Only a few more days," I say. "Are you traveling this summer?"

"Yes," he says. "I'm going to visit my grandparents in Linz in two days. My mother is French but my father is Austrian. And then I go to Tuscany," he says.

"To collect more art?"

"No, for *vacances*. Uh . . . vacation," he says. "My family has a house near Castiglione della Pescaia. Tuscany is beautiful in the summer." He pronounces beautiful as beaut-ee-ful.

"I'm sure it is."

"I will be in America in October. I have meetings with Sotheby's in New York."

"You certainly are busy," I say.

"Not too busy to take you for dinner tomorrow night."

"Sorry?" I say, startled.

"I would like very much to take you for dinner tomorrow. Unless you have other plans?"

The hot French guy is asking me out? Is it already time

for me to have another kissing adventure? What do they call snogging in France?

Oh. French kissing. Obviously.

I look over at Leela, who's walking silently next to Kat.

I'm not sure she will love the idea of me leaving her. Actually, I'm pretty sure she'd hate it. And also, I'm not sure I'm ready to kiss someone new so quickly when I was just making out with Jackson two nights ago. "I'm sorry— I don't think I can leave my friends. But thank you. That would have been fun."

He puts his hand over his heart. "Do you have a boy-friend like Kat?"

"No, it's not that." Jackson is definitely not a boyfriend. I lower my voice. "My friend Leela just broke up with *her* boy-friend, and I don't want to abandon her in the city of *amour*."

"You are a good friend," he says solemnly. "Where are you going next?"

"We haven't finalized it yet," I say. "Probably Barcelona. We fly out of Rome."

"Oh! Well then you must come see me in Tuscany," he says.

"Leela and I are traveling together."

"You both must come. Plus Kat. I have many rooms. It is a beautiful property." He says beaut-ee-ful again.

"Thanks," I say. "Maybe we will."

A free and beaut-ee-ful place to stay in Tuscany is not a bad invitation.

We stop in front of the apartment. "*Enchanté*," he says, kissing me on both cheeks. He smells like aftershave.

I wonder if I should have said yes to the date.

"Good-bye," I say, and follow my friends inside the building.

"Omigod," Kat cries. "He's, like, in love with you. I knew you guys would hit it off. Did he ask you out for tomorrow?"

"He did," I say.

Leela's face clouds over.

"But I said no," I add quickly.

Kat frowns. "What? Why?"

I trail behind her on the stairs, extra careful in my heels. "Because we have plans for tomorrow. We're going to the Eiffel Tower! And the Arc de Triomphe! And we still haven't had fondue!"

"But that was your chance to have a fabulous fling on your European adventure!" Kat cries.

"I already had a fling on my European adventure," I say.

"She had two flings, actually," Leela says. "Don't forget Charlie."

"Charlie hardly counts," I say, giggling. "I kissed him and ran away."

"More details, please. And who was the second fling? Does he count? I love it!"

"Leela's ex-boyfriend's friend," I say. "And he counts."

"Oooooooh." Kat swoons. "Was he hot?"

"Very," I say.

"Are you going to see him again?" she asks.

"I doubt it," I say.

Kat makes a sad face. "Tragic."

"He's a man whore anyway," Leela says, with a wave of her hand. "She can do better."

"Then she should have hooked up with Alain!"

I laugh. "I'm not going to make out with a different guy in every city."

"Why not?" Kat asks. "Please let me live vicariously through you. Alain is amazing. And you look spectacular in that dress. You're keeping it."

"No!"

"Yes."

"But—"

"No buts."

"Thank you," I say, kissing her on the cheek.

Kat yawns. "I'm wiped. I can't believe they asked me to be at work tomorrow at nine. I wish I could play hooky with you. Are you sure you'll be all right?"

"We've navigated three other countries," Leela says, putting her arm through mine. "I think we'll figure it out."

Tip: Make your reservation to see the Eiffel Tower at least two months in advance.

Otherwise you'll be MOL! (Merde Out of Luck.)

★ ★ ★

The sun streaming through the windows wakes me up at eight the next morning. Leela is still sleeping. Her stuff is all over the living room, so I start tidying up. Kat won't care, but if you stay in someone's living room, you should probably not make it a total pigsty, right?

"Morning," Leela says. "What are you doing?"

"Folding your clothes," I say.

"I love you," she says. "Thanks."

Leela is very messy but not the kind of messy person who enjoys being messy. She loves things clean. She just doesn't seem to know how to clean. Whenever I was at her house, her mother was always tidying up for her. "I don't know how you find anything," I say.

"I don't," she says. "And everything I brought is dirty. We have to do laundry tonight."

We say good-bye to Kat and then put on our Toms, shorts, T-shirts, and sunglasses. It's a walking day. A hot walking day. And we have a lot to see. The Eiffel Tower. The Arc de Triomphe. Notre Dame.

We're saving the Louvre for tomorrow.

We walk across town to the seventh arrondissement where the Eiffel Tower is. It's a ridiculously long walk, but at least we get to see the city.

Surrounding the tower is the Champ de Mars, which is a grass meadow. Tons of people are sitting around on picnic blankets or playing ball. "Amazing," I say, looking up. "It's so tall!" I check my book for details. "It's over a thousand feet. Did you know it was built to be an entranceway to the World's Fair?"

"I did not," Leela says. "I guess that's why it looks like an entranceway."

"The lookout is the highest in Europe! This is so exciting!"

"But look at those lines," she says, taking off her sunglasses. "How long is it going to take to get up there?"

"I don't know," I say. I have a bad feeling about this. I make my way toward the front of the line, and get the attention of one of the security guards. "*Bonjour*," I say. "*Excusez-moi?* How long is the line?" My French is pretty bad.

"*Quatre heurs et demis*," he says, barely looking at me.

"Four and half hours," Leela translates.

Shoot. "Are you kidding me?"

"*Non*," he responds. "*Peut-être cinq heurs*."

"I really want to take a picture from the top," Leela says.

"Oh, look, there's a restaurant," I say. "Maybe we can make reservations to eat? Then we'll get up. We can come back tomorrow if there's nothing today."

"Good idea," she says.

I lead us to the restaurant awning. "*Bonjour!* Leela, I'm guessing your French has gotten even better since you moved to Montreal? Can you ask if we can get a table in the next two days at the restaurant? Any time."

She translates for me.

203

The woman laughs and responds.

"They're booked until November," Leela translates.

"Crap," I say.

"*Merde*," Leela says. "I really, really want to see it."

"So let's wait," I say.

"Seriously?" she asks. "You want to wait four and a half hours?"

No, I do not want to wait four and a half hours. But I want her to be happy. "If you want to see it, we'll stay."

"I'm not waiting four and a half hours."

"Maybe it won't actually take that long. Why don't we join the line and see if it moves?"

We join the back of the line. We wait twenty minutes. It doesn't move.

Leela sighs. "I wish we had made a reservation."

My back tenses. As head planner, I can't help but feel guilty.

Leela hops from foot to foot. "This doesn't seem worth it. Let's get out of here."

"No," I insist. "If you want to go inside, let's stay."

"Forget it."

"No! You want to go inside!"

"No, I want to get out of here. Come on."

She starts walking in the other direction and I follow.

As we walk through the park, we pass a middle-aged couple fondling each other on the grass. A second later, we pass two teenage boys kissing.

"Is it my imagination or are people making out every-where?" Leela asks.

"I see it too," I say. "It is the city of love."

"What does that even mean? What's so romantic about this place? Waiting in line for four and a half hours to climb a metal structure?"

"You're right. Nothing is romantic about Paris. I hate Paris," I say.

She laughs. "Everywhere I look people are kissing. I kind of want to punch them in the face. And then take a nap."

"We can go home if you're tired," I offer. I still feel bad that she didn't get to see the Eiffel Tower.

"Never mind. I just hate romance. Let's keep going. Where to next? Why haven't we had any cheese yet?" She claps her hands. "Oh! Oh! Can we go to that famous street?"

"Can you be more specific?"

"You know. Where all the designer stores are."

I look it up in the book. Oh! "Champs-Élysées. And hey, it seems to lead right to the Arc de Triomphe. And that has a view."

"Perfect," she says.

"So we'll walk down the street and it will be amazing and we'll feel glamorous and we'll buy scarves—"

"It's way too hot for scarves."

I wave her comment away. "And then we'll climb up the Arc and you can take glorious pictures that we can post everywhere looking windblown and fabulous."

"I do not look fabulous," she argues. "I'm all sweaty."

"Sweaty, windblown, and fabulous," I say. "Let's go."

The Champs-Élysées is even more glamorous than we imagined.

It's also packed with tourists. Tourists carrying Louis Vuitton bags and wearing high heels. One woman in a full leopard pantsuit and gold stilettos almost knocks us over with a giant Chanel bag.

"How can they shop in those?" Leela wonders. "My feet hurt, and I'm wearing flats!"

"Maybe French women are born with stronger calf muscles," I say.

"It's like Fifth Avenue in New York," she says. "But Frenchier. More cafés and more perfumeries."

"Yeah," I say. I've only been to New York once.

"Look!" she shrieks. "Sephora!"

She practically skips inside, eyes alight. "This is amazing," she breathes. "Paris Sephora. This must be the flagship store! Sephora is from Paris, you know. Oh, wow, it doesn't get any better than this. I'm just going to . . ."

Her voice trails off as she wanders inside.

"I'm going to try and find some Wi-Fi," I tell her. "'Kay? Did you hear me? I'll come back."

She nods, distractedly. "Take your time."

I stand outside a café that claims to have Wi-Fi. My

three bars darken. Perfect.

I look at my phone. A missed FaceTime from my mom.

It just came in and it's ten thirty here, which makes it . . . four thirty at home. In the morning. That's not good. My shoulders clench.

I try to FaceTime her back.

It connects.

"Mom?" I say breathlessly. "Are you okay?"

She's sitting at her desk. The computer light glows against her face, casting weird shadows. "Hi, honey," she says. Her smile looks forced. "How are you? I miss you!"

"I'm fine! How are you? Why are you up? Is everything okay?"

"Just couldn't sleep," she says. "So I decided to do some work. Thought I'd call you and see how you are. See if it's a good time to catch you."

This isn't totally unusual, but it still makes me nervous.

"Where are you?" she asks.

"Paris," I say. "Leela is buying lipsticks."

"Are you traveling well together?" she asks.

"Pretty well. We're with Kat now, too."

"Oh, great. And . . . do you know how to get around?"

"Yup," I say. "Thanks to your guidebook."

"Good, good," she says. Her forehead wrinkles. "You're not worried about getting lost?"

"No," I say. After years of driving everywhere, I never worry about getting lost. "How's it going with Addison? Are you guys okay? Did you go out today?"

If she doesn't go out all day she can't sleep at night. I know this. Addison should know this. Why doesn't my sister seem to know this? She needs to get out. This is exactly what I was worried about!

"We're fine," she says. "Everything is fine. Don't worry about me. Send more pictures! I want to see what you're up to."

"Love you," I say.

"Love you, too," she says. I disconnect and stare at the phone.

I message my sister.

Why is Mom up at four in the morning? Is everything OK? Did she not go out today?

Addison doesn't answer, which makes sense since it's four in the morning.

I rub my temples. Why did my mom call me anyway? She knew I'd worry. The very act of calling me at four in the morning was designed to make me worry. So why call and tell me not to worry? She says she's proud of me for going away but then wants me to worry? What does she want from me? Does she want me to worry or not?

I try to calm down. I stuff my phone in my mini-backpack and return to the store. Leela has a metal basket full of stuff.

"How's it going?" I ask.

"Amazing," she says. "I found some treasures here.

Treasures! Can I have two more minutes? Just like two or three. Then we'll go."

"Sure," I say. "No worries."

She takes another twenty. But whatever, we're not in a rush. Outside, she hands me a lipstick. "For you," she says.

"Oh! You didn't have to do that."

"I know. But I wanted to. It's the perfect pink for you. Trust me."

I give her a hug. "Thank you."

We walk toward the Arc de Triomphe, which we can see in the distance. It's basically a white statue that looks sort of like a horseshoe.

"There it is," I say. "Very impressive."

We walk toward it but we can't figure out how to get to it. There are cars driving in what seems like a circle around it and no crosswalk.

"Are we missing something?" I ask. "Is there a *Star Trek*–like teleporter we're not seeing?" It's hot. I'm tired.

"We can figure this out. There are people there. I can see them."

It's true. I can see people there. But how did they get there?

"Oh! Look!" Leela says, pointing to what looks like a subway entrance. "Maybe that goes under the traffic into the Arc."

"You're a genius," I say. "Let's go."

We go underground, and it indeed seems to be a pathway to the Arc. When we pop up on the other side, I ask the scary question. "How long is the wait?"

"*Dix minutes*," the woman says.

"Did you hear that?" I say. "*Dix minutes!* That's ten, right?"

"Yup," says Leela.

"Is there an elevator?" I ask.

"*Non*," she says.

"Let's see how Leopard Pantsuit Lady does this in her stilettos," Leela says.

"She's not doing this," I say. "She's going to have her helicopter take her to a private dinner on the Eiffel Tower."

"Lucky bitch."

We follow a family with two young kids up the stairs. There are no windows. Just a circular staircase going up and up and around and around. The stones are square and spiral. Each step has a small rubber mat on it and there's a brown metal railing on the left side.

Hmm. My heart slowly starts to pound. Louder. And faster.

Is this going to be a problem? Is it going to be a repeat of what happened in the Tube? At Anne Frank's?

Am I going to have to turn around again? I can imagine what my mom would tell herself. *You can turn around! You don't need to go up there!* I try to block her voice out. But are these stairs ever going to end? Am I just going to keep walking up and up and up forever? No. It's going to end. We're at least halfway up, aren't we? It didn't look that high up when we were outside. I'm just hot. And tired.

My heart beats even faster.

Am I having a panic attack?

My heart is hammering. My mouth is dry.

What if I stop breathing? What if I pass out? How would anyone save me? How would they get here?

Shut up shut up shut up.

Need air.

"Lee?" I whisper. "I don't think I can do this."

She doesn't hear me, so I raise my voice as loud as I can, which isn't much louder. "Lee? I have to stop!"

She spins around. "What? Why?"

"I can't breathe. I have to go back."

She takes three steps down to me. "Are you okay? Do you want water? What's wrong?" She takes her water out of her bag and thrusts it into my mouth.

I take it gratefully, and drink fast. "Thanks. I'm not sure I can make it."

"Do you want to turn back?"

"Maybe," I say. That's all I have to do. Turn around. Go back down the stairs. I don't have to keep going. My mom doesn't push herself to leave the house. Why should I push myself to see a silly view?

"Do you want me to see how much more there is?" Leela asks.

I nod. Good idea. "Okay."

I stand in place while she disappears up the steps. I have a plan. I'm not throwing in the towel yet. Just taking a break. And then I'll know what I'm dealing with.

I can still turn around.

But if I turn around now, I might never try to see a view again. And then what if all flights of stairs start to look daunting? Will I refuse to go anywhere that doesn't have an elevator?

Plus, I didn't panic on the stairs at Anne Frank's. I panicked in the house. Am I never going to be able to go into small spaces again either?

Forget elevators. They're too small. I'll have to live my entire life on ground floors with high ceilings.

Then I'll really become my fucking mother.

Leela comes back a few minutes later. "I can see the light. It's about ten more flights. What do you want to do? We can go back down if you want. But I think you can do it. Actually, I know you can do it."

I take a deep breath. My heart is still beating fast. But not as fast.

I am not becoming my mother. I am going to push through this. It's only ten flights. I can do it.

My heart continues to slam against my chest, but I take deep breaths and keep going. One foot in front of the other. I'm doing this. Leela takes my hand and squeezes it.

As soon as I see the light up ahead, I know that I did it.

It's over. I panicked, but I did it. I take a huge breath of air when I step off the stairs and into a big room that opens to the outside. "Please tell me that was it."

"Yes," she says. "We're done. You did it! You triumphed at the Arc de Triomphe."

"I thought I was going to die," I say. My heart is still beating out of control. "How are we going to get down? Is there a fireman's pole?"

She puts her arm around me. "No."

"Can I jump?"

"Probably not. But going down is always easier," she says.

My legs are still shaking. "I think I had a panic attack. Maybe?"

Her eyes widen. "Are you sure?"

"No? I don't know? I think it happened before. On those Tube steps? Remember? And possibly at the Anne Frank house."

"I'm so sorry. We could have turned around."

"No. I'm actually glad we didn't." Now I know I *can* do it.

We step outside. Ah. A breeze! It's nice up here. We lean against the spiked railing and look through. It's like we're in the middle of the world and the streets all shoot out from where we're standing. In the distance, I see parks and towering office buildings and the Eiffel Tower.

I wish my mom could see it. She's never been to Paris and she'll probably never come, either.

My heart aches. My poor mom. She misses out on so much.

Paris is so beautiful. London is beautiful. Amsterdam is beautiful. There are so many places to see. Yet her world is shrinking to the size of a snow globe.

And yet every day my world gets bigger. I want it to be huge.

I watch the tiny people and colorful cars, all out and about. Working. Living. Maybe I could come back one day. Maybe *I* could live here. Not forever, but for a year. A year abroad, maybe? University of Maryland has an exchange program. I could do it. I did this. If my mom makes it through this month, maybe I could do that, too?

If my mom makes it through. *If.*

But what if she doesn't? What happens then? Am I going to spend the rest of my life taking care of her? Am I never going to move out? Am I going to live in the same bedroom for the rest of my life, sleeping in the same bed, staring at my glow-in-the-dark stars? My sister will go away to college and have a life but I'll have to stay at home forever?

Is it my responsibility to take care of her? There's nothing physically wrong with her! She can drive her own car if she wants to! I *triumphed*. Why can't she?

"Let's take a selfie," Leela says, interrupting my rambling thoughts. "With the Eiffel Tower in the background."

She lifts the phone and holds it up. "Say 'triumph,'" she says.

I push my concerns away and force a smile. "Imagine if we'd waited four and a half hours for the Eiffel Tower and then I stopped halfway? Never mind, I think they have an elevator."

"Stop talking, I'm trying to take a photo!"

I kiss her on the cheek, and she snaps the picture.

Since I know I made it up, the walk back down is easy. We head to Île Saint-Louis because *Travel Europe* says they have the best ice cream.

I order *nougat au miel* and Leela gets *fraise*. I take a stack of napkins. We walk back over the bridge and sit on a bench and look at the Notre Dame Cathedral.

"How are you feeling?" she asks.

"Mostly better," I say. I hesitate. "I'm just worried, you know? That I'm turning into my mom."

She turns to me. "Syd, a little anxiety isn't a panic attack. Everyone has anxiety. It's normal. It's your body responding to *actual* danger. Like being chased by a lion."

"Do I often get chased by lions?"

"No, but our species used to. We have anxiety to heighten our senses so we can react and hide from danger, or so we can fight the danger. The problem with your mom is that she sees danger when there really isn't any."

"Like at the grocery store." I lick the side of my cone. The ice cream has started to drip down the side.

"Exactly," she says.

"Because there are no lions at the grocery store."

She laughs. "Right."

"But she worries that if she goes she'll have a panic attack."

"Yes."

I try to understand. "You're saying my mom avoiding the grocery store because of panic attacks is like a caveman avoiding a forest because of lions."

"That's what I'm saying."

"So panic attacks have become my mother's lions."

"Exactly," she says, nodding. "Except cavemen were right to avoid lions. Lions can actually kill you. Panic attacks can't."

Right. We sit in silence eating our cones. By the time we're done, she looks like she has a strawberry goatee.

I hand her a napkin.

"Thank you."

"How do you know this anyway?" I ask.

"Psych 101, baby. It's a required course for marketing majors. Teaches us how to manipulate people."

"Good to know," I say. I pause. "But . . . there was no lion chasing me up the Arc de Triomphe."

"No, but there were a lot of steps. And it was hot. Your heart was thumping. Your adrenaline was rushing. Add in all your fears about leaving your mom and turning into your mom and of course you got freaked out."

"And what about at the Anne Frank house?"

"Same. You were thinking about the Holocaust, death, being forced to live in an attic, your mother, you were hungover, maybe the room was small, maybe there were stairs . . ."

216

"There were stairs," I say.

"I'm sure it pushed *plenty* of your buttons."

"I think it did." I smile at her. "Thanks."

She winks. "Anytime."

I hand her another napkin. She's still a strawberry mess. "What do you want to do now?" I ask.

"Laundry," she says. "I'm out of underwear."

"My bras are disgusting."

"What if we pick up stinky cheese and bread and wine—"

"And macarons," I add in.

"And macarons, obviously, and we go back to the apartment and do laundry and relax? It's so hot out and we did a lot today."

"That sounds perfect," I say.

"Good," she says. "Lead the way."

We type in the key code and use the key Kat left us since she said she has to work late tonight and we'll be on our own for dinner. We went to a *boulangerie* and picked up a huge still-warm baguette. Then we stopped by a tiny *fromagerie* where bricks of cheese lined the walls and bought blocks of Camembert, Brie, and two others called Cantal and Fourme d'Ambert. Finally, we went in to the corner *épicerie* and bought a bottle of rosé. We're going to do our laundry, eat bread and cheese and drink wine, and go to sleep early. We're wiped. My feet are burning and blistered, despite not wearing gold stilettos.

We're laughing when we open the door.

"Hi!" Kat says. She's wearing a bathrobe and her hair is wrapped in a towel.

"*Bonjour!*" I say. "I thought you were working late!"

"I got out early," she says. "Did you have a fun day?"

"We did," Leela says, smiling. Her arm is linked through mine.

"Spectacular! I'm so glad. I just got home, but we have to get moving! Go shower or bidet or whatever. We're meeting a group of people in Oberkampf. It's very cool. You're going to love it. It's like the Williamsburg of Paris."

"We bought stuff to eat for dinner," Leela says.

"So don't eat! Just drink."

"I'm kind of zonked," Leela says, and turns to me. "Aren't you tired?"

"Yeah, but . . . we're in Paris. We should go out," I say. "Don't you think?"

"We've gone out every night for the last week and a half. I thought we could stay home and have an early night. We have a million things to do tomorrow. The Louvre. Musée d'Orsay, Sacré-Coeur. Plus we have two more nights here. Staying home one night isn't going to kill us."

"But . . . but . . . it's only nine," Kat says, looking baffled.

"But I'm tired," she snaps. "So's Sydney."

"I . . ." I look back and forth between them, feeling a little like I'm the rope in their tug of war. "I'm not really sure what to do here? I want to hang out with both of you?

I want to stay in and I want to go out?"

"You want to go out," Kat says, her eyes shining. "You can stay home when you're in Maryland. You're in Paris! Don't you want to eat French food and drink more wine and maybe see my handsome boss again?"

"Well . . ." She does have a point. "Let's go out for a bit."

Leela crosses her arms. "We bought dinner! We have bread! And cheese! We've been spending so much money. We don't need another dinner out."

"I'm sure Alain will pay," Kat says. "He always pays."

"Why don't we eat the bread and cheese now and then we can meet up for a quick drink," I say. "Compromise?"

Leela takes a step back, pursing her lips. "Honestly, I'm wiped. I'll stay home by myself. You go. It's fine."

It does not sound fine.

"Oh! I have an idea!" Kat says. "You're too tired to go out? Why don't I invite everyone over here instead? We'll have a party. It'll be great. Spectacular. Yay party!"

"Oh," Leela says, biting her lip. "But—"

"No buts! I should have thought of this before. We'll invite everyone over to toast your arrival and have wine and cheese and your baguette! Let me go text everyone. Leela, can you just move your stuff to Syd's room, and we'll close the door and fold up the bed?"

She runs off before we can comment.

We're both silent. I force a smile. "Excited?"

Leela rolls her eyes. "Can I wear my pajamas to the party?"

"Um, no," I say. "Unless they're really cute pajamas?"

"My *My Little Pony* sleep shirt?"

"Not that kind of cute."

"Then no. I'm out of clean pajamas too, actually. Do you think we can do our laundry during the party?"

"I don't see why not," I say, brightening. "Look at that, multitasking!"

"Hmmph," she grumbles.

I hold out the Brie. "Cheese?"

The party is in full swing. There are a whole bunch of people in the living room, drinking wine and halfheartedly aiming their smoke exhalations out the windows.

Leela is talking to a Parisian named Pierre in French. Her hand is on his knee. She is smiling. Smiling! Woot!

I am sitting between Alain and Kat on what only an hour ago was Leela's pullout bed. They are debating the best hotel in New York. "I like the Plaza," he says. "It is the best, *non*?"

"Why? You have to stay in SoHo next time. You have to. Stay at the Mercer or something. So much cooler. You're not a fifty-year-old man!"

He leans closer to me. "Where is your suggestion, Sydney?"

"I am not an expert on New York hotels, I'm sorry to say."

"But you will come visit me?"

"Maybe," I say, laughing. This guy definitely isn't shy.

My phone buzzes beside me. It's Addison on FaceTime.

"Excuse me," I say.

"Hi," I say, her picture coming into focus. Her hair is wet and in a ponytail. "Just got home?"

"Yeah," she says. "Where are you? It's loud."

"At Kat's," I say. "She's having a party. One sec, let me find someplace quieter." I pass the washer, where I can see all our clothes bunched inside. Leela started it before the party. I step out of the apartment into the hall and leave the door unlocked. "Hi!"

"So how's Paris?" she asks. Her tone sounds kind of bitter. "Nice lipstick."

"Thanks," I say. I'm wearing the one Leela bought me. It really is the perfect pink. "Paris is good. How's Mom? She called me in the middle of the night. Are you taking her out for some fresh air?"

"She's not a dog, you know."

I flush. "I know that, thank you. But she needs to go out. Otherwise she's up all night. Can't you just take her for ice cream? The Baskin-Robbins is five blocks away. It's an easy walk."

"What she needs to do is go to a doctor!"

"We tried that. It didn't work."

"Then she needs to go to another one! A shrink!"

"Great!" I know I'm yelling but I don't care. It's not like anyone inside can hear me. "Take her!"

"She won't go! She's insane."

"I'll be home on August second. I'll take over. You just

221

have to help her for a few more weeks."

"I think she's getting worse."

"It's too loud here. I can't hear you."

"Sorry, I don't want to keep you from your party," she snaps, and then hangs up.

I stare at the blank screen. Great. Just great. I try calling back but she doesn't answer. I open the door and go back inside.

My phone beeps again. An iMessage.

Hi.

There's a number but no name. Who is it? It's a 778 area code. What is that?

Who is this? I type in.

You've forgotten me already? So much for we'll always have Amsterdam.

My heart stops. Jackson?

Did you meet someone else in Amsterdam?

Yes. He works at the Pink Dolphin. Texting is too PG for him though. We FaceTime.

I smile to myself and wait for him to type back.

Jackson: Funny. I got your number from Matt's phone. I guess Leela called you once. OK that I used it?

Me: Yes.

Jackson: Where are you?

Me: Paris. You?

Jackson: Berlin.

Me: We're pretty far from each other.

222

Jackson: Nine hours by car. Two days and nine hours by bicycle. How's Paris?

Me: Magnifique. I think that means magnificent but I'm not a hundred percent sure. How's Berlin?

Jackson: Gut.

Me: How's Matt?

Three dots. And then three dots. Then nothing. Then three dots.

Jackson: How's Leela?

Me: You didn't answer my question.

Jackson: You didn't answer mine.

Neither of us is typing. I don't see the three dots.

"Syd? Where are you?" I hear Kat ask.

Me: I gotta go. Have fun. Gute nacht.

Bonne nuit, he writes.

"It was nice to see you," Alain says. He hugs me good-bye. "I am sorry I have to leave, but I have an early breakfast."

"It was nice to see you too," I say.

He kisses me on both cheeks, and I let his lips linger.

I could totally make out with him right now. Well, I can't really because there are still twenty people here and the apartment is not that big and Leela's mess is all over my room, but I could kiss him, couldn't I? So what that I've been texting with Jackson? It's not like I'm going to ever see him again. I am in Paris and Jackson is in Berlin and Alain is French and gorgeous and not kissing him would be a crime. A *crime*.

I turn my head just a little bit so that, there we go, his lips are gently touching mine. I lift my hand so that it's on the back of his neck and now we're really kissing and he tastes like wine and he pulls me closer to him and now his hand is on my back and his lips are moving against mine and this was definitely a good idea, it really was, we're kissing, we're kissing, we're *French* kissing, and you know what, my room isn't that messy . . .

He pulls away and smiles down at me. "Unfortunately, I really must go. But maybe you will come see me in Tuscany? Kat has all my information." He pronounces it *inforrr-ma-sion*.

"Maybe," I say. "It's a definite possibility."

"Then good night," he says. "*À bientôt.*"

I close the door behind me and exhale.

I tell a very drunk Leela she can share my bed. The living room is just too disgusting with wine and cigarette smoke to sleep in.

"We'll clean it tomorrow," Kat says.

"That was fun," Leela says. "And I saw you kissing Alain! Was it *magnifique*?"

"It was pretty good," I admit.

"You kissed Alain?" Kat screams, throwing her arms in the air. "How did I miss that? Are you going to see him again?"

"I don't know," I say. "He invited us to Tuscany. We'll see."

"I'm going to try and call Gavin. Night." She blows a

kiss, and disappears into her room and closes the door.

"Did you hear my French?" Leela asks. "It's pretty good, huh? Isn't it?"

"It is," I say, handing her two Advil and a glass of water. "Have these. We have a big day tomorrow, right?"

"Right," she says. "We're going to see the *Mona Lisa*. Mona. Mooooona! I can't wait to see her. I wish I had her. Wouldn't it be cool to have the *Mona Lisa* in your bedroom?"

"That would be cool."

"Don't worry. I'm not going to steal it or anything."

"I don't think you could steal the *Mona Lisa*. I'm pretty sure it'll have tight security."

"Good point. Very good point! Where would I put it, anyway? There's not much room in my suitcase. It's already hard to zip."

"Yes. Maybe I can put it in my backpack?"

"You're such a good friend!"

"I am."

"You take good care of me. It makes me feel very loved." Her head lolls from side to side. "You're my best friend, you know."

"I know."

She opens her eyes. "Am I your best friend?"

"Of course you are," I tell her.

"More than Kat? Do you like me more than Kat?"

"Shh," I say. "You're being really loud."

"So? Does that matter? Don't you want her to know that

I'm your best friend?"

Seriously? "Yes, I will tell her you're my best friend. Okay?"

"Good. And for the rest of the trip it's just us, right? You and me?"

"Just us. Unless you're planning on meeting up with Matt again," I can't resist adding.

"I'm not. And no Kat either."

It's not like we have definite plans for Kat to join us again. Unless we really do go to Tuscany. But one step at a time.

"Where are we going next?"

"Barcelona," I say.

"Right! Tomorrow?"

"Not tomorrow. Monday or Tuesday?"

"Okay. But can we go somewhere cold?"

"Huh?"

"Barcelona is really hot. I don't think I can do more hot. Let's go somewhere cold."

"Like Switzerland?"

"Yes," she says. "Switzerland! Good night." And with that, she passes out.

And the plans change again. I look at my phone to see if Jackson texted.

He didn't.

Our last few days in Paris are hectic but fun. On Sunday, we visit the Louvre and see the *Mona Lisa*.

"She's not *that* special," Leela says.

"*Travel Europe* says that the only reason she's so famous is that she got stolen. Otherwise no one would even know this painting existed. And now she's the most famous painting in history."

When I still haven't heard from Jackson, I decide to text him.

Me: How hard would it be to steal the Mona Lisa?

Jackson: Not that hard. You should try it.

And then:

Jackson: Do you think Drecksak is an insult?

Me: It does not sound like a compliment.

We sneak messages back and forth and back and forth.

On our last day, Leela and I visit the Palace of Versailles, and then meet Kat for a fondue dinner. We start with bread dipped in cheese, move on to pieces of steak, and then end with strawberries dipped in chocolate.

"I need to get a fondue set for res," Leela declares, her mouth full of cheese.

"Res?" Kat asks.

"My dorm. They call it res in Canada."

"Do most people live in a dorm sophomore year?" Kat asks.

"Most people get apartments," Leela says. "But dorm living is so much easier, you know?"

"Maybe we should get an apartment," Kat says to me.

Leela snorts. "Yeah, right."

"Why not?" Kat asks.

Leela looks at me and then at Kat. I can see her registering the situation. She looks back at me, her eyes almost gleeful.

She doesn't know about your mom? I imagine her shouting, *I know something you don't know!*

"What?" Kat asks.

"Nothing," Leela says, but she's smiling. Seriously?

I want to wipe the smile off her face. "Yeah," I say. "Maybe we should."

"We could get a place right near campus!" Kat says. "I have a ton of cool furniture in storage in New York from when my parents moved, so we wouldn't even have to buy too much stuff. I signed up for another year in the dorm, but there's a waiting list so I bet I could get out of it."

Leela dips her strawberry back into the chocolate. "I think it's a great idea," she says.

My neck and back feel hot. Does she really?

"So were you able to get in touch with Gavin the other night?" I ask, switching the subject.

Kat gets a dreamy smile on her face. "Yes. He's good. It's color war."

"What's color war?" I ask.

"It's camp Olympics. But there are only three teams, and each team has to wear the same color. He's head of the blue team. He's lucky it's a good color on him. Want to see a picture?"

"Yes," I say, and out comes her phone.

"Doesn't he look cute?" she asks.

"He does," I say.

She puts her phone down and sighs. "I'm going to miss

you guys. I wish you were staying longer. Maybe I'll meet you guys for a weekend? Tuscany?"

I think about Alain. I think about Jackson.

"We'll see," Leela says, smiling tightly. "We're going to Switzerland next. Not sure how long we'll be there. And then who knows?"

"Yeah," I say, dipping another strawberry in chocolate. "Who knows."

INTERLAKEN, SWITZERLAND

The Basics: Do you like skiing, hiking, and banking? Then Switzerland is for you!

Don't worry, there's lots to do if you're a lazyass, too.

"I will miss the cheese," I say sadly. I stretch back in my train seat. It's going to be a while. Around five and a half hours and we have to switch trains in Bern.

"So will I," Leela tells me. "Does Switzerland have any good cheese?"

"Swiss cheese?"

"I don't really like Swiss cheese," she says. "Do you?"

"I don't mind it," I say. "With good mustard, rye bread, and a crunchy piece of lettuce."

She shakes her head. "It has too many holes. Why would I want my cheese to have holes in it? What is the reason for the holes? I am paying for the cheese. Not the holes."

"I see your point," I say.

Leela turns to me. "So how come you never told Kat?"

"About what?"

"About your mom? I know you don't really talk about it, but you and Kat seem close. I'm surprised."

"It just never came up," I say. "We hang out on campus. She's never been to my house or met my mom."

"Never?" she asks.

"No."

She nods. "I'm not going to lie, part of me likes that I'm the only one who knows."

This would probably be a good time to tell her that I told Jackson, and that we're still in touch, but I don't. I know it would upset her.

I've left my Wi-Fi off on the train so Leela won't see his messages come through.

"Omigod, look," she says, peering out the window. "It's like we're in the end of *The Sound of Music*."

Out the window, we see a blue sky behind high snow-capped mountains. We snap some pictures. Then some selfies.

"Should I just cave and get one of those selfie sticks?" she asks.

"No," I say. "They're so embarrassing."

"Say cheese," she says.

"Swiss," I say.

"Thanks for switching the plans again," she says. "You're the best."

"No problem," I tell her. "I don't mind." It's pretty here.

We get off at Bern, then get on another train headed to Interlaken. When Leela's in the bathroom, I send one of the selfies to Jackson. He sends me back one of him sitting at a picnic table, holding a frothy glass of beer. He's smiling. I save it to my phone.

> Tip: The official languages of Switzerland are Italian, German, French, and Romansh.

No, that wasn't a typo. Romansh is a real language—it comes from Latin. And in case you're wondering—no, Swiss is not a language.

"Omigod, smell," Leela says.

Sniff, sniff. "It smells like—"

"Mint gum!" she cries.

"And leaves!"

"And spring!"

"And fresh water!"

"And snow!"

We take more pictures and more deep breaths before going inside.

Our hostel is basically a backpacker commune. It looks like a huge chalet in the middle of a mountain that has everything you could possibly need. The rooms are upstairs and downstairs is a massive restaurant/sports bar.

After getting a quick tour of the hostel, we take our large

keys and head up to our dorm room to put down our stuff. The room is huge and sparse and all the furniture is wood. It smells good even in here.

We head back downstairs and study the posters everywhere about all the stuff we could do. Skydiving! Rappelling! White-water rafting!

"Do you think there's a spa?" I ask.

"No," Leela says. "I do not. Which is too bad because I could use a facial. I'm breaking out."

"Me too," I say. "I think I left my face wash in Belgium."

"So what are we going to do here?" she asks.

I shrug. "Yodel?"

We step out through the double doors and onto the terrace. There's a pool table and a foosball table.

"Now can I yodel?" I ask.

"Do you know how to yodel?"

"Yodel-ay-hee-who!" I sing.

"You're killing it."

"Shall we go drink and eat at the sports bar?"

"We totally should."

Our eyes take a second to adjust to the dimness of the restaurant. There are long wooden tables everywhere like we're in a lunchroom cafeteria. There are four large television screens, all playing soccer games, or football, as it's called here.

The travelers are all in groups. I hear a mix of French, German, and Spanish.

"Let's find the English speakers," I say.

"And then what?" she asks.

I throw my arms up. "And sit with them!"

"Seriously? Remember what happened last time you tried that?"

"Yes. But this is different," I say.

"Why?"

"Look around," I say.

She looks. And then she sees what I'm noticing. The people around us are 90 percent men.

"Oh," she says.

"Yeah. I think we'll have an easier time here."

"Okay," she agrees. "Let's scope it out and then decide where to go."

We stand by the bar trying to look nonchalant about our scoping.

"Okay," I say. "Table at the back. I think I detect some Aussie accents."

Her eyes widen. "Ohhhh, Aussies! So what do we do?"

I think about what Kat would do. "We just walk over and say, 'Hi, we just got here, can we join you?'"

Leela twists her ponytail. "What if they say no?"

I give her a look. "They won't say no."

We study the table. There are three of them. Two guys and one girl.

Leela bites her fingernail. "What if the girl hates us? What if she wants all the boys for herself?"

"Then we leave. Let's do it!" I lead the way and march over to the magical table. I feel Leela behind me. "Hi," I say, a little too loudly. "We just arrived. Would you mind if we sit with you?"

They stare at us for a half a second. "We would love if you sat with us," the girl says, and scoots over.

The Aussies are the best. The best.

They are: Lachlan, Gabriel, and Sienna. Sienna and Gabriel are twins. They're tall and pale and blond with matching high cheek bones. Lachlan is just a bit taller than me, about five six, and, he tells us, Chinese-Australian.

All three live in Brisbane but are on a gap year, meaning they took off twelve months to travel before going to college, starting in January, since our winter is summer in Australia. They started in Asia and got jobs in Phuket but are now mostly just traveling through Europe.

They make jokes, include us in their conversation, and are clearly having the most fun out of anyone at the bar.

"Why didn't we have a gap year?" I ask.

"You don't?" they ask.

"Just summers off," Leela says. "It doesn't seem fair."

"Technically, no one stopped us from taking a year off," I point out. "There's no law. Americans *do* do it."

"Another beer?" Lachlan asks.

I look at Leela and smile, and she smiles back. We did it! We made friends! Traveler friends! How cool are we?

"So are you guys coming rafting with us tomorrow?" Gabriel asks.

"Sure," I say.

"Really?" Leela asks.

"No? Too scary?"

"Rafting isn't scary," Lachlan says. "Today we went sky-diving. That was scary."

"You jumped out of a plane?" I ask, incredulous.

"No, from a canyon," Sienna says. "I honestly thought I was going to die. I'm not sure I will ever do that again. But rafting is relaxing. We're just sitting on a raft. Getting some sun. It'll be a total blast."

I look at Leela. "What do you think?"

She shrugs. "Sure. Why not?"

Tip: Enjoy a fabulous day rafting on the Lütschine. The scenery is gorgeous!

You might want to wash out your wet suit first.

We somehow are convinced to buy two activities for a bargain price. White-water rafting on Wednesday and paragliding Thursday. We're not exactly sure what paragliding is, but the Aussies promise it'll be a "ripsnorter," which I'm told is a good thing.

We sleep in, have brunch, and then get picked up outside the hostel at one p.m. We all climb into a van that drives us down mountains for thirty minutes to the rafting base. I take about a hundred pictures along the way. It's like we're driving through a postcard.

That's when we have to gear up. And by gear up, I mean get dressed in a full-on, soaking wet suit. Ankle to chest.

"I kinda wish we had done the morning trip," I say. "At least the suits would have been dry."

"Yeah, but then we would've had to get up at seven."

"Good point," I say, as I trip over the wet suit leg.

After we put on the black wet suits, we're given bright red life jackets and even brighter yellow helmets.

We leave our cell phones in our storage lockers so they don't get smashed or wet, and then get safety training from a German-sounding guy named Florian, who will be our leader.

We are told not to panic, to stay in the boat, and to hold the paddle by the shaft.

Leela and I giggle at the word *shaft*.

"Um, excuse me?" I ask. "What happens if we fall into the water?"

"Don't fall in the water," Florian says.

"Um. Yeah. But what if we do?" Leela asks.

"Toes up!" he barks.

"Huh?"

"Keep your toes up! Rocks are dangerous. Keep your toes up and stay near the boat. If you get far from the boat, swim to shore. I will pick you up. Don't worry."

"I'm worried," Leela mumbles.

"You will have an exciting afternoon!" he screams.

The Australians cheer.

We're given paddles, and since it's eight per boat, the six

of us are ushered into a bright orange raft with a mother and her son from London.

"Are you sure this is for beginners?" Leela asks.

"Don't worry, love, I'll take care of you," Lachlan says.

Leela's eyes widen at the word *love*.

They were sitting pretty close last night. Oooh. This is just what she needs. A fling with an Australian!

I'm on the left side of the boat, with Leela in front of me. It starts off slow, but very quickly we are swerving back and forth like clothes in a washing machine, with frothy water attacking us from all sides.

"Bump!" Instructor Florian yells as we jump over a rock.

We go flying but all manage to stay inside.

"Bump!" he yells again a second later.

OH. MY. GOD. The raft soars into the air, freezing water splashing in my face. I try to hold on, to grip the paddle, and to NOT FALL OUT.

We're still in the air. Now we're at a ninety-degree angle, and my side of the boat is almost underwater.

OH MY GOD OH MY GOD OH MY GOD.

We're going in we're going in we're going in . . . I try to grip my paddle and NOT FALL OUT but I can't hold on I can't hold on I can't hold on.

SPLASH.

I go headfirst into the water.

I pop up beside the boat, which is still at a ninety-degree angle.

"Are you okay?" Florian asks me. "Toes out of the water!"

I lift my legs so I don't hit any of the rocks at the bottom, and so he doesn't yell at me again.

"I'm fine," I say. I lunge toward the side of the raft. Holy crap, that was insane. "Where's Leela?" She's not in the boat. "Leela?!"

I spot her on the other side of the river. "She's floating off! Leela!"

She continues to drift away from us. Holy shit. Holy shit. HOLY SHIT.

"What do I do?" she yells.

I have to help Leela! How do I help Leela? I reach out to swim toward her, but Florian grabs my arm. "Absolutely not. Can you even swim?"

"Not well," I admit, starting to panic. "But someone has to help her!"

"I'll get 'er," Lachlan says. He jumps out of the boat and swims toward her. He has major arm strength. Impressive.

"Stop!" Florian cries. "You return to the raft! We will get her! Toes up, toes up!"

I watch, relieved, as Lachlan swim-lunges toward Leela.

He picks her up and scoops her in his arms and swim-walks back to the raft.

"Are you okay?" I ask, throwing my arms around her.

"Okay?" she asks, eyes glinting. "That was the most fun I've had in weeks."

"I'm so happy to get out of this," I say, peeling off my wet suit when we get back to the locker room.

"Me too," Leela says. "I totally peed in it."

"No, you didn't!"

"Yes, I did. I was in the water for like twenty minutes!"

"You were in there for five minutes."

"Well, I didn't think Lachlan was going to come rescue me and I had to go!"

"That's gross," I tell her.

"I'm sure the water cleaned it out."

"I'm so glad I'm not wearing your wet suit next."

By the time we get back to the hostel, it's after six. We're exhausted.

"Hostel bar in an hour?" Sienna asks us.

"Definitely," Leela says.

"We have friends!" I chirp to her. "Aussie friends! Isn't it amazing?"

We shower. I change into a white T-shirt and my jeans—which, AHHHHH, somehow still have the jam stain. Leela is in a matching outfit, without the jam stain. We head back down to the bar.

"Hey!" our new friends call when we get down there. "We saved you seats."

"They saved us seats," I whisper.

"I heard," she says. "I would like the seat next to Muscle-Arms."

"You may have it."

We join them and see that they already have a pitcher of

beer and glasses for us.

"We just ordered raclette," Sienna says. "It's like nachos with potatoes. Also burgers. I'm starving."

"Are we eating here?" I ask.

"Yup. We could go out but isn't it so much more fun here? And have you tried the burger? It has bacon and tomato chutney and caramelized onions. It's delicious."

"I have not. But I definitely will," I say.

"Sounds good to me," Leela says, then gets up to get a glass of wine.

My phone buzzes.

Jackson: Still in Paris?

I lower my phone under the table.

Me: Nope. Still in Berlin?

Jackson: Nope.

Me: Where are you?

Jackson: You first.

Me: I'll give you a clue. I just went white-water rafting.

Jackson: Switzerland!

Me: Yes. You?

Jackson: I'll give you a clue. I'm eating nakladany hermelin. I probably did not spell that right.

Me: I have no clue. Vienna?

Jackson: Wrong! Prague.

Me: But what is it?

Jackson: Guess.

Me: Lamb stew?

241

Jackson: Pickled cheese.

Me: That's disgusting.

Jackson: I'm enjoying it actually. It goes well with a Bevog Hagger. That's Austrian beer.

"Here you go," the waitress says, putting down our raclette.

"Are you texting Addison?" Leela asks.

I shove my phone back in my bag. "Yes." I reach my fork over and grab a cheese-covered potato. Mmm.

Actually, I haven't heard from my mother or sister in a few days.

"Hey! Eli!" Lachlan calls out.

There's a new guy standing by our table. "My favorite Aussies!" he says.

"They let you tossers in here?" Sienna says, batting her expertly mascaraed eyelashes. "I thought they keep out the riffraff."

The guy, Eli, looks around our age. He's only about a head taller than I am, and thin but not too thin. He has a round face, light brown hair, one dimple, and he's wearing a Yankees baseball hat and an NYU sweatshirt. He's cute. Hello, American!

"Hello, American!" I cheer.

Eli smiles and pulls up a backward chair. "Hello."

"How do you know our fellow countryman?" Leela asks the Aussies.

"We met in Budapest," Sienna says, pronouncing it Budapesht.

"I loved Buda," Eli says. "And Pesht. Are you ladies going?"

"Nope," I say.

"Why not?" he asks, shaking his head. "You have to go to Budapest."

"We only have three weeks left," I say. "We can't go everywhere."

"It's a shame. Beer is really cheap in Hungary," Lachlan says.

"Everything is cheap in Hungary," Sienna says. "It's hard to go hungry in Hungary."

"I had an entire steak for, like . . ." Gabriel calculates the conversion in his head. "Four euro. And it was ace."

"Not as good as this hamburger," Sienna says.

"But your hamburger is fifteen euro," Gabriel says.

"Can I get anyone a drink?" Eli asks.

"Yes," we all say.

"What would you like?" he asks.

We ask for another pitcher of beer and one glass of chardonnay.

"I'll help," Gabriel says, and goes with him to the bar.

"He's cute," Leela says to me, pointing her chin toward Eli. "You should go for him."

"He is cute," I say.

"Sorry, love," Sienna tells me. "He has a girlfriend."

Oh well.

When they come back, I ask, "So, Eli, where are you from? How long are you traveling for?"

"Long Island. And I'm traveling for seven weeks."

"We have a few friends from high school who go to NYU," I say. "Any chance you know Ellery Morganstein?"

"No," he says.

"Jeremy Dooth?"

"Nope. It's a big school."

"I know," I say. "But it's a small world. I hear you have a girlfriend."

"I do," he says, blushing.

"Is she here too?" I ask.

"No," he says, and sighs. "She's a camp counselor."

"Yeah? What camp?" I wonder.

"Blue Springs. In northern New York."

"Shut up!" both Leela and I yell.

He jumps back. "What?"

"Our friend's boyfriend is there too!" I say.

He looks surprised. "Really?"

"Yes!" I say. "Swear."

"What's his name?"

"Gavin," I say. "Lawblau. Does that name sound familiar?"

He shakes his head. "I don't think so. I'll ask her next time we talk. If I can ever get in touch with her."

"Yeah, I've heard cell phone service at camp is spotty."

"It's horrible. The whole place is a dead zone."

"That must suck. If it makes you feel better, it sucks for our friend Kat too," I say.

"What's she doing this summer?" he asks.

"She's working in Paris. We just came from her place."

"It's gorgeous," Leela adds. She takes a sip of wine. "Like insanely gorgeous. Near the Latin Quarter. So, are you traveling alone?"

"No, I'm with my cousin Yosef. He's showering."

"Another American," I say. "Excellent."

"He's Israeli, actually," Eli says. "My aunt met her husband while backpacking in Israel and stayed there. He's traveling for the year. He just got out of the army."

"Hear that?" I whisper to Leela. "Another Israeli. You get a second chance."

Two hours later, when Yosef finally joins us—that must have been a super long shower—we haven't moved from our spots. Yosef has the same round face and one dimple as his cousin, but looks like he's in his early twenties, has a scruffy beard, and darker hair and skin. Also he's clearly more built.

He checks the soccer score and then joins us. "*Shalom*," he says, nodding.

"Yosef, meet Leela and Sydney."

"Hi," we say.

Leela is checking him out, clearly into him.

Excellent.

He nods at her, checking her out. I think he's into her too.

"Do you speak English?" she asks him.

"*Ken*," he says.

"That means yes, guys," I say. "I went to Hebrew school."

"So, Syd," Lachlan says, like we're old friends. "Do you have a fella?"

"Me? No." I think of Jackson. What's wrong with me? He's not my boyfriend. He's just a guy I almost slept with and send flirty messages to.

"And you?" Lachlan asks Leela.

"Nope," she answers, twisting her hair behind her shoulder.

He leans a little closer to her. I'm pretty sure Lachlan's into her too.

Yay! Now Leela has two potential guys to hook up with. How can I move this along?

"Maybe they have girlfriends," Sienna says. "Maybe they're together."

"We're not," I say quickly.

Lachlan leans in closer to Leela. "Have you ever been with a woman?"

Leela clears her throat. "No. But it's on my bucket list."

I almost spit out my drink. "It is?"

"Of course it is. It's not on yours?"

"No," I say. "I mean, it wasn't. Should it be?"

"You have to try everything once," Sienna says, smiling at Leela.

"Have you?" Leela asks.

"Oh yeah," Sienna says. "I don't discriminate based on

race or gender or age."

"Her last boyfriend was sixty-four," Gabriel says.

"He was forty-six," she corrects, and takes a sip of her beer.

"Did he have gray hair on his balls or what?" Gabriel asks.

"You're being disgusting," Sienna says, making a face. "And you would have screwed him too if you could."

"It's true," Gabriel says. "I would have. He was *hot*."

"And what's your story, Gabriel?" Leela asks.

"Men only." He smiles.

"Do you have a boyfriend?" I ask.

"I did," Gabriel says. "But we broke up before I left for the trip. Which was for the best."

"He made a special friend in Croatia," Lachlan says.

He sighs. "True. But now that ship has sailed. All the way to Greece."

"And what about you guys, Lachlan and Yosef? You attached to anyone back home?" I make eyes at Leela and enjoy watching her squirm in her seat.

"Nope," Lachlan says. "I travel freely."

"*Lo*," Yosef says.

"That means no," I say to Leela.

Leela leans closer to Yosef. "You were really in the army?"

He nods. "Every Israeli must be in the army."

"How old are you?" Leela asks.

"Twenty-one."

Lachlan leans forward in his seat. "I was in the army too," he says.

"You were not, you big liar!" Sienna says. "Stop trying to impress the American girls."

At the end of the night, my phone buzzes again when I'm in the bathroom getting ready for bed.

Jackson: hiiiiiiii. What ya doing?

Me: Are you drunk texting me?

Jackson: I am.

Me: Aren't there any real live girls to talk to?

Jackson: Yes. But I keep thinking of you.

I stare at my phone.

Me: Yeah?

Jackson: Yeah.

Me: I keep thinking of you, too.

Jackson: I wish you were in Prague with us.

Me: Yeah, the four of us hanging in Prague. That would not work out.

Jackson: Where are you going next?

Me: Not sure.

Jackson: When are you leaving?

Me: Not sure. Leela's having fun, so we'll probably stick around for a few days. But Jackson . . .

Jackson: Yeah?

Me: I wish I were in Prague with you, too.

After we say goodnight, I message my sister.

Me: How's everything going? Is Mom OK?

I wait twenty minutes for her to answer, but she doesn't.

★ ★ ★

Ow, ow, ow. Every muscle in my entire body is sore. I feel like I've been in a car accident. I grimace and not from the pain. I should not, definitely not be making light of a car accident when Jackson's mother died in one. But seriously, my whole body hurts. "Can't move," I squeak out.

"I'm not sure I can go paragliding today," Leela says. "I don't think I can stand up, never mind jump from the sky."

"We have to," I say. "We paid already. It was a special!"

"No! Listen!"

"To what?" I hear a pitter-patter against the windows. "Is it raining?"

"It is!"

"That means it's canceled!"

"Yes!"

"Wahoo!" I cheer. "We better get a refund."

"So what are we going to do instead?"

"Go to the bar?"

"It's eight a.m."

"Let's go back to sleep and then go to the bar?"

"Umph," she says, and we both go back to sleep.

Tip: There are so many amazing things to do and see in Interlaken, even when it rains. There are caves to explore. There are indoor ropes courses. There are ice rinks. There are bowling alleys. Don't just sit around—get active!

We spend the whole day in the bar.

For brunch we have French toast. For lunch we have chicken fingers. We take a break halfway through the day to watch the Aussies play soccer in the rain. We stay dry under the terrace awning.

Then we go back inside. Eli lends us his cards and we play Asshole and Rummy 500.

It's the best day ever. And we never leave the Wi-Fi zone.

It's hard to text back and forth with Jackson with Leela watching, but I do my best. I tell her I'm writing Addison. Addison who has not responded to my last three messages.

I email my mom to check in, and she finally writes back.

I'm fine! Your sister has been out and about. I hear her come home at night but haven't spent much time with her.

I message Addison, again.

Can you please, please just take care of Mom for two and a half more weeks? You said you could handle it!

"Where are you going next?" Leela asks Eli during our third game of Rummy 500.

"South of France," Eli tells us. "Tomorrow. Then Spain and Portugal. You?"

"We have no idea," I say. "We fly out of Rome on August second."

"Did you already do the South of France?" Gabriel asks.

"No," I say, and take a nacho from the plate that I don't even remember ordering and then pick up a card. No set. I need the eight of clubs. "We were thinking of just going straight to Italy."

"You have to go to the South of France," Sienna cries. "That's the entire point of going to Europe."

Leela snort-laughs. "I thought the whole point was seeing museums and castles."

"Don't you want to go to the beach?" Eli says.

"I could use a beach," Leela says.

So much for cold weather.

"We're gonna go tomorrow, too," Sienna says. She slams her glass of beer against the table. "And you're coming."

"We are?" I ask.

"Yes," she declares. "We are all going to Juan-les-Pins. Best place on the Riviera for backpackers."

"See?" I look at Leela. "Backpackers. I bet these people have actual backpacks, too. Am I right?"

"Of course," Lachlan says. "Don't you?"

"Not all of us have such incredible upper-body strength," Leela says, batting her eyelashes.

"Oh, please," I say.

"So are you coming or not?" Sienna asks. "If you're not, you may be banished from our table."

"You're leaving tomorrow?" I ask.

"Yes," Lachlan says. "Tomorrow. We won't take no for an answer."

I turn to Leela, and ask in a low voice, "What do you think?"

"I think we're going to Juan-les-Pins," she says. She puts down a set of eights, flips over her winning card, and smiles.

JUAN-LES-PINS, FRANCE

The Basics: Right between Cannes and Nice is a sandy-beached slice of heaven called Juan-les-Pins.

Get ready to take off your bikini top and get some sun. Hope you're not shy . . .

"So how many trains do we have to take exactly?" I groan at the train station.

"Four," Lachlan says. "Interlaken to Bern, Bern to Basel, Basel to Cannes, and Cannes to Juan-les-Pins." He says Cannes like cans. I'm pretty sure that's not how it's supposed to be pronounced.

"This is going to be insane," I say.

"It'll be worth it," Sienna says. "Promise."

We get on the train at eight a.m. Lachlan, Sienna, Gabriel, Yosef, and Eli better entertain us.

I take out my phone and connect to the Wi-Fi on the

train. No message from Jackson.

I decide to write him.

Me: Hey! On train. On our way to Juan-les-Pins . . . how's Prague?

There's no answer. Which makes sense, since he's probably still asleep. My sister's definitely still asleep. But why didn't she text me back again last night? Where has she been?

I put my phone down.

"Who wants to play Rummy 500?" Eli asks.

"Me!" I say, and scoot over to his seat.

Two trains, seven games of Rummy 500, all of *Girls On Fire,* and three of Sienna's Australian tabloid magazines—*Woman's Day, Who,* and *Take 5*—later, six hours have passed and I still haven't heard back from Jackson or gotten a message from Addison.

Since it's nine a.m. at home, I put in my earphones and call her on FaceTime.

"Yes?" she says. The connection is shaky.

"You're alive!" I say. "I was beginning to worry you ran away from home."

"I'm fine," she says. She ties her hair back in a bun.

"How's Mom?"

"Fine."

"Have you been . . . going out?" I don't want to be too specific since I'm in public.

"Oh yeah, yesterday we went white-water rafting."

253

I feel stung. "I guess you looked at my pictures?"

"Yup."

I lower my voice. "So you didn't go out?"

"Not yesterday. I had plans with Sloane."

"Who's Sloane?"

"She's a friend."

I've never heard of this alleged friend. "So what did Mom do all night?"

"I don't know. She's a grown woman, you know that, right?" She's looking away from the phone. "Where are you, anyway? On a yacht on the Mediterranean?"

"No. I'm—"

The screen freezes. I disconnect and try to connect again. It rings but she doesn't answer. Great.

A message from Jackson pops up. Finally!

Jackson: Hey.

Me: Hey!

Jackson: Are you really on your way to Juan-les-Pins?

Me: Yup. Why?

Jackson: Um . . . that's where we're going too.

My heart soars.

Me: Seriously?

Jackson: Yeah. Matt wanted to go to the beach.

I'm thrilled. But . . . I look at Leela. She's laughing at something Lachlan said. She's finally having fun. If she sees Matt, it's going to upset her, if not ruin her time in France.

Me: I'm not sure what I should do? Maybe I should tell Leela.

She might want to do something else.

Jackson: Don't tell her.

I hesitate.

Me: That is so wrong.

Jackson: I won't tell Matt either. They don't even know we're talking to each other. It's not our fault we're ending up in the same place. It's a popular stop.

Me: Maybe they won't even see each other?

Jackson: Where are you staying?

Me: It's a hotel. La Lune.

Jackson: HAHAHAHA

Me: No way. Same? How is that even possible?

Jackson: It's a popular hotel?

Me: So we're going to be in the same hotel at the same time?

Jackson: Seems that way. Don't tell. I won't either. I want to see you.

I hesitate. Does this make me the worst friend ever? Possibly. But it's not like I *invited* them to come. He was already going. What am I supposed to do—tell him not to come? That doesn't seem right. And maybe we won't even see them. If I tell her they're coming, she could freak out and want to get off the train right now. And I don't even know what country we're in.

I hear more laughter from across the aisle. Leela is sprawled across the seat and her feet are in Lachlan's lap.

She'll be fine.

I'm not telling her. I can't. If I do, then I'll have to admit that I've been in touch with him for the last week.

Also I want to see him. My whole body warms up. I *really* want to see him.

I type, OK.

My heart hammers. What am I doing? Am I just going to sleep with him? I know he's a player. Am I being played? Do I care?

Three dots.

Jackson: See you soon ;)

By the time we arrive, it's already seven. We walk the three blocks to the hotel, hand over our passports, and check in.

"Nice," Leela says.

"It's pronounced *niece*," I say.

"Huh?"

"It was a joke. 'Cause we're near Nice? The place? Get it?"

I'm losing it. I'm giddy with nerves. Are they here? Maybe. Omigod, how did I not tell her? She's going to freak. I should have told her. Now it's too late.

My body tingles at the idea of him.

I want to see him. I can't wait to see him.

I hope he's here.

"*Votre chambre est sur la deuxième étage,*" the woman says. She holds out two large silver keys. "*Vingt-trois.*"

Why are all the keys on this continent so enormous?

"*Merci pour votre aide,*" Leela says.

"Your French has really come in handy," I say.

"You speak French?" Sienna exclaims. "Extra plus!"

The woman checks in our friends and hands out their keys.

"Let's meet downstairs in half an hour," I say. "Then we'll try and find a place for dinner."

"Perfect," everyone says.

Our room is small, with two single beds, one against each wall, a window, and a tiny bathroom. "I'll shower first," I say, and step into the bathroom.

There's no actual shower stall. There's just a small drain on the floor in the corner, and a handheld shower faucet beside the toilet. You get what you pay for.

By the time I'm done showering, the toilet paper, sink area, and my towel are all soaked.

"Sorry," I say. "You're up."

My phone buzzes as I'm debating what to wear. I put on the navy tube dress that Kat lent me and then insisted I keep.

The message is a picture of a Google map from about an hour away by train. Nine hours by walking. Three by bicycle.

Text me when you get here . . . I write back.

"That wasn't a shower," Leela says, stepping out. "It was more of a hose."

"Seriously," I say. My heart pounds as I tuck my phone into my new clutch.

★ ★ ★

257

All seven of us are sitting outside at a place called La Princesse, about two blocks from the beach. I beg the hostess to give me their Wi-Fi password.

His text comes in when I'm halfway through my Nicoise salad.

Jackson: At the hotel. Where are you?

Me: At a place called La Princesse.

Jackson: Should we come?

Me: I don't know. She might freak.

Jackson: I have to see you.

Me: Do you think I can sneak out of dinner?

Jackson: Yes.

I look up at Leela. She's twirling her hair and laughing at something Lachlan says. Then she laughs at something Yosef says.

OK, I write back. Meet me outside room 23 in ten.

My heart racing, I drop my phone into my purse and jump up.

"Leela," I say. "I'm having some family issues I have to deal with. I need to call home."

"I can come with you," she says, pushing back her chair.

"No, no," I say. "I won't be gone too long. Actually, if I don't come back, just meet me back at the room later?"

"I don't mind coming with you," she says, still standing.

"No, honestly. I need privacy anyway. You stay here. Have fun."

"Where are we going after this?" she asks the table.

"Le Spectacle down the street," Lachlan says. "It's a tiki

bar! It's supposed to be wild."

"If I'm running late, I'll meet you there, then," I say. I leave twenty euros on the table. "Cover me if I'm short?"

"That's more than enough," Sienna says. "No worries. We got this. Hope everything is okay."

I grab my clutch and hurry down the street and back to the hotel. I step into the lobby and run up the two flights of steps.

He's standing in front of my room.

My heart stops.

He's wearing jeans and a black T-shirt and his hair is damp. He's staring right at me.

He smiles. He reaches his hand up and puts it in my hair and now we're kissing. We're kissing fast and his hands are on my back and my hands are pulling him closer and closer and it's him, it's him, it's Jackson.

"One sec," I say, pulling back, getting the massive key from my purse, unlocking the door, and tugging him inside. He keeps kissing me and falls on top of me and off comes my tube dress and his black shirt and his jeans and it's Jackson, it's Jackson, it's Jackson, and everything else comes off, too.

Tip: Don't miss the sizzling nightlife in Juan-les-Pins!

Unless you have something even hotter to do.

"Hello," he says afterward.

I smile. "Did we forget to say hi?"

He laughs. "I think I forgot what my name is."

"That was a little bit crazy," I agree.

"That was a lot crazy," he says. He kisses the inside of one of my wrists and then the other.

"So where does Matt think you are?"

"I told him I was going for a walk."

"What room are you guys in?"

"Twenty-four."

"Twenty-four? You're in the room next door?"

"Yup." His eyes crinkle with laughter. "My bed is actually right on the other side of this wall."

I sit up. "We should clean. Leela's going to come back."

All of our clothes plus a condom wrapper are in the middle of the floor.

"Text her and see where she is," he suggests.

When I take out my phone there's already a message from her saying that I should come to the tiki bar.

I type back: **Am wiped out. Have fun! See you later!**

I turn back to Jackson and say, "Where were we?"

"Is everything okay with your mom?" Leela asks me the next morning as soon as I wake up.

"Uh-huh," I say, not looking at her. "How was the bar?"

"Insane," she says.

"Did anything happen with you and any of your boys?"

"Not yet. I'm still debating which one. Lachlan is clearly the most adorable, but Yosef's so dark and dangerous. And then there's Eli—"

"I thought he has a girlfriend?"

"He does, but he's still a flirt. They all are. Which one do you want? I don't need all of them."

"Oh, don't worry about me," I say quickly. "You can choose."

"You really should have met us after you got off the phone."

"I was tired," I say.

Jackson and I had fallen asleep. We woke up when we heard Leela and the crew outside the window belting out a round of "Ninety-Nine Bottles of Beer on the Wall."

"See you tomorrow," Jackson had said, giving me a kiss. He closed the door behind him.

He opened his own door a second later.

"Dude!" I heard through the wall. "Did you get lost? I went to look for you on the beach! I met some guys from London . . ."

Jackson tapped the wall between us, once. Twice. I fell asleep facing where I imagined his lips to be.

"Come on," Leela says now, opening the curtains. "We're meeting everyone on the beach."

"I need coffee," I tell her.

"There's an adorable *boulangerie* next door. How do I look?"

She juts out her hip. She's wearing a bright red bikini.

"Hot," I say. I unpack my black one.

"Make sure to put sunscreen on your boobs," she tells me.

"*Exqueeze* me?"

"We're going topless."

I shake my head. "Who are you and what have you done with my best friend?"

Our travel buddies have turned her into a new person! So what if she bumps into Matt? She's going to be fine. Absolutely fine. She won't even care. And maybe she won't even see him. They could keep missing each other. It's possible, right?

I want to see Jackson though. My body tingles remembering last night. I want to see him *soon.*

When we leave our room, our beach towels in hand, our floor is quiet. It's ten a.m. I'm guessing our neighbors are still sleeping.

After we get our coffees and croissants, Leela insists we take a selfie.

"Say *croissant!*" she says.

"Croissant!" I say.

"Are you going to post? You haven't taken enough pictures."

"I'm trying not to rub the trip in my sister's face."

"Really? I would think you should do the opposite."

Huh? "You think I should rub it in her face?"

"I think you should show her how much fun you're having so she feels you left for a good reason. Isn't it so much worse if you left and have a sucky time?"

"I guess," I say, taking out my phone. I lift my arm and

angle it so it gets both of us plus a sliver of the water in the background. Snap. I am still picking up the Wi-Fi from the hostel so I post it with #goodmorningriviera.

We finish our food, carry our towels, and head down the beach to find the rest of our group.

Up close, the beach is gorgeous. The water is a calm blue-green and the sand is soft and smooth. There are sunbathers everywhere. To the right there are fancy blue hotel umbrellas from the Ritz, and to the left are umbrellas and chairs from some European hotel, but in front of us are just people sitting on beach chairs and bright towels right on the sand.

And everyone is topless. Apparently, it's not a rumor about French people. All I see around me are breasts. Big breasts, small breasts, lopsided breasts, old breasts, young breasts.

It's hard not to look at all the breasts.

Breasts and men's Speedos. "Look at what the men are wearing," I say under my breath.

"Banana hammocks!" Leela cries. "They're everywhere. They really don't leave much to the imagination, now do they?"

"Nope," I say.

"There they are," Leela says.

"The banana hammocks?"

"No," she laughs. "Our friends." She points a few rows over. "They are wearing regular bathing suits."

"Thank goodness," I say. "But Sienna is topless."

"Morning, gorgeous," Lachlan, says, waving.

"Hi, handsome," Leela says.

"What about me?" Yosef asks.

"Hello, stud," Leela says.

"I'm getting jealous," Gabriel says.

Sienna lowers her sunglasses. "You guys are *never* this nice to me," she complains.

"Who wants to put lotion on my back?" Leela asks.

"Me!" Lachlan calls out.

I lie down on my towel and take a sneak peek at my phone. No wireless. Argh. How do I know where he is? Is he still sleeping? It's already noon.

Maybe I can pick up the signal from one of the other hotels?

I play around a bit. Move my towel to the left. Score! Free hotel Wi-Fi!

But still no text from Jackson.

Hmph.

Should I be concerned that I slept with a guy and haven't heard from him since? No. Maybe?

I check the picture I posted of me and Leela. Twenty-four people liked it. My sister isn't one of them. Kat is. There's also a comment from her. "You're in the South of France?!"

Leela turns to me. "Are we doing it?"

"Doing what?"

"Taking off our tops!"

I look around self-consciously. "I feel like I'm in *Girls Gone Wild: Croissant Edition*."

"We have to do it," she says.

"Why?"

"Everyone else is! Even Sienna is."

"You can do it without me," I tell her.

"No way. Either both of us, or neither. We're in this together, baby."

"Okay, fine," I grumble. "Let's do it. But I'm going to be super subtle about it." I lie on my stomach and carefully unhook the back of my top. There we go. It's off. "Did it."

"I can't see your boobs," she says. "That's cheating. Turn around!"

I look over at her. "Your top is still on!"

"I'm taking it off. Don't get your bikini bottoms in a twist." She copies my move and lies on her stomach and unhooks her top. "Here we go," she says. "We'll flip on the count of three. One."

"Two."

"Three!" she squeals.

We turn over.

And see Matt and Jackson standing right in front of us.

Jackson is wearing a pale blue swimsuit, sunglasses, and no shirt. Ah, that smooth chest. I want to run my hands all over it.

Matt is in a green checkered suit and a white button-down.

The next few minutes play out like a horror movie. Leela screams. Loudly.

Lachlan and Yosef jump up.

Sienna yells, "What is it? Is it a bee?"

"What's wrong?" Lachlan asks.

"It's him!" Leela yells, pointing at Matt.

"Is there a problem?" Yosef asks, standing up. "He bothering you, Leela?"

Matt's face clouds over. "What the hell? Who are these guys?"

At this point Eli, Gabriel, and Sienna are standing too.

Jackson steps closer to Matt.

"*Al tid-ag,*" Yosef says, and I have no idea what he means but his arms are spread protectively and everyone on the beach is staring.

"*Les Américains sont fous,*" says an old topless woman with a cigarette dangling from her wrinkled lips.

"Everyone calm down," I say, standing up. Of course it's only after I stand up and the Riviera breeze hits my breasts that I remember that I too am not wearing a top. *Merde.* It's like I'm having that dream when your teacher calls on you in class and you start talking and you realize that you're butt naked. Except this is actually happening and at least nine people are staring at my boobs. Including me.

"Hold on," I say. I grab my towel and wrap it around myself, post-shower style. "Okay. That's better. Everyone relax. Guys, these are our friends Matt and Jackson. We know them. Matt is Leela's boyfriend."

"Ex-boyfriend," Leela snaps. "Definitely ex." I expect her to put her shirt back on or grab a towel too, but she

266

doesn't. In fact, she lowers her hands so her boobs are at full attention. She smiles.

Matt just stares. He can't look away.

They are pretty amazing boobs. Big yet perky. Naturally dark. Possibly the best on the beach, I'll give her that. Maybe I should go on the pill.

"What are you doing here?" Leela asks him.

"What am I doing in Juan-les-Pins?" he asks.

"Yes!" she screams.

"What are *you* doing here? You never said you wanted to go to the South of France!"

"Neither did you!"

"We changed our plan. Jackson wanted to come."

I look up at Jackson. He did?

Jackson blushes.

Did he change his plans to come here? To see me?

I think back to our messages. Did I tell him I was coming here before he told me he was? Yes. I did. That means he switched his plans. To see me.

I flush.

"Hi, Syd," Jackson says.

"Hi, Jackson," I say, smiling. "How have you been?"

"Pretty good," he says, smiling back. "You?"

"Can't complain."

He's wearing sunglasses, but I can still see his eyes.

"Can we join you guys?" he asks.

"Of course," I say.

Leela says, "No!"

"We can go somewhere else," Matt says quickly. "It's a big beach."

No! Stay! Don't go! Jackson, I want you to rub lotion all over my topless body!

"Bye," Leela says, turning her back on them.

"I guess we'll see you later, then?" Jackson says as Matt storms off.

"Bye," I say sadly.

He gives me a wave and follows his friend.

"That was unbelievable," Leela says. She turns to me and lowers her voice. "Do you think he's following me?"

"Huh?" I say.

"Do you think he saw my posts and came to try and get back together?"

"Maybe?" I say. I don't want to burst her bubble and tell her the truth.

"He needs to get his shit together," she says. "And leave me out of it. I'm done with him. Did he see the two guys who are basically fighting over me? I mean, come on. Lachlan could crush him with his super arms and Yosef could torture him to death. Matt's a total tosser."

"A tosser, huh?"

"Yes. Ugh. I don't know what I ever saw in him." She sits back down on her towel and lies on her back, boobs exposed. "I don't even care if he's here. I love France. He's not going to ruin this for me. Nobody is."

Okay, then. She sounds pretty adamant. The girl might protest too much, but if she says she's fine, then that's what I'll go with.

I turn on my side. There's already a message from Jackson.

That went well.

Ha! I type back.

Jackson: When can I see you again? Meet me in like thirty minutes by that big white hotel?

Me: The Ritz?

Jackson: Um . . . yes.

Me: Did you get us a room?

Jackson: That is a great idea. Should I try?

Me: I'm kidding! The rooms are probably five hundred euros a night.

Jackson: Yeah, but we only need it for an hour. So that's twenty euros.

Me: I'm not sure the Ritz has hourly rates.

Jackson: Good point. OK, we'll just meet there and then we'll take a walk.

Me: Sounds good. Thirty minutes.

I see I missed another message. This one's from Kat.

Kat: You're in the South of France ???? 🇮🇹

Kat: I thought you were going to Switzerland!

Me: We were in Switzerland. Now we're here!

Kat: OMG I love the South of France! Where are you? 🇮🇹👙👒

Me: Juan-les-Pins.

Kat: I love that beach! 🖤 I passed by a few summers ago when we went to St. Tropez! 🛥 ☀

Three dots. I wait.

Kat: 💡! When are you there until?

Me: Till . . . not sure!

Kat: I'm going to come meet you! 😍 Buying my ticket right now! 💵 🎫 🚅 See you soon!

Wait. What? Did that just happen?

Me: You're coming? Here?

Kat: Yes! Alain is gone! I'm barely working anyway. I'll just throw some stuff in a bag and go to the train station. Will be there by dinner! Try and get me a room wherever you are! 🛏 K?

What am I supposed to say? No, don't come? Yes, I know you let me and a perfect stranger stay at your gorgeous apartment but please don't come to the same hotel as us in the South of France. My other best friend doesn't want to share me.

Me: K!

Kat: So excited! See you soon! 🎉

Now what? I probably shouldn't hit Leela with *another* surprise visitor. I sit up. "Um, Leela?"

"Mm-hm?"

"Remember that picture you made me post?"

"Yes."

"Well, Kat liked it and now she's getting on a train."

She lowers her sunglasses. "She's coming to Juan-les-Pins?"

"Yes."

"When?"

"Now?"

She sighs. "Today just keeps getting better and better."

"Sorry," I say. "But I know something that will make you laugh. Look to your right."

She sits up and looks to her right. There on a towel, is a man lying on his stomach wearing a *thong* banana hammock.

"Omigod, the string goes right up his butt." She laughs. "You're right. That is hysterical."

Jackson and I make out by a juice bar.

"I want to take you for dinner tonight," Jackson says.

"Like a date?"

"Exactly like a date."

"But Kat is coming."

"I know. She can hang with Leela," he says.

"That is not going to go over well," I say. "Okay, here's the plan. You eat with Matt. I eat with the crew. Then we all meet up at some bar. She can't blame me for going home with you if I meet you in a bar, right? She's the one who set us up in the first place!"

"Absolutely," he says. "You make perfect sense." He kisses me again.

"I have to go back in two minutes."

He pulls me against him. "Give me thirty minutes and let's go to my room at the hotel."

"Cool it, horndog," I say. "Wait until tonight."

His voice is low. "I can't wait until tonight."

"Oh, you'll wait," I say. I run my finger up his arm and then down the front of his smooth chest. I stop right before the elastic of his bathing suit. "See you later."

"You're leaving me?" he says, laughing. "I don't think I can walk."

I blow him a kiss, lower my sunglasses, and let him watch me walk away.

I'm waiting at the train station when Kat gets off, sunglasses perched on the top of her head. She's wearing an off-the-shoulder yellow jumpsuit that I already know is going to annoy the hell out of Leela because it's so perfect. She's not wearing a backpack or rolling a suitcase. She's holding a Louis Vuitton weekend bag.

"Hi!" she exclaims, throwing her arms around me. "I'm so glad I'm here. This is so fun! We're going to have the *best* weekend."

We catch up as we walk to the hotel. "Alain keeps texting me about you," she says. "He's obsessed. He really wants us to come to his place in Tuscany next week."

"I . . . I can't," I say.

"What? Why not?" She lifts up her sunglasses. "Omigod, did you meet a guy?"

"Kind of," I say.

"Kind of? Wait a sec. Someone from home?" Her eyes

widen. "No. Wait. Is it that guy from Amsterdam?"

"Yes. Jackson. Leela's ex's friend. How did you guess?"

"I could tell you really liked him. Is he here?"

"Yes."

"The ex too?"

"Yup," I say.

"Is he back with Leela?" she asks. "Maybe that will get the stick out of her ass."

"Kat!"

"I'm sorry," she says. "I'm really trying with her because I know she's your bestie, but she's making it tough for me. That's why I decided to come. I want her to like me."

"You're amazing," I say, meaning it. "And you're right. She has been a pain, but she's been much better since we made these friends in Switzerland—you're going to love them. And I really don't know what to do about Jackson. I snuck back to the hotel to meet him last night!"

"No way."

I blurt out the whole story. At first, I feel guilty spilling my guts to her when I'm basically keeping everything from Leela, but I have to talk to someone about all of this, and right now that person has to be Kat.

Her eyes are bright. "Love it. You're like Romeo and Juliet!"

"Not quite."

"Close enough. It's so sexy! I'm so jealous! Maybe I should have some secret sex."

"Kat!"

"I'm kidding. I wouldn't. Swear. Gavin is the best. But this is great. I am totally going to help you. I love it. I have just the dress."

We all meet up in the lobby at eight.

Somehow, Leela and Matt haven't crossed paths at the hotel. Thank goodness we have bathrooms and showers in our rooms. Tiny bathrooms and showers, but still. No one wants to run into their ex in the bathroom. No one wants to run into the guy they just started sleeping with in the bathroom either.

"Hi!" says Kat to the Aussies. "I'm Syd's friend from school. So great to meet you."

"It's good to meet you too," Lachlan says.

"Yes," says Yosef. "It is."

Leela's face squishes into an unpleasant expression.

"Hi," says Eli. "Do you go to the University of Maryland, too?"

"Omigod!" I say. "Eli! This is my friend who I told you about. Her boyfriend is at the same camp as your girlfriend."

"What?" squeals Kat. "No way! What's her name?"

"Samantha," he says.

"Is she the same Samantha who Gavin was color war captains with last week?"

He looks confused. "Oh! Yes, she was a color war captain. Wait, what's your boyfriend's name again?"

"Gavin."

His forehead wrinkles. "I don't remember her mentioning him."

"It has to be her. How many color war captains named Sam can there be?"

"What does he do there?" Eli asks.

"He's a sailing instructor," Kat says. "What about Sam?"

"She's a counselor for the little kids. Eight- and nine-year-olds."

"He sleeps in a junior bunk too. That's so funny! Such a small world!"

They continue talking as they walk up ahead and I fall back with Leela. "Everything okay?"

"Now it is," she says. "As long as she stays with Eli and leaves me with my men, everything will be just fine."

"You're not a very good sharer," I say.

"You speak the truth. Although I would be more than happy to share my men with *you*. Either one. You say the word. At least that would help me decide."

"I'll pass," I say. "Enjoy them both."

"Both? But why? They're cute. Kiss one of them. You haven't kissed anyone in, like, two cities."

"Yeah," I say, not looking at her. "I will have to look for some kissing opportunities."

"Now you're talking."

I maneuver the seats so that she's sitting between both of them for dinner. Eli sits next to Kat and I sit on the other side of her beside Sienna.

When we're done with the meal, I ask, "So! Where to now?" I have already asked for the Wi-Fi password, so all I have to do is message him.

"To the bar," Sienna says.

"Which bar?" I ask.

"There's a beach bar a few blocks away that looks pretty happening," Lachlan says.

"Do you know what it's called?" I ask.

Lachlan shrugs. Apparently not.

"To the beach bar a few blocks away!" Sienna calls out. "Onward."

I message Jackson that we're on our way to the beach bar a few blocks away.

Jackson: Can you be more specific?

Me: I'll find out more when we get there.

The crew makes about a hundred stops along the way, and the bar is more like fifteen blocks away, but finally we arrive.

There are tons of people sitting on loungy wicker chairs under red awnings outside. Since there doesn't seem to be an empty table, we go inside where French rock music is blasting. A long wooden bar lines the room. "We made it!" Eli cries. "I was beginning to doubt this place's existence."

"Never doubt me," Lachlan says. "I always deliver. Eventually."

The bar does not have Wi-Fi. Crap. Now what?

"Can I borrow your phone?" I ask Kat. "You have 3G or 4G or whatever it's called in France, right?"

"Yup," she says.

I text the name of the bar, Le Chateau, to Jackson with a note that says, It's me!

See you soon, he writes back.

I order a Kir Royale and try to appear nonchalant while I wait. I talk to everyone, but I'm not really listening. I'm watching the door. And waiting. And watching.

And then there he is.

My heart stops. And blows up again.

He's here. He looks so good. Green shirt, dark jeans. His eyes are searching around the bar and then he sees me. He smiles.

"Hi," he mouths.

"Hi," I mouth back.

He looks away and slowly heads to the other end of the bar, with Matt behind him.

I take a sip. I want to see him again right now! But I can't give myself away. I take another sip.

"Wanna take a walk?" Kat says to me.

"Hmm?"

She wiggles her eyebrows. "A walk? Check out the room?"

Leela is deep in conversation with Lachlan but I lean over and say to her, "We're just taking a walk around the bar!"

She nods distractedly and we turn around the corner.

"Is he here?" Kat asks me.

"Yes."

"Spectacular! Can't wait to meet your man."

"Just remember that Matt doesn't know that Jackson knew I was here."

She shakes her head. "This is all so twisted. I love it."

We find the boys ordering beers.

"Hi, stranger," Jackson says.

He pulls me toward him and I let my lips brush against his cheek. The kiss lingers a few seconds longer than it should.

He keeps his hand on my back.

"Hi," I say.

"Can I get you a drink?"

"Have one already, thanks. This is my friend Kat. Kat, Jackson. And Matt."

"Nice to meet you," Kat says, smiling. "I've heard *all* about you."

"She has," I say.

Matt's cheeks are sunburned. "What's up," he says. He looks from Jackson to me and then back to Jackson. "I guess I know why we had to come here. And to the South of France?"

"I don't know what you're talking about," Jackson says. Then he leans closer to me and whispers, "He's on to me."

"Where's Leela?" Matt asks, craning his neck.

"On the other side of the bar," I say.

"Is she with those guys?" he asks.

"She is."

"Who the hell are they, anyway?" he barks, and takes another chug of his beer.

"People we met in Switzerland," I say.

"You're just hanging out with some random dudes you met in Switzerland?" he asks.

"Yes," I say.

"So where are you from?" Kat asks. She is good at changing the subject and smoothing over awkwardness.

"He's from Toronto, and I'm from Vancouver," Jackson says. "But we go to McGill."

"Oh, right," Kat says. "I love Montreal. It's so adorable!"

"You're adorable," Matt says, smiling.

I give him a look. "You're not allowed to flirt with Kat. Just so we're clear."

Matt throws up his hands. "Why not? Leela can flirt with guys from who knows where, but I can't tell your friend that she's adorable?"

"I have a boyfriend anyway," Kat says. "If that makes you feel better."

"It doesn't," he says, and waves down the bartender. "I'm getting a shot. Who wants one?"

"No, thanks," I say. Kat and Jackson shake their heads no.

"Four shots of vodka," he orders.

"No, I said—" I try to protest.

"Don't worry," Jackson tells me, his hand still on my back. "He'll do them on his own."

"You sure you don't want?" Matt asks when they come. We all nod.

"All right. Then I'll give them to my new friends."

"Who are your new friends?" I ask, bewildered.

"Leela and her boyfriends," he says, and starts carrying them through the room.

"I'll go," Kat says. "To make sure they don't kill him. You guys have fun!"

They disappear in the crowd.

"That's going to be trouble," I say.

"Not our problem," he says.

A minute later, we hear a cheer on the other side of the room and see them all raising their shot glasses. Including Leela. I guess the peace offering worked.

Jackson steps closer to me. "Can we get out of here yet?"

"Let's go."

We run out the door and down the beach. We find a white plastic beach chair that's been left behind on the sand, and I sit back between his legs, resting against him, facing the ocean.

The breeze off the water kisses our faces.

"This is nice," he says.

"Yup," I say.

He plays with my hair and my body sinks into his.

"Syd . . ." he says. His voice trails off. "I like you."

"I like you too," I say.

"I don't normally do this," he says.

"Do what? Follow a girl across a continent?"

"You don't know the half of it," he says, and laughs.

"What do you mean?"

"I was going to surprise you . . . in Switzerland."

"Huh? You were?"

"Yes. We took an overnight train from Prague. And I was about five minutes from Bern when I got your text saying you were on your way here."

I sit up. "No way."

He laughs. "Way."

"So, you just got on another train?"

"We just got on another train."

"That's . . . that's . . ." I don't know what to say. Crazy? Romantic? Instead of saying anything, I turn around and kiss him hard on the lips. When I pull back, I say, "I'm glad you came."

"Me too."

I laugh again. "I just can't believe you traveled all that way to see me."

"I just thought, well, if I don't do it then I might never see you again. And I wanted to see you again. At least for a few more days."

I squeeze his hand again. "How did you get Matt to leave Switzerland?"

He smirks. "I told him it was too cold, and then I asked him if he wanted to see topless girls on the beach instead."

"And that was enough?" I ask.

"Oh yeah."

"Do you think he's upset? Now that he figured it out?"

"Maybe. But he got to see topless girls, didn't he?"

I elbow him in the stomach. "He did."

"I think he misses Leela, too. He knows he messed up."

"Twice."

"Twice," he repeats.

"How did you end up traveling with him, anyway?"

"It was last minute," he says. "Matt said he was going and that I could crash with him."

"Lucky," I say. "What were you supposed to be doing?"

"Going back to Vancouver. Working for my dad."

"He's a doctor, right?"

"Podiatrist."

"You turned down taking care of feet to come to Europe? Shocking!"

He looks out at the water. "He's pretty pissed off, actually."

"Oh." I squeeze his hand. "Sorry."

"No, don't be. I just wanted to get as far from home as possible," he says. "I couldn't spend the whole summer there."

"Do you guys not get along?" I ask.

"Not really," he says. "I'm not the favorite son."

"Who is?"

"My older brother Jonathan. He's the golden boy.

Seriously. My dad actually calls him Golden Boy."

"What's your middle brother's name?"

"Aidan. My dad calls him Silver Boy."

"And what does that make you? Bronze Boy?"

He shakes his head. "Pewter Boy."

"You're kidding."

"I'm not."

"That's awful," I say, horrified.

"They all think it's hilarious. They think I'm the family fuckup. Remember, I'm the one who kills frogs."

"I'm going to call you Platinum Boy," I say. "Platinum's even better than gold."

"What's *your* sister like?" he asks.

"I think she hates me right now," I say. "Since I kind of ran away from home, too."

"Yeah, well, it sounds like you needed a break from your family."

I tense. "I came because your friend pulled a number on my friend, remember? Not because I needed a break."

"You didn't need a break? From everything you've told me, it sounds like you needed a break."

"I . . . I guess I did need a break," I admit.

He pulls me closer to him. "Maybe it will be good for your mom," he says. "You being away. Not having you to depend on all the time."

"Maybe," I say. "Or maybe everything will go to shit."

"Also possible," he says.

I laugh.

"Hey," he says. "Let's go to Monte Carlo."

"Huh? What? When?"

"Tomorrow," he says.

"Just for the day?"

"Yes. The two of us. We'll take the train out in the morning and come back at night."

"But what will I tell Leela?"

"That you're going with me for the day. She'll understand."

I doubt that. But it's my trip, too. And maybe it would be good for her and Kat to have some one-on-one time?

We hear loud talking and laughing down the beach. In English.

"Is that them?" I ask.

"I think so."

The whole crew of them, including Leela and Matt, spot us at the same time.

The Aussies start hooting. "It's the lovebirds! We found them!"

"Well, hello," Leela says, wiggling her eyebrows. "Unfinished business, I guess?"

She winks at me and I realize I'm relieved she's not mad.

"We're going swimming!" Gabriel says.

"They're wasted," I say.

"Yes," Jackson says, still holding me on his lap.

"But we don't have our suits on," Leela says.

"So we go without suits," Lachlan says. "Come on, guys. Let's do it!"

"Do you think it's cold?" Kat asks.

"I'm not sure I want to do this," Eli says.

"We're all being such wimps!" Sienna screams.

Without saying a word, Yosef drops his pants and boxers. He tosses off his shirt. He's walking to the shore butt naked.

"Omigod," Leela says.

"I'm coming, too!" cries Sienna, and tosses off her dress.

Kat giggles like crazy, and steps out of her jumpsuit. She leaves on her bra and thong. "Come on!" she says to Leela, who hesitates before squealing and following her. This is crazy. How many shots did they have?

Lachlan, Gabriel, and Eli go next.

Leela turns to me. "Sydney, you better get in here!"

I stand up.

"Are we doing this?" Jackson asks.

"We are."

I take off my dress, but leave on my bra and polka-dot undies, and run down the beach. I hear Jackson behind me. I dive into the water and know he's with me.

I put my arms around his neck. "Hi," I say.

"You look good wet," he says.

I kiss him, hard. "You taste good wet. Salty."

"Matt! You're the only chickenshit. You better get in here!" Leela cries.

"It looks cold!" he says.

"Don't be a baby!" Leela yells. "What happened to no regrets?"

He strips off his jeans. He hesitates before taking his shirt off, but then he does that too. I remember what Leela said about his chest. I can see a small indentation where the muscle should be but I doubt I would have noticed if I hadn't been told.

"Real men take it all off," Gabriel yells. Matt strips off his boxers too.

"Geronimo!" he shrieks as he runs into the water.

The water is calm and we all splash and laugh until a few minutes later someone starts yelling at us in French. Giggling and shivering, we grab our clothes and make our way back to La Lune.

"You can have my room," Kat says to me as we walk back.

"Really?" I ask.

"Yeah. I'll sleep in your bed. Go have fun."

"You're the best," I say. I contemplate asking Leela if she's okay with it, but technically she did the same thing to me back in London. So I think it's fair.

I pull Jackson by the hand. "I got us a room," I say.

"Is it by the hour?" he asks.

"It is not. We have the *whole* night."

"We are going to have to think of a whole lot of activities to fill the whole night," he says.

"I think we can swing it," I say, and lead him up the stairs.

When we wake up the next morning, I have nine messages.

Leela: You gave Kat your bed?

Leela: Seriously?

Leela: She's your friend, not mine!

Leela: Whatever. It's fine. Hope you're having fun.

Leela: You owe me!

Leela: You up yet? What are we doing today?

Leela: Should I wait for you?

Leela: I'm going to wait for you.

Leela: I'm in the room. Waiting for you.

"Morning," Jackson says, kissing me on the lips.

"I have morning breath," I tell him.

"So do I," he says. "Want to get some breakfast and then we'll look at the train schedule for Monte Carlo?"

I look down at my phone. Leela is clearly freaking out. And she would want to see Monte Carlo, too. And it's not really fair to leave her with Kat, is it? Kat is *my* friend, not Leela's. "About that . . . how would you feel about a group date?"

MONTE CARLO, MONACO

The Basics: Monaco is a city-state on the French Riviera. It's known for its casinos, wealthy people, royal family, and yachts.

Look, there's Princess Alexandra! Just kidding. You're not going to see any royals up close. And you probably don't know who Princess Alexandra is anyway.

Two hours later, our entire crew is on the train. Me, Jackson, Matt, Leela, Kat, Lachlan, Sienna, Gabriel, Eli, and Yosef.

"We can act like we're alone," Jackson says. "We'll just pretend they're an annoying family of eight."

Kat and Eli are playing cards, and Leela is giving Yosef a shoulder massage. Matt is talking to Gabriel and pretending not to notice that Leela is giving Yosef a shoulder massage. Leela is clearly trying to rub in the fact that she has two hot guys into her and that she and Matt are *over*. At least she doesn't seem too upset that he's coming along. Or that Jackson and I are getting together again.

When the train pulls up to the station, we all cheer.

We are all dressed to impress. The casino we're going to has a no shorts and no flip-flops rule. The guys are wearing pants, button-downs, and their dressiest shoes, and the girls are all wearing dresses and our prettiest sandals. I'm wearing Kat's navy tube dress again. We all brought our passports too, since Monaco is technically another country, but we didn't need to show them on the train.

When we finally get to the Monte Carlo Casino, we're all speechless.

"It's gorgeous," Leela says.

"Huge," says Matt.

It looks like a golden castle.

"I think I'm in heaven," Eli says, admiring the line of expensive cars in the long driveway. "Look at that Aston Martin. It's the most beautiful thing I've ever seen."

"I'm totally going to tell Sam you said that," Kat jokes, poking him on the shoulder.

"Second most beautiful," he clarifies.

Still speaking in hushed, reverent tones, we step into the atrium.

"It's like a church!" Kat exclaims.

The floor is white marble and the walls look like they're made of gold. There are columns everywhere, and chandeliers, and the ceilings are sky-high.

We each pay the ten-euro entrance fee and head inside.

We enter what's called the Salle Renaissance.

Sienna jumps up and down. "Pokies! I love pokies." She's

pointing to the slot machines.

"I'm finding the poker table," Eli says.

"I want to play roulette," Kat says.

Lachlan looks at his phone. "Okay, guys, it's two p.m. Let's all meet here at seven."

"Seven? You're going to gamble for five hours?" Sienna asks, incredulous.

"I want to get my ten euros' worth!"

"I read about a place called Brasserie M," I say. "It's on the harbor. Should we meet there?"

Everyone agrees.

"But my phone won't work if you can't find it," I say. "I don't want anyone getting lost."

"Don't worry," Jackson says, taking my hand. "They'll find it. Or they can text me."

"Okay," I say gratefully. "What do you want to do?"

He tilts his head to the side. "How do you feel about roulette?"

Tip: Monaco is one of the richest places in the world. If you're lucky, it could rub off on you!

But it probably won't.

After Jackson and I buy ten euros' worth of chips each, I've pretty much used up all sixty of my euros for today. I will have to dig into tomorrow's budget for dinner. Or maybe I can win some money at this place? That would be nice.

We go upstairs to the Salle Blanche, which is gorgeous. Satin drapes adorn the walls, and gold chandeliers hang over the roulette tables.

"Let's go outside," Jackson says, and we go onto the terrace. The floor is marble even outside, there are still chandeliers, and there's a never-ending view of the harbor, palm trees, and blue water.

"Wanna play?" Jackson asks, standing behind me and wrapping his arms around my waist.

"Are you usually lucky?" I ask.

He kisses the side of my neck. "I'd like to *get* lucky."

"Focus, Jackson, focus."

"It's hard. You are seriously hot right now. Have you seen what you look like in that dress?" His hands run along my bare shoulders, sending shivers down my spine.

I turn around and press myself against his body. I can feel every part of him despite our clothes. I wrap my arms around his neck and our eyes lock.

"Hi," he says.

"Hi."

"I think we're supposed to play roulette now," I say, my breathing heavy. "Isn't that why we're here?"

"I'm here to watch you in that dress. And to watch you take it off later."

"One step at a time. C'mon. Let's go, I've never done this before."

"You've never done what before?" he asks, pressing against me even harder. "Gotten frisky in public?"

291

"I've never played *roulette* before," I correct him. "Have you?"

"No," he says, leading me toward one of the tables. "But I've seen enough James Bond movies to figure it out. Do you have a lucky number?"

"No," I say.

"Then let's bet on two."

"Why two?" I ask.

"The day we met. July second."

My heart melts. "You remember when we met?"

"Of course. Baggage *re*claim at Heathrow. Feels lucky to me."

"Let's do it," I say. "What are the odds?"

"Thirty-five to one."

"So if we bet five euros, we make a hundred and seventy-five euros?"

He raises an eyebrow. "That was quick."

"I'm good at math," I say. "And if we bet two chips—ten euros—that's three hundred and fifty euros."

"And if we bet all four chips?"

"That's seven hundred euros," I say.

He leans over and whispers into my ear. "We could get a room at the Ritz."

"Or fund the next week," I say, turning toward him.

"Let's do it," he says slowly, watching me. "Let's go all in."

I'm suddenly not sure if we're just talking about the bet. "Yeah?"

He nods. "Yeah."

I place all four chips on the black two. My heart races. Imagine if we win? I know the odds are against us, but it could happen. We could get lucky.

With the bet.

With us.

I bite my lip. If we win, maybe it's a sign that this isn't just a summer fling. That what we have is real. Is it possible? Could we be *real*?

The dealer spins.

It goes around . . . and around . . . and around . . . it's slowing down. It's getting close. It's on the two. It's on the two!

And it rolls past the two and onto red twenty-five.

The dealer takes away all four of our chips.

My heart sinks. We didn't win. We're not lucky.

Jackson sighs. "It was a long shot. But I thought maybe we had it."

"We're out of chips," I say. I feel a lump in my throat. What did I expect? That we were going to hit the jackpot, get rich, and stay together forever?

"I hate roulette," Jackson says.

"Me too," I say. "At least we only lost ten euros each."

"Why don't we walk around Monaco," he says, running his thumb down my arm. "Explore. Find a secret spot. *Pretend* we have a room at the Ritz."

"Okay," I say, and take his hand. "Let's go. It's almost four."

Suddenly, I don't want to waste a second.

★ ★ ★

"How'd you do?" I ask Sienna and Gabriel when they sit down at our table at Brasserie M.

Jackson and I play footsie under the table.

"Up two cocktails," she says. "Purchased by a dashing Persian man before Gabriel showed up and scared him off."

"Sorry," he says. "I tried to tell them I was your brother. I wouldn't have bothered you, but I was down thirty euros and needed some cash."

"You?" I ask Lachlan.

"Even," he says.

"I'm down twenty euros," Leela says. "But Matt's down fifty, so I win. Where are Eli and Yosef?"

"I hope they didn't get lost. This place wasn't that hard to find, was it? Did you check your messages?" I ask Jackson. "Can they not find us?"

"Don't worry about them," Kat says. "Eli is on a lucky streak. I think he's still at the casino with Yosef, although Yosef is just cheering him on."

"He doesn't seem like much of a cheerer," I say. "He's kind of subdued."

Kat laughs. "Oh, he's cheering. Eli was up a thousand euros. We might not see them tonight."

Wow. Now that's lucky.

Jackson and I order the Nicoise salad and chicken paillard to share. Leela has a Caesar salad and a pizza. Kat orders *fois de veau*, which she tells me is calf's liver.

I can't help but make a face.

Halfway through the meal, Eli and Yosef show up, with wide Cheshire cat smiles on their faces.

"Good news?" Jackson asks.

They nod, eyes wide.

"How good?"

Eli pulls out a wad of colorful bills. "I won four thousand euros."

We shriek.

"You did?" Leela cries.

He nods.

"That's insane," I say.

"Congrats!" we all cheer.

Kat gives him a high five.

"Mazel tov!" I call out.

"I hope you know what this means," Eli says.

"What?" Kat asks.

He drops a pile of colored money on the blue tablecloth. "Dinner's on me."

A cheese plate, two chocolate mousses, two soufflés, three tiramisus, and four bottles of Moët & Chandon Brut Impérial champagne later, Eli pays the bill with a flourish and we shuffle onto the beach.

"Let's take a picture," Kat says.

"I will take it," Yosef says.

"No way," says Leela. "I want you to be in it. We all have to be in it."

"Excuse me," Kat says to a passing couple. "Will you take a picture for us?"

"*Bien sûr*," the man says, and takes her phone.

"I want it too!"

"So do I!"

"Let me give you my phone!"

"I'll send it to everyone," Kat says.

We stand against the railing and scrunch together.

"Make sure to get some of the yachts in the shot," Leela instructs.

"Maybe I should rent a yacht," Eli says.

"You didn't win that much money."

"No kidding. That dinner cost me half of it."

Leela stands between Yosef and Lachlan, and puts her arms around both of them. Sienna puts her arm around Gabriel, and Eli puts his arm around Kat. Matt stands beside Jackson.

Jackson pulls me into him, his chin resting against the top of my head. My body fits into his perfectly.

"*Un! Deux! Trois!*" the man says.

"Take a few," Kat says. "Like ten."

Snap. Snap. Snap. "*C'est bon.*"

"Thank you!" she says, and we all disband.

Jackson takes my hand.

"The next train leaves in fifteen minutes," Sienna says.

"Let's go back," Leela says.

"You guys can sleep in my room again," Kat tells me.

Leela opens her mouth to say something, but then seems

to change her mind. She smiles at me instead.

"Who wants to go skinny dipping?" Lachlan calls out.

"Again?"

"Again!"

Jackson and I hold hands the whole way home. Kat sends the picture to all of us, and those of us who have accounts and Wi-Fi post it online. Even Matt posts it. Hashtags include #monaco #rivieradreams #noregrets and #strikingitrich.

JUAN-LES-PINS, FRANCE (Again)

The next day, July 19, is more sun and more ice cream.

It's also Addison's birthday.

After the beach, when they should just be getting up, I email my mom.

Doing anything special with the b-day girl? I ask.

She's going out with her friend Sloane, she writes back.

I try to catch Addison on FaceTime, but she doesn't answer. I message her instead.

Me: HAPPY BIRTHDAY! 🎂 🎉 🎈 🎁 Look what I got you!

I snap a picture of the Paris snow globe I bought her the week before. I haven't been able to find one in Juan-les-Pins. Even though Jackson has been helping me look. And I forgot to get one in Switzerland.

Me: I hope you have an amazing day. Love you.

She doesn't answer. I take a shower.

"I'm hooking up with one of them tonight," Leela tells me as we get ready.

"Which one?" I ask.

298

"I haven't decided yet," she says. "It'll be a game-time decision."

"You're debating between Yosef and Lachlan, right?"

"Yes . . ." She hesitates.

"Not Matt. Right? Not Matt?"

"Not Matt," she says. "I'm done with Matt. It's not just all the shit he pulled. I don't like *myself* when I'm with him, you know? I become the worst version of me. Whiny. Jealous. Controlling. It doesn't feel good."

"Wow. Okay then." I'm proud of her. "It sounds like you're ready to move on."

"I know. I'm going to! I'm ready." She applies her lipstick in the mirror. "Hey, do you think Kat hooked up with Eli last night?"

"No, definitely not," I say.

She shrugs. "They were getting a little cozy on the train home. I just wondered."

"She loves her boyfriend."

"Then why did she leave him to go to Paris?"

"Because she wanted to go to *Paris*. And he was going to camp anyway."

"Okay," she says in a singsong voice. "If you say so."

We do another group dinner. This one involves *moules frites*.

"Do you think this one is too closed?" Leela asks me. "Or can I eat it?" She is sitting to my left at our long, rectangular table.

"I wouldn't," I tell her.

"What are you talking about?" Sienna asks.

"If a mussel is too closed, you could get food poisoning because that means it's not cooked all the way," I explain.

"Yikes," says Sienna.

Leela dips a piece of bread in her sauce instead.

"More wine?" Lachlan asks her.

"Sure," she says, smiling at him.

"I think we're going to take off tomorrow," Eli says to Kat, who he's sitting beside.

Kat frowns. "Already? How come?"

"We have to get to Barcelona," he says. "And then Portugal. Then Yosef is flying to Brazil, and I fly home."

"Are you going straight to camp?" Kat asks. She twirls a strand of hair around her fingers.

"Almost," Eli says. "I fly into New York and then I'm going to drive up the next day. Will I see you there?"

"I don't leave Paris until August tenth," she says. "Gavin's gonna try and come to NYC for a night to see me when I get back."

"Yeah, Samantha's going to take a day off when I get there. We're going to get a room at a B and B in the Hudson Valley."

Leela takes a sip of wine. "I hope it's nicer than La Lune."

"Oh, it will be," Eli says. He taps his chest pocket twice. "I've got my winnings now."

The waitress comes and refills our glasses with bottled water. None of the restaurants offer tap.

"What about you guys?" I ask the Aussies.

"We fly out of Heathrow," Sienna says. "So we're going to Paris next, then Amsterdam, and then London."

"That's our trip in reverse," I say.

"What about you?" Lachlan asks me.

"We fly out of Rome," I tell him as I open another mussel.

"Me too," Matt says.

"Can't wait," Leela says, rolling her eyes.

"I thought we were friends again," Matt says to her, and blows her a kiss.

"Best friends," Leela says, smiling sweetly. She finishes her glass of wine, and pours herself another. She turns to Jackson. "Are you flying out of Rome too?"

He shakes his head. "I fly out of Athens."

"You do?" I ask.

"Yeah," he says. "Air Canada was having a special."

"When do you leave?" Leela asks.

"Two weeks. Same day you leave Rome."

"We're all splitting up," Sienna says. "How sad!"

At the words *splitting up*, I tense.

Jackson puts his hand on my knee. We look at each other. Splitting up.

We're splitting up.

We haven't discussed it, but we've both known it was coming. After Juan-les-Pins, we go our separate ways.

"Hey, Syd, where are we off to next?" Leela asks.

"I don't know," I say, my mouth dry. I take a sip of water.

"This is our fourth night," she says. "We're not going to stay more than five, are we?"

"At some point I might have to go back to work," Kat says.

"I don't know," I say again. I take Jackson's hand. I don't let go.

"*Excusez-moi?*" Leela says to the waiter. "Can we get another bottle of wine?"

About an hour later, we're all walking down the beach. Leela is singing. Loudly. Then suddenly she stops.

"I don't feel well," she says, swaying.

"Let's sit down," I say.

She plops right down in the sand. "My tummy hurts. I think I ate a bad mussel. Did I eat a bad mussel? Doesn't it sound gross to eat a mussel? Yosef has muscles, and I wouldn't want to eat them."

"She's drunk," Matt says.

"Yeah," I say. "I think I should take her back to the room."

"Don't let Matt see me get sick," she begs.

"I won't," I promise, even though, obviously, he heard that.

We leave the rest of the crew on the beach and Jackson and Kat help me carry Leela back to the hotel.

Matt offers to help but Leela screams, "No way." He challenges Lachlan to an arm wrestle instead.

Tip: Rosé is even cheaper than water in the South of France!

That doesn't mean the wine is cheap. It just means the water's expensive.

I unlock our door, put her on the bed, and hand her a bottle of water.

"Drink this," I say.

"Where's Matt?" Leela asks.

"On the beach," I say.

"Good. Good, good, good," she says. She frowns. Her face is flushed. "He's not going to hook up with Kat, is he?"

"No," I say. "Kat's right here."

"Oh," Leela says, staring at her. "Hi, Kat."

"Hi," she says, waving. "Also, I would never do that. Never."

"Good," Leela says, head bobbing. "What about Sienna?"

Sienna had been chatting up a Swedish girl on the beach.

"I think she's going the other way tonight," I say.

"Also good," Leela says. "Jackson, tell him not to hook up with anybody, 'kay? Can you go now? It's girl time."

He sighs.

"Thanks for helping me bring her up," I tell him, walking him to the door.

"Of course," he says. "Come to my room in five?"

"Will do," I say. "I just need to make sure she's okay."

"I can stay with her," Kat says. "You can take my room with Jackson."

"No!" Leela cries. "Stay with me, Syd. Don't leave. I miss you. I miss you so much. All year I missed you. Will you braid my hair? You're so good at braiding hair. Has she ever braided your hair, Kat?"

"No," Kat says.

"I'll come get you," I mouth to Jackson.

He closes the door behind him.

I try not to feel too aggravated. I want to be hooking up with Jackson, not braiding someone's hair. I try to calm down. She needs me. Leela has always been there for me. And anyway, friends come first.

"Okay," I say, sitting behind her on the bed. "I'll braid your hair. But you have to drink more water."

She takes another sip and then says, "The room is spinning! It's magic!"

"The magic Lune," I say, brushing her hair with my fingers.

"Lune means moon you know," Leela says. "Not loony."

"The magic moon," I say. "Do you have an elastic?"

"The bad mussel is back," Leela says. "It's coming back right now. It's—"

"The bathroom!" Kat says. "Go to the bathroom!"

"She's not going to make it!" I cry. "I meant to move over the garbage! Where's the garb—"

But it's too late. She pukes all over a bag. You've got to be kidding me. The smell is noxious.

"I hope that's *her* bag," Kat says. "The duffel-suitcase is hers, right?"

"Yes," I say, relieved. I do not want half-digested mussels all over my snow globes and clothes. And my jeans are already stained enough.

"Come on, Leela. Stand. You have to go to the bathroom."

We help her up and walk her to the mini-bathroom. I lift up the seat.

"My hair," she says. "I don't want puke in my hair."

"I'm going to braid it," I tell her.

"French?"

"Of course," I say.

"Thank you," she says. "Thank you for everything. I love you. I'm sorry I've been a bitch. This trip has been so messed up. First, I was supposed to be on it with the love of my life, and then he screwed me over and then you came along, which was amazing, don't get me wrong, but then Matt keeps showing up everywhere, and it's just been hard. I can't escape him! I know he's here by accident and I'm trying to pay attention to Yosef and Lachlan but I can't really because Matt is here. And I still love him! Even though it hurts! Even though he's an idiot! I know he makes me miserable, trust me, I know he brings out the worst in me, but he's so cute with his little sunburn. And Kat is the super-amazing person who is so much better at everything than me and now she's here too. It's just too much."

"It's going to be okay," I say. "We'll figure it all out."

On that note, she vomits once more while I hold her hair.

I don't make it to Jackson's. Leela makes me promise I'll stay, and I do.

Also, I'm pretty sure I don't smell my freshest.

Jackson stays in his room, Kat goes to hers, and I sleep in my original bed. I knock twice on the wall.

He knocks back, knock, knock, knock.

My phone pings.

Jackson: Sneak out for a kiss?

Me: K

I carefully and quietly slip on my flip-flops and sneak out of the room.

He's waiting in the hallway.

"You're not leaving tomorrow, are you?" he asks.

"No," I say. "Definitely not."

"But the day after?"

"I don't know. Maybe."

We're both silent.

"So this is it?" he asks. "On Wednesday, we just say good-bye?"

"I guess," I say.

"Syd, I don't want this to be good-bye. Let's keep traveling together."

"The four of us?" I ask. "I wish. But we can't—being

around Matt is making Leela miserable."

"Then you travel with Leela and I'll travel with Matt and we'll meet up at the end of the trip. Just the two of us. In Greece."

My heart stops. "Greece?"

"Yeah. Maybe you could change your flight home. Instead of leaving from Rome, you can meet me in Greece and fly home from there."

"But . . . I can't ditch Leela."

"Just for a few days."

"She'd kill me."

"So travel with me for a few days now, and she can hang out with the Aussies."

My heart sinks. "She's not going to travel with people she barely knows. And anyway, they're going the wrong way."

"Can't she travel with Kat?"

"Kat is my friend, not hers."

"I'm guessing she's not going to want to travel the three of us."

"Nope," I say sadly.

He sighs. "So this is it?"

"I'm sorry. I wish it wasn't. But I can't leave her. She needs me."

"Well, I *want* you."

I shake my head. I can't leave Leela. I just can't. "We can't always get what we want," I say. "Look, we'll do something special tomorrow night. Just us. For real." I feel the lump in my throat again and kiss him lightly. "Good night."

"Night," he says. I can hear the defeat in his voice.

I still feel his lips when I climb into my bed and close my eyes.

My FaceTime starts ringing at 7:10 in the morning.

It's my sister.

I connect. "Hello?"

She doesn't say anything. Nothing. The camera is not even facing her. What is she doing? What time is it there? It's six hours earlier. So that makes it 1:10 a.m.

"Addison? Addison! Addison!" I yell.

"Syd?" I hear. "Hello?"

"Pick up the phone!"

I hear tumbling, and then she's pointing the camera at herself. "Hi!"

"Happy birthday?" I say.

"Thank you!"

"Where are you?" I ask. It looks like she's on a street.

"Out!" she says. She's smiling and laughing. She can't hold the camera straight.

Goose bumps cover my arms. "Are you drunk?"

"Are you?" she answers back.

Shit. "I'm nineteen and in Europe. You're sixteen and in America."

"Seventeen today," she sings.

Leela is sitting up in bed, wide awake.

"You're not driving, are you?"

She doesn't answer.

"Addi! Who's driving?"

"Um . . . Sloane!"

Who is this goddamn Sloane? "Did she drink too?"

"Um . . ." Addison drops the phone on the pavement. "Sorry! One sec!"

"Listen, Addi?" I say. "You have to call a cab."

"We don't have any money," she says.

"Do you have Uber on your phone?"

"No," she says. "I think my phone's going to die. Soon."

"Call Dad," I say. "He'll come get you."

"No," she says. "I can't call Dad. Shit. What do I do? Can you come get me?"

"Are you kidding?"

"You promised. You said you'd come home if I needed you. I need you!"

My head pounds. "Addi, how drunk are you? I can't fly home to pick you up. It would take me a day to get to you."

"I can't believe you just left me. And that you won't help me!"

"Call Dad! Now!"

"No. I don't want to call Dad. I want to call Mom."

My heart races. "She won't drive. If you don't want to call Dad, call Sloane's parents!"

"She won't call her parents. She says she's fine to drive. But . . . I don't know . . ."

"Don't let her. DO NOT get in that car." I am panicked.

"My phone's going to die in, like, a minute. I'm calling Mom."

She disconnects.

Fuck. I stare at my phone. What's happening?

I call her back. She doesn't answer. Shit. Should I call my mother? What do I do? I message Addison again.

Me: What's happening?

Me: Addison?

Three dots.

Addison: I told her she has to come get me or Sloane's driving. She said she's coming.

I stare at the phone.

Addison: Phone going bye.

"What's going on?" Leela asks.

"My sister is drunk and with some person I don't know who is also drunk, and they just called my mom to pick them up."

Leela sits up. "Your mom's going to drive? Isn't that good?"

"Is it? She hasn't driven in years. And what if she has a panic attack while she's on the road? I'm sure she's freaking out. I'm going to kill my sister." I'm breathing faster and faster and my heart is thumping. Am I going to have a panic attack? For real?

"It's going to be okay," Leela says. She comes over to my bed and puts her arm around me. "It is. Your mom is going to get them. Everything is going to be fine. Can we call your

310

mom and see how she's doing?"

"She doesn't have a freakin' cell phone anymore because she doesn't leave the house. I don't even know if she still has a valid license."

"Let's call your sister back, then." She takes my phone and tries to get through on FaceTime. There's no answer. She tries calling her number. It goes straight to voice mail. "I think her phone is off."

"It's dead," I say. "What do we do?"

She squeezes my shoulder. "We wait."

It's two hours later, and I still haven't heard anything.

Leela is sitting beside me, wrapped in a towel.

I'm freaking out. "They could be in a ditch somewhere. It's three thirty in the morning there."

"They're not in a ditch," Leela says. "I bet your mom picked Addison up, they went home, and now they're fast asleep. That's why they didn't answer your call."

"But why wouldn't they call me?"

"Because they're sleeping." She looks around the room. "Come on. Let's get out of here. This room is depressing and smells like puke."

"That's because you vomited all over your suitcase."

She winces. "Yeah. Sorry about that. I will find a way to wash everything today. But for now, we really have to get out of here."

I shake my head. "I don't want to leave. What if they call?"

"Go shower. I will watch the phone. I will not let it out of my sight. Then we will find a place with Wi-Fi and coffee."

I shower. I drench everything in the bathroom but I don't care. I put on shorts and a T-shirt and we go.

Jackson's room is quiet. He's somehow still asleep when I've been up for centuries.

We go down to the *boulangerie* and order coffees. I buy a *pain au chocolat*, but I'm too nervous to eat, and Leela is too hungover.

"Should I try calling the house again?" I wonder.

"I'm sure they're just asleep."

"Is it wrong that I'm Googling *car accidents, Maryland*, and *three women*?"

"Stop Googling," she says. "Gimme your phone."

I hand it over.

"I'm looking at your pictures," she says, and scrolls through my photos.

I take a small nibble of the *pain au chocolat*. But I'm really not hungry.

"Love this shot of us in Switzerland," she says. "We look shockingly good in wet suits." Her forehead wrinkles. "Wait. Why do you have a picture of Jackson in Berlin?"

Oh shit.

"It's not Berlin," I say.

"Your PhotosMap is telling me that he took this in Berlin. I'm so confused. Was he sending you pictures from Berlin?"

312

Crap. "Yes."

"You were in touch with him?"

I close my eyes. "Yes."

"I don't understand. Why didn't you tell me?"

"Because you wanted nothing to do with him," I say.

"Yeah, but . . ." Her voice trails off. She stares at me. "Did you plan to meet him here?"

"No," I say quickly. "I only found out he was coming when we were on the train. And then I didn't want to tell you because I thought you might not want to come. . . . I'm sorry. I should have told you."

"Yeah," she says, her voice tight. "You should have told me."

Neither of us speaks.

"There you are!" we hear. We look up to see Kat at the entrance of the *boulangerie*. "What's shaking, ladies?"

I guess it's time to tell her how fucked up my family is.

"My sister got drunk last night and my mother had to drive to get her in the middle of the night but she hasn't driven a car on her own since I was twelve. She doesn't drive at all, actually. She doesn't even leave the house, and now I haven't heard anything from them for hours." I take a breath. "*Pain au chocolat?*"

"Whoa," Kat says, sitting down beside me. "So that's why you didn't go away to school. To help your mom. And why you were being weird about potentially moving off campus with me?"

313

I nod.

She gives me a hug. "I am so sorry. Are you okay? Is there anything I can do?"

A message pops up on my phone.

Addison: Did I call you last night?

"It's her!" I FaceTime her right away.

"Mmmph," she says.

"Omigod, Ad, I've been worried sick! What happened? Are you okay?"

Leela and Kat are mouthing things at each other.

"I'm fine," she says. She looks exhausted. And hungover.

"Did Mom come to get you?" I ask.

"She did," she says.

I don't believe it. "That's incredible. She actually drove?"

"No! She tried to drive, she got in the car, she even turned on the ignition, but then she started to panic and turned it off."

"So what happened?"

"She called a cab. And she went with the driver to get me, and then picked us up. We dropped Sloane off first, and then came home."

"Wow. Still. She got in a cab. That's impressive. She hasn't been in a cab in years." I'm proud of her. "And she didn't have a panic attack along the way?"

"No, she *did* have a panic attack. The driver had to pull over. But she eventually got back in the car."

"So you were all fine?" I ask.

"We were all fine," she says. "She says I'm grounded for life, but we're fine. Syd, I don't feel well. I'll call you later, 'kay? I just wanted to let you know I'm okay."

"Thanks. Happy birthday. Love you."

"Love you, too."

We hang up. Leela and Kat are watching me.

"All good?" Kat says.

I nod. And then I burst into tears.

We go back to the room to change into our bathing suits.

"Are you mad at me?" I ask Leela.

"Yes," Leela says, looking everywhere in the room except at me.

"I'm sorry I didn't tell you."

She sighs. "I just can't believe you'd screw me over for a silly fling."

I lower my voice. I don't know if he's next door or not. "What if it's not a fling?"

She shakes her head. "Syd. It's a summer fling."

I hesitate. "He asked me to go to Greece with him."

"What?" She turns to me. "He did not."

"He did."

"Do you want to go?" she asks.

"Well . . . I said no. I'm not going to leave you by yourself."

She nods. "Thank you. Because I don't want to *be* by myself.

"I *said* no."

"I'm glad you agreed not to ditch your best friend, a person who you've supposedly missed all year, to travel with someone you barely know and will never see again. That seems like the right move." Her voice is dripping with sarcasm.

Does she have to be so mean about it?

There's a knock on the door. "Ladies? It's me," Kat says. "Are you ready to go to the beach?"

"Come in," I say, opening the door.

"I saw Jackson downstairs," Kat says, shifting the turquoise beach bag on her shoulder. "He's looking for you. That boy is crazy-pants about you."

"Of course he is," Leela says. "It's still summer."

"What happens when you leave?" Kat asks. "Are you guys breaking up?"

"We can't break up if we were never officially together," I say quietly.

"You're not going to try and make it work?" Kat asks. "Gavin and I stayed together even though we're on different continents. You don't just break up because you're apart. Not if you have something special."

Leela snort-laughs. "Come on. There's no way Sydney and Jackson could have a long-distance relationship."

I flush.

"Why not?" Kat asks defiantly. "They could so!"

Leela looks at me. "First of all, you are the worst at

keeping in touch. The *worst*. I could never get hold of you."

"I was busy!" Can't she cut me some slack?

"I know you were busy. I'm not *mad* at you for being busy. I'm just saying that if you were too busy to text me back, your best friend for a million years, do you really think you're going to have time to make a relationship with Jackson work?"

I don't answer. She's not wrong.

"And even if you did, would you really trust him? He slept with like twenty-five girls last year, and those are just the ones I happen to *know* about."

Every time she talks about him, the number of girls he's slept with rises. "He didn't have a girlfriend then."

"Yeah, well, are you sure he even wants a girlfriend?"

My chest tightens. "I don't know."

"Do *you* even want a boyfriend?"

"I don't know!" I've never really wanted one before. It was always too complicated. And anything with Jackson would be even *more* complicated.

"And not just any boyfriend," Leela continues. "A long-distance boyfriend. Are you sure you want one of those? You didn't seem to want a long-distance best friend."

Ouch.

Kat's lips are in a thin line. "Leela, you're being a bit harsh, don't you think? Sydney had a lot going on. More than I even knew. I've lost touch with most of my New York best friends too. But that doesn't mean they're not my best friends. And long distance can work. I'm living proof. Gavin and I have been apart all summer."

Leela's eyes shoot venom at Kat. "Are you? You and Eli were getting a little cozy on the train from Monaco. And where did you sleep last night?"

Kat's face flushes. "In my room! Alone! Eli and I were talking. We're *friends*. We were bonding over the fact that we both miss our significant others! Nothing happened! Why would you think anything happened?"

Leela crosses her arms in front of her chest. "Okay. I'm sorry. But just because you're well-behaved doesn't mean Jackson will be. He's going to hurt her. And she doesn't need that. And anyway, it's not like she's going to visit him—" Her voice stops abruptly.

"She might," Kat says.

Leela just shakes her head. "She's never come to visit me once."

"You know I wanted to," I say, my voice cracking. "And I'm here, aren't I?"

"Yeah, but you still check your phone every five minutes," she says.

"I'm trying to look out for my family!"

"Yeah? Or were you texting Jackson?"

She's not wrong. I was texting Jackson. But I was also trying to keep tabs on my family. I can't just forget all about them. They need me.

"Maybe you'll be able to make it work long distance,"

Leela snaps. "At least you write *him* back." She grabs her bag, shoves her feet into her flip-flops, and storms off.

I sigh.

"Whoa," Kat says. "She's pissed off."

"Well, I'm pissed off, too." Pissed off and tired. My sister scared the hell out of me. And maybe this thing with Jackson is just a fling. But I don't need Leela making me feel like shit about it.

I give her five minutes to calm down and then find her on the beach.

She's sitting on the sand, facing the ocean.

I sit down beside her. I don't say anything.

"I'm sorry," she says. "I was being a total asshole. Again."

"Yes," I say. The water laps our ankles. "You were. But I should have told you about Jackson. And I should have been there for you this year."

"I missed you," she says. "And I know he's going to break your heart, Syd. I know him. I do. He's going to hurt you. And I don't want you to go through what I'm going through with Matt. It sucks and you have enough shit to deal with." Her eyes are wet.

I look out at the water. "I want us to have fun. I want you to have fun. I want us to have fun together."

"I know. I think I need to get out of here. It's too hard for me to be around Matt even with Lachlan or Yosef around. They're nice and cute although Yosef's a little intense and Lachlan talks too much, but mostly they're not Matt, you know? And I'm totally leading them on, and I'm even leading Sienna on. Yesterday on the beach I think I patted her ass when I was drunk and now she's avoiding me . . . I just need to go." She sounds like she's begging. "Can we leave? Please? Tomorrow morning?"

The thought makes me dizzy. "Tomorrow? Where do you want to go?"

"Venice! Rome! Florence! Tuscany! There's so much to see in Italy. We've been here for four nights already and tonight is going to be night five. That seems like a lot of time to stay in one random beach place. I know leaving Jackson will be hard, but . . . you have to say good-bye eventually, right?"

She's right. I *know* she's right. But I kind of hate that she's the one to make me do it. "I guess."

"So we can leave tomorrow?"

"All right. I'll tell Jackson."

"Why don't you spend the night with him? Just you guys? Since it's your last night."

Gee, thanks, I almost say, but don't.

I find Jackson by himself, lying on a towel in the sand, reading *The Beach*.

I sit down beside him and fill him in on what happened with my mom and sister.

"You should have found me," he says. "I heard noises in your room, but I thought it was just Leela getting sick."

"Nope." I squint in the sun. I don't have my sunglasses.

"So is everything okay now?"

"I guess. Hopefully Addison will never be an idiot again and everything will go back to normal."

"I guess she's the Pewter Girl in your house," he says.

"No, she's not," I say quickly. "I would never call her that."

"Well, maybe now that your mom got into a cab, she'll be more mobile. Or maybe it was a first step. Maybe she'll start getting better."

I shake my head. "She's not going to get better. She had a panic attack in the cab. The whole thing probably made it worse. Now she'll never get in a vehicle again." I shake my head. "I have something else to tell you. Leela wants to leave tomorrow."

He stares out at the water. "But *you* don't have to go. You could stay."

"Here? Forever?"

"Yes. I'll stay with you. We'll rent an apartment on the beach and open a store."

"What would we sell?" I ask.

"Snow globes," he says.

"I can't find a single one here!"

"All the more reason to open a store." He puts his arm around me, and I inhale the scent of suntan lotion and him. "I'm going to miss you," he says.

"I know," I say, and he laughs.

★ ★ ★

We have dinner, just the two of us, at a small bistro by the water.

He orders a bottle of wine, and I think back to Amsterdam. We laugh and joke and share another Nicoise salad, a cheese plate, and a ratatouille. We're going all in on French food.

"So this is it," he says, taking a final bite of the ratatouille. "The last supper."

"I guess so."

"And Greece is completely out of the question?"

I sigh. "I can't go to Greece. I'm flying out of Rome."

"So I'll go to Rome with you," he says. His eyes are hopeful.

"Leela would hate that. I just can't do that to her. She'd be miserable."

"Syd, it's not your responsibility to take care of her," he says. "It's not your responsibility to take care of everyone."

I'm not sure if he's talking about Leela or my family. "Friends take care of each other," I say. "People take care of each other. It *is* my responsibility."

"Does Leela ever take care of you?"

"Yes! She was with me all morning when I was freaking out."

"You stay home when she's sick. You plan everything. You practically carry her bags. It seems like she's taking advantage of you. You know, I was with Leela all year, and

322

she was fine. She had Matt and her sister and she took care of herself."

"You don't understand," I say, my cheeks burning. "I can't just leave her after everything she and I have been through. And I'm not going to just ditch my best friend for a fling."

He stares. "Is that all this is?"

I sink into my chair. I'm so tired. I can't deal with all this in one day. "Isn't it? Am I ever going to hear from you again once the summer's over?"

He looks surprised. "Why wouldn't you ever hear from me again?"

"Didn't you sleep with like twenty-five women this year? Have you spoken to any of *them* again?"

He looks down at his plate. "Is that what you think this is?"

"I don't know what this is!"

"Well, neither do I."

My head hurts. "Do you think we should be a thing? Is that what you want? You're going to call and text me every night from school instead of drinking too many Molsons and hooking up with random girls? Really? When something happens with me, when my mom freaks before my sister's high school graduation, and won't come inside, or has a panic attack halfway through, are you going to drop everything to be there for me? Is that what's going to happen? No. We live in different countries. This isn't going to work. I'm not saying I don't want it to, or don't wish

323

it could, but it just isn't. I don't have the energy to worry about you too."

"I don't want you worrying about me at all," he says. He doesn't say, you wouldn't *have* to worry about me.

"We both know the truth," I say. I make my voice sound strong, but my legs are shaking. "Tonight? This is it."

"Okay," he says, looking at his hands. "This is it. Then let's get out of here."

I offer to split the bill, but he pays.

"Thank you," I say. I reach to hold his hand, but he pretends he doesn't see me do it.

We silently walk back to La Lune.

"Let's go to Kat's room," I say. "She gave me her key."

I lean over to kiss him but he pulls back.

I feel like I've been slapped. "What? You don't want to?"

"I want you to come to Greece with me."

"I can't," I snap. "I just told you that."

We both stand there. Staring at each other.

"So you're not going to come to Kat's room?" I ask.

"I don't think so," he says, his voice cold. "Maybe it's easier to call it right now. While I'm mad."

Is he serious? I feel like I'm in free fall. "You want to say good-bye like this?"

"Easier, no?"

My eyes fill with tears. He looks away.

"Okay," I say. I lean over and kiss him on the cheek. "Good-bye."

"*Au revoir*, Sydney."

I go upstairs and open the door to my room. Leela is already there. She's folding clothes. "I cleaned my bag and did a wash. I threw in your dirty clothes, too. They're on your bed."

There's a pile of undies and T-shirts on my white sheet. "Thank you," I say, surprised.

"I wasn't expecting you," she says, folding a shirt. "Everything okay?"

"You should roll it," I say. "It won't get as wrinkled."

"Oh. Okay." She unfolds the shirt and tries to roll it.

"Let me help," I say, and do it for her.

"So what happened with Jackson?"

"It's over." I sit down on my bed. My legs are still shaking.

She sits down next to me. "I'm sorry."

"Are you?" I ask, hearing the bitterness in my voice.

She sighs. "Of course I am! You know I didn't want you to get hurt."

My head hurts.

"Do you want to talk about it?" she asks.

"No."

"Okay."

We're both silent. I hear a bottle breaking on the street and then shrieks of laugher.

"Do you want to talk about where you want to go tomorrow?" she asks.

Greece, I think, a bitter taste in my mouth. But I'm not going to Greece. I'm taking care of Leela, instead. Just like I didn't go away to college so I could take care of my mother.

"Syd?" she presses.

I pull out my *Travel Europe* from my small backpack, and flip to the map of Europe. "Italy?"

"Finally! Yay. Can we go to Venice?" Leela asks.

"Too far. It's on the eastern side."

"Milan?"

"Too expensive," I say. "And I'm running out of money." At my last bank withdrawal, I had less than eight hundred dollars left. I am cutting it very, very close.

"Florence?"

"Yeah," I say. "Okay. We can go to Florence. And Pisa is on the way."

She pauses. "Do you want to invite Kat to come?"

I wasn't expecting that. "Really?"

"I don't mind. She's growing on me. I apologized for saying what I said about Eli. It's none of my business anyway."

"What did she say?"

"She said it was no biggie. I think she's FaceTiming with Gavin right now, actually. So should we ask her to come with us? Do you think she can get more time off work?"

"Seems likely," I say.

I hear movement in the room next to me. I freeze. Then laughter. Then the door closes. Is he going out? Now? We just broke up, and he's going out?

"Macarons?" Leela asks. "I have some in my bag."

"Yes, please," I say, and take a bite. I will miss you, macarons.

Among other things.

PISA, ITALY

The Basics: Pisa is in Italy. It has a tower. It is leaning. That is really all you need to know.

"This is all we do here?" Leela asks.

I am taking a photo of her lifting her hand in the air to make it look like she's holding the tower up.

"This is it," Kat says. "And I literally took the exact same picture when I was seven."

"It's so hot," Leela complains, wiping her hairline with the back of her hand. Then she downs a bottle of water in one gulp. "Can we find a bathroom? I have to pee."

"Yes," I say. "And then I need to get a snow globe. I'm guessing it will feature a leaning tower."

"I need to eat," Kat says. "I'm starving."

The tower is in a small walled-off park. We walk around it and find the bathrooms behind a cathedral. They cost eighty cents to use.

"Rip off!" I say. "Can you wait? We're going to find a restaurant for lunch. You can use the bathrooms there."

"I can't wait," Leela says, paying the eighty cents at the bathroom's reception desk before waiting in line.

"At least when I pay eighty cents in the States to pee at a Starbucks, I get a coffee out of it," I say. Oh well. I decide to pee too, just in case.

The bathrooms are clean. They should be for eighty cents.

I pee quickly and then press the pee flusher. That thing really makes a lot of sense.

After washing our hands, and our faces, we leave the walled area and head into the market area.

"Snow globes!" I cheer.

"McDonald's!" Leela cheers. "Can we get french fries? Please? Pretty please?"

"Yes, definitely," Kat says, licking her lips. "I would kill for a burger."

Mmm.

The line is long, but that doesn't stop us.

"So now that we're in Italy," Kat says, "are we going to visit Alain?"

Alain. I haven't thought about Alain since Paris. "I don't know," I say.

"He likes you," Kat says.

"I'm not sure I'm ready for that," I say. "I need to decompress from Jackson."

Kat nods. "No pressure."

"*Ciao*," says the cashier.

"Hi," I say. "Do you speak English?"

"A l*eetle*," she says.

"Can we get three Cokes, three burgers, and three french fries, please?"

She nods and rings us up. "Keep receipt for toilet code."

"*Grazie*," Kat says.

"See?" I say. "Told you. We could have waited."

"Would have if I could have," Leela says, shoving a french fry in her mouth.

We drop into a booth and I grab my burger. "We forgot ketchup!" I cry, straining my neck to spot the ketchup pumps. "Where is the ketchup?"

Kat points to menu on the wall. "It's twenty-five cents."

"No," I whine.

"Yes."

The line is too long.

"Forget it," I say, stuffing another french fry in my mouth. "I'm too hungry. In this case, I can't wait."

FLORENCE, ITALY

The Basics: Florence, home to the Statue of David, is Tuscany's most famous city.

Sure, David's naked torso is the highlight, but Florence also has gorgeous medieval churches! And cheap leather purses! And heavenly gelato! And OMFG the pizza!

The room at the hotel we stay at in Florence is tiny, with molding on the walls and high ceilings. It looks like it's about a thousand years old. Our room is on the first floor, which is actually the second floor since, like everywhere else in Europe, the ground floor is floor zero.

There is no air conditioner. Our iPhones tell us it's ninety-seven degrees Fahrenheit outside. We are hot. We are smelly. We share a wall with a family of Americans. They are loud. They are cranky. It is their first stop abroad and their children haven't adjusted to the time difference yet. Newbies.

The good news is there's free Wi-Fi. The bad news is there are no messages from Jackson. Not that I was expecting any. There's a heaviness in my chest, but I try to shake it off.

When I see a text from my sister I feel better.

Addison: We went to get ice cream yesterday.

Me: Walked?

Addison: Drove.

Me: You drove?

Addison: Nope. SHE DID. Well, halfway.

Me: ????????!

What the hell?

Addison: It's been kind of crazy here.

Three dots. I wait.

Addison: Mom was really upset after my birthday.

Me: No kidding.

Addison: Not just at me. She was upset with HERSELF. For not being able to pick up her drunk daughter.

Me: Really?

Addison: Yes! She started to cry and said something had to change. So we made an appointment with an online therapist.

Me: Seriously?

My mother agreed to talk to a therapist? My knees feel jiggly and I sit down on the bed for support.

Addison: Yes! She lives in New Jersey. But you can talk to her on Skype. Sloane told me about the one she used to talk to, so we Googled online therapists and made an appointment with Dr. Walters. We didn't even have to leave the house!

Me: I can't believe she spoke to an actual therapist.

Addison: I know! Dr. Walters said that if she really wants to get better she should try and do a little bit of what terrifies her every day, with increasing difficulty. So the first day she got into the car, turned on the ignition, and drove to the end of the driveway. That's it. Today she drove halfway to Baskin-Robbins! Tomorrow she's going to try to drive the whole way. And she said she might consider trying another type of anxiety pill. Maybe . . . She's thinking about it at least!

Me: Wow. Just. Wow.

Addison: I know. Yay! I gotta go. Love you!

I stare at my phone in disbelief. I can't believe it. My mother is getting better. My sister is *helping* my mother get better. I feel relief. I feel hopeful. I feel ecstatic.

I also feel queasy. How come I couldn't help her get better?

An hour later, I'm still in shock. When I tell the girls what happened they cheer.

"That's fantastic!" Kat squeals. "Now come on! We've got things to do. This is going to be amazing. I want to get a leather jacket and a purse. The leather here is cheap. And the food is spectacular. All we're going to eat is pizza and gelato. You're going to die when you have the pizza. Die."

333

I try to focus on the good news and push away the feelings of weirdness.

We get takeaway pizza at a place called Mangia that *Travel Europe* swears by.

"Omigod," Leela says. "My mouth just had an orgasm."

"Amazing," Kat says. "Where does it say is the best place to get gelato?"

At the place where we end up, right down the street, there are rows and rows of flavors with Italian and English labels—flavors I would never think of turning into ice cream, like cinnamon, which is sandy-colored; melon, which is pale orange; ricotta and fig, which is white and brown. They also have, um, Viagra, which is bright blue. I think I'll skip that one. We each try a few tasters and I end up with a sugar cone of *cocco*, which is coconut, and melon. The gelato is creamy and thick and looks and tastes more like frozen icing than it does ice cream, but mmm. I will have to try some other flavors tomorrow.

"I feel like I'm in *Eat, Pray, Love*," Leela says, licking her cone of Nutella and coconut. "Except we started with love, then went to eat, and we totally forgot about the praying."

"We have been pretty pathetic on the church and museum front," I admit.

"But we're in Florence," Leela says. "We'll make up for it here. That's all we'll do. Learn, pray, eat. I'm done with loving."

Me too.

Tip: Watch out for hidden costs at restaurants.

You know that lovely free basket of bread your waiter always brings to your table? It's NOT free. Check the bill. They charged you three euros for it. Tricky bastards.

So the next day we do what one is actually supposed to do when one travels through Europe.

We see stuff.

Well, first we stop at a leather market so Kat can buy an orange leather jacket and a yellow leather purse, and Leela and I can buy black leather gloves for our dads.

Then we see stuff. First, we visit the halls of the Uffizi Gallery, where we see many paintings titled Madonna-something.

"Masterpieces always make me feel so attractive," Kat says. "Beauty really is in the eye of the beholder."

"It's true. We're totally as hot as these women," Leela says. "But nobody has ever tried to paint me."

Next we walk over to the Duomo.

"Isn't there another Duomo in Milan?" I ask.

"*Duomo* just means Italian cathedral," Kat says. "So there are a few. I think this is one of the most famous ones, though. I was in Milan two years ago."

"Of course you were," Leela says. "Is there anywhere you haven't been?"

"I haven't been to India," she says. "I would love to go to India."

"Wow, I've been somewhere you haven't?" Leela says. "I'm in shock!"

"Where did you go?" Kat asks.

"Mumbai," Leela says. "My dad's parents live there. I went for a summer once."

"That was the longest summer of my life," I say.

"I missed you too," she says. "Remember all the postcards I sent?"

"I still have them," I tell her.

"Wow," Leela says, as we stand outside the cathedral. It's a massive Gothic structure built out of green, white, black, and pink stones. It looks like a mosaic. It's amazing.

We try to buy tickets at the cathedral but are sent down the street to the museum. They are fifteen euros each, but include entrance to the cathedral, the dome, the museum, the baptistery, and the bell tower.

We start in the cathedral. After thirty minutes in line, we're finally allowed in. More gorgeousness. The ceilings are sky-high and the cathedral is filled with paintings, portraits, frescoes, statues, and stained-glass windows.

"If I ever get married," Leela says, "I want it to be here."

"You think they do weddings?" I ask.

"Of course," Kat says. "If you're Catholic."

"I'm not Catholic," Leela says. "Are you?"

"Yup," Kat says. "I guess it will be *my* wedding here,

suckers. You guys can be guests, though."

Next up we wait in line for the dome.

Once we get inside, I see the sign in Italian and English: *Visitors are required to climb 463 steps.*

463 steps?

"Syd?" Leela asks, looking at me. "What do you want to do?"

If my mom can go to Baskin-Robbins, then I can do this. I take a long sip of water. "Let's do it."

The stairs are absurdly narrow, it's hot, and my legs start to shake at about stair two hundred. Maybe I'm just in better shape after three weeks of carrying forty pounds of clothes and snow globes on my back, or maybe it's because I *know* I can do it, or maybe it's because the frescoes along the way are gorgeous, but I make it to the top. We all do.

We stand outside, and enjoy the wind on our sweaty faces. The view is three-hundred-and-sixty degrees around Florence. We look out over all the red roofs and beige and yellow houses and cobblestoned streets and the water and surrounding mountains.

I feel strong. I feel brave. I feel lucky.

"Nice," Leela says, linking her arm through mine.

Kat snaps a photo of us and says, "Spectacular."

The next day we visit the Accademia Gallery, where we check out the ultimate piece of art: the statue of David.

He's made of white stone, surrounded by glass, and looming at the end of a long hallway.

"What do you think?" I ask.

"He's kind of small, you know?" Leela says.

"He's seventeen feet!" I exclaim.

"That's not what I meant. His, *you know* . . . is small. If you were making a statue of a prominent biblical figure, wouldn't you make him better endowed?"

"His balls are pretty big," Kat says, studying his nether regions. "He's just not erect."

"Michelango should have sculpted Goliath," I say. "I bet he would have been well-endowed."

"We have dirty, dirty minds," Leela says.

"Take a picture of me with it so I can send to Gavin," Kat says. "Make him jealous. Or not jealous since Gavin's is so much bigger. Proportionally, of course."

"Much more info than I wanted," Leela says.

"Oh, come on," Kat says. "You just broke up with your boyfriend. You're legally obligated to tell us what a small penis he has."

"It's true," Leela says. "Matt does have a small penis. Also it's tilted to the left. Okay, let's take a picture of ourselves in front of David and make them all jealous."

We stand together and Kat takes the photo.

"Say *small penis*," Kat says.

"Small penis," we repeat.

Snap.

"Let's take a few more," Leela says.

"You know," I say, "*Travel Europe* says there are actually three statues of David in Florence."

"Does that mean we can each have a David of our very own?" Kat asks.

Snap. Snap. Snap.

"Oh, that's good," Leela says. "We're all laughing. We look like we're having a great time."

"Aren't we?" Kat asks. She shrugs. "I'm having a great time."

Leela scrolls through her phone. "I want to have a better time than our idiot ex-boyfriends are."

"*Our* idiot ex-boyfriends?" I repeat.

"Yeah. Losers."

She seems to like that we're in this together now. It's us against them.

"Why don't you stop looking at Matt's photos," I say. "Then you won't know if they're having fun."

"But why has he suddenly become an active poster? And why are they on a boat?"

"A boat?" I repeat, trying to keep my voice light.

"Yeah. I think they're still in France," Leela says. She says the word with disgust.

"Never mind," I say. "I don't want to know."

She keeps scrolling.

"Oh, let me see," I say, even though I know it's a bad idea. She hands me the phone and then I see it. The two of them with a group of women in black bikinis.

"Crap," I say.

"Who are those girls?" Kat asks, peering over my shoulder.

"They look like models," Leela says.

They really do. There are three of them and they have long dark hair, large boobs, and toned stomachs. I hate them.

"How the hell did our boys meet the Kardashians?" Leela asks.

"Omigod, they do look like the Kardashians," I say.

"No, they don't," Kat says. "You girls are a million times more attractive than them. Plus, you are smarter, funnier, and kinder."

"And you know that for a fact?" I ask.

"I do," she says.

"One of these girls is *actually* a model," Leela says. "Look." Since Matt tagged her, we flip to her account and see shot after shot of her in various come-hither poses.

Unfortunately, she's also the one who has her hand draped across Jackson.

"I guess he's moved on," I squeak out.

"Bastard," Kat growls.

"Such a player," Leela says. "This should make you feel better that it's over. I really hope you used condoms."

"Leela," Kat warns.

"What? Just saying."

My whole body is tense. He already met somebody else? Two days later? *Two days?* I should not have looked at the photo. I don't want to think of him. It's over. It was a fling. Time to move on.

"What do you want to do?" Kat asks. "Make him jealous? Should I take inappropriate pictures of you with the David statue?"

"No," I say, forcing out a laugh.

"The only way to get over him is to hook up with someone else. You know it's the truth," Kat says. "You have to get the feel of him off your body."

"You want me to just hook up with some stranger?" I ask.

"No," she says. "I was thinking, since we're in Italy, Tuscany actually, maybe now you'll want to visit Alain."

Leela lowers her sunglasses. "Do you think he really wants us to come?"

"He certainly does," Kat says. "Should we go?"

I hesitate. "I don't know." He was cute. And sweet. And we shared a pretty great kiss. . . .

"Yes," Leela says. "I think we should go."

"I thought we were having a girls' trip?" I turn to Leela. "I thought we'd given up on love?"

"Florence is really hot," Leela says. "And I'm almost out of money. Does Alain have a pool?"

"Yup," Kay says. "And a chef."

"A chef?" we both shriek.

"Should I double check with him if we can come?" Kat asks. "He might have invited other people."

Leela fans herself with her hand. "Please do. I'm melting."

"I'm not going to have to sleep with him, am I?" I say.

"I'm not sure I want to sleep with him."

"You don't have to sleep with him," Kat says. "Very funny. He's texting back. He's there. He wants us to come. He has lots of extra rooms. What do you think?"

"One of you is going to have to sleep with him if I don't want to," I joke.

Leela nods. "Deal."

I laugh. "Now let's go find me a snow globe of David's tiny penis and we can go."

Tip: *Villa* is the Italian word for country house.

A really, really nice country house.

Alain is waiting outside the train station in Grosseto. He's standing beside a black Mercedes. Casual—like it's no big deal. Actually, maybe it isn't in Europe. A lot of the cars are German. Even some of the taxis are BMWs.

My heart flutters and sinks at the sight of him. He's sweet and he's cute and he likes me and he's here. But he's not Jackson.

"Sit in the front," Kat whispers to me.

"Stop whoring me out," I whisper back.

"I am so happy you came," he says, giving all three of us kisses on both cheeks.

"We're happy to see you," Kat says.

"You will love the villa."

"I love that you *have* a villa," Leela says.

"We are not far from the sea. Later this week we will take a boat to Elba and Isola del Giglio."

"It all sounds great," I say, climbing into the front. "Thank you for inviting us."

We all chatter as we drive through rolling hills and pass olive trees and occasional vineyards.

"This is amazing," Leela says, her face pressed against the window.

"It is," he says.

About twenty minutes later, we pull up in front of his house.

It's huge. It's only two floors but it's spread out on a cliff and blends into the horizon.

A woman in a white uniform joins us outside.

"Luciana will take your bags," he says. "Lunch is waiting for us."

As we walk through the house, we all make faces at one another. It's gorgeous. The ceilings are high, the entrance-ways are arched, the floors are marble. Europeans really love their marble.

"What a stunning place," Kat says.

"Yeah," I repeat.

"Omigod," Leela says.

"Yes," Alain says. "It is nice. Now come eat. Lunch is on the *terrasse*."

We walk through the kitchen to the most beautiful spot

in the entire world, hands down. The terrace overlooks the valley below and the mountains in the distance. To the right is a perfectly still, pale blue infinity pool.

"This is heaven," Leela says. "Did our train crash? And now we're all here?"

"You had trouble on the train?" Alain asks.

"No," I say. "She was joking."

On the glass table are plates and plates of food. Salad with juicy-looking tomatoes. Platters of cheese. Crusty bread. Grapes. A plate of some sort of sliced meat that I won't eat because it's probably ham. Three bottles of prosecco, which, he explains, is Italian champagne.

"*Mangiamo*," he says.

"That means let's eat," Kat says.

After lunch, we unpack.

"Now you relax," Alain tells us. "I must work, but you enjoy the pool. I will join you for dinner at twenty hours."

"Sounds good to me," I say. Twenty hours. Eight p.m. it is.

Relax it is.

All three of us spread out on the poolside chairs. They're the fancy long kind with thick white pillows.

It's quiet. No phones. No music. Nothing but silence.

"Why does he have so much money?" Leela asks. "And do you know the Wi-Fi password here? My 3G is having issues."

"Stop checking on Matt," I say. "Enough. You've got to disconnect."

"Disconnect to connect?" Kat says. "I hate that saying."

"Is that really a saying?"

"It is."

"She has to do it, though," I say.

"Fine, I won't check," Leela says, putting her phone down on the glass side table. "So why's Alain so rich?"

"Family money," Kat says. "Old family money."

"So if we hadn't shown up he would have been here by himself? With just his staff?" I ask. "Is that weird?"

"I'm sure he has friends here," Kat says. "He's here a lot. And he definitely still likes you. In case you're wondering."

"He's still attractive," I say. "And I'm definitely in love with his house."

"You may as well see what happens," Kat says. "Why not, right?"

Jackson is why not. I push the thought away. Jackson is on a yacht with Kardashian models. He's not worrying about me, so I shouldn't be worried about him. End of story. Now where's that prosecco?

Luciana makes pasta from scratch and Alain invites some friends over and we all drink and eat and are merry.

Alain flirts with all of us, but he sits next to me.

I'm not quite ready for something to happen again, so after dinner I say good night with the other girls and go back to my room. He doesn't make a move.

I'm not sure if I want him to make a move.

We all go to sleep in our beautiful down beds, the heavy blinds pulled and the air-conditioning blasting.

We wake up the next day and return to the pool.

"I could live like this," Leela says. "Should we just stay here until it's time to go home? It's only nine days."

"I guess since I'm with Alain, it counts as work," Kat says. "Do you know I'm getting school credit for this?"

"Of course you are," Leela says with a laugh. "Can I be you when I grow up?"

All is great until Alain shows up at the pool.

He's wearing a blue banana hammock.

All of our eyes widen to the size of pasta bowls.

"He totally pulls it off," Kat whispers.

"I'm not sure anyone can pull that off," Leela whispers back, giggling.

I can't decide if it grosses me out or turns me on. He does look good in it. He doesn't have the statue of David's problem, that's for sure.

That night, Alain drives us into the town, and we end up at a restaurant called Oliva, which is on a cliff overlooking the town of Castiglione della Pescaia. We sit at an outdoor table, which overlooks the pedestrian-only streets and the harbor behind it. Stars blanket the black sky.

When the waiter comes, Alain proceeds to speak in Italian.

"Why are Europeans so international?" I ask. "I can barely speak English and Alain is fluent in at least four languages."

"Do you ladies trust me?" he asks, looking around the table at each of us.

"Yes," Kat says quickly. "Absolutely."

"I will order for everyone, then?" he asks.

We nod.

"But no snails," Leela says. "And nothing snaillike. Promise?"

"I promise," he says, but he makes a worm motion with his fingers. "I am kidding."

I relax into my chair. It's nice to have someone else make the plans. It's nice to be taken care of, for a change. I take another deep breath and then an even deeper sip of the bright orange fizzy Campari spritz cocktails that he already ordered for us.

Plate after plate of food arrives. Appetizers (cuttlefish, prawns, mussels), then pasta dishes (lobster spaghetti, burrata ravioli, pici pasta with tuna), and then finally the *piatti principali*, the main dishes (branzino, Florentine-style steak, and duck). It's way too much, but every bite is like a delicious surprise, and we eat it all.

"Who wants gelato?" Kat asks.

"Me!" says Leela. "We'll be back!"

Giggling, the two of them run down toward the packed pedestrian-only streets, leaving us standing by the railing.

"It is a beaut-ee-ful night, yes?"

"Um, yup."

"Shall we walk?"

"Sure," I say.

He puts his arm out and I take it.

We walk.

I can do this. I am with a handsome Austrian–French man in Italy. He's sweet. He ordered dinner. He has a gorgeous house. The stars look like glitter paint on a black canvas. Now *this* has fling potential. He is a mystery. I don't know how many girls he slept with this year. I don't know his horrible family nicknames or that he snores. I know nothing about him except that he is rich, European, young, handsome, a good kisser, and well endowed. It couldn't be a more perfect fling. I mean, seriously. This is what summer romances are made of. Jackson who?

"I hired a boat for tomorrow," he says.

"Wow. That sounds wonderful." I'll take Jackson's French boat and raise him an Italian one.

He nods. "Yes. It will be."

His arm is around me. The moon is full. He is standing over me. He is about to kiss me again. He is about to kiss me again! What do I do? Do I stop it? He's not Jackson! I wish he were Jackson. But Jackson's gone.

He leans down and presses his lips against mine.

His lips are soft. He tastes like tomato sauce and red wine.

He does not taste like Jackson.

But it's a nice kiss.

I hear Leela's giggle and look up to see Leela and Kat licking their ice cream cones on a bench.

My cheeks burn.

I wave.

They both wave back. Kat turns away from us.

"We should take them home," Alain says, staring at them.

"Yeah," I say.

He takes my arm and walks me back to the car.

I sit in the front. It's like we're playing house. I'm the mom, Alain is the dad, and Leela and Kat are the kids in the backseat who giggle and whisper to each other all the way home.

A few days ago they kinda hated each other and now they're two peas in a pod. Part of me is happy they're getting along. Part of me feels left out.

I want to be one of the kids in the backseat.

"Glass of wine?" Alain asks me. The four of us are sitting on the terrace. The moon shines, the stars are still bright, and the air smells like lemon and olive oil.

I see Leela and Kat making eyes at each other.

"I'm tired," Leela says, jumping up.

"Me too," says Kat. She slowly stretches herself out of her chair like a cat.

"Good night," Alain says. "Sleep well. Sydney, you will have another drink with me?"

"Sure," I say. Why not?

And then it's just the two of us.

I know what's going to happen. Do I want it to happen? I don't really care, if I'm being honest.

Alain turns his chair so that it's directly facing me. His left knee bumps up against mine. "I am coming to New York in the fall. Maybe I can see you?"

"Oh. Um, I don't live in New York," I say, running my finger against my wine glass.

"Where do you live?" he asks.

"In Maryland. It's about a five-hour drive."

He leans over. Closer and closer. My heart is thumping. It's a beautiful night. In a beautiful place. With a beautiful man.

He kisses me.

It is a fine kiss. It is a nice kiss. But he's not Jackson.

I can't.

I pull back. "I think I'm going to go to bed."

"Okay," he says. "We go to bed."

"No, no, no," I say, flustered. "Sorry. Um. I want to go to bed. By myself? See, I'm really tired. And I . . . I kind of have feelings for someone else? A guy I met in London?" I'm not sure why my sentences are coming out as questions, except for that this whole conversation is super awkward.

At first he says nothing. Then he leans back and sighs. "I understand. If I'm being honest, I care for someone else too."

"An ex?" I ask.

He shakes his head. He motions to Kat's bedroom window. "Your friend."

"Oh!" I say. I realize I'm not that surprised. "That's . . . she has a boyfriend."

"I know. And evidently she is not interested in me because she is pushing me to date you."

"I think she's pretty crazy about her boyfriend," I say. "I'm sorry. Again."

"Me too," he says. "But thank you for being honest. I appreciate that. *Bonne nuit.*"

I go into my bedroom and knock on the door to the bathroom I'm sharing with Leela. "You up?"

"Come in," she says.

I open the door. Kat and Leela are sitting on the bed chatting.

"Did anything happen?"

"We kissed," I say.

"That's it? How come?" Kat asks.

"Because I'm not over Jackson. And it turns out Alain's into *you*."

Kat blushes. "Me?"

"Yes."

"He told you that?" she squeals.

"He did."

"He really likes me?"

"Yes," I say. "You're not interested in him, right, Kat?"

She doesn't answer.

"Kat?" I ask again.

"No," she says. Her face is white. "Or yes. I don't know.

351

He's very attractive. And he's so generous and smart and . . ." She turns around and buries her face in her pillow.

"You like him?" Leela asks.

"I don't want to like him!" she says. "I'm in love with Gavin. But Gavin is across the world and every time I'm in the same room as Alain I want to jump his bones. What's wrong with me?"

"Nothing's *wrong* with you," I say. "It's normal to be attracted to more than one person."

"Is it, though?" she asks. "All I think about is sex when I'm around him. Sex, sex, sex. It is not right to be thinking about having sex all the time with one man when I'm with someone else. That's wrong."

"So break up with Gavin," I say. "And have sex with Alain." I'm friends with Gavin at school, but my loyalty lies with Kat. I want her to be happy.

"Break up with him by phone?" she asks. "That's horrendous. And I do love him. And it'll crush him. And how stupid would it be to break up with my loving, amazing boyfriend back home to hook up with some guy—even a handsome French guy—who I will never see again after the summer? That's just bad planning. Plus he's kind of my boss! I'm not the type of girl who sleeps with her boss!" She turns to Leela. "What do you think I should do?"

"Honestly?" Leela replies. "I think we should leave."

"You want to leave this magical, air-conditioned villa?" I ask, incredulous.

"Yes. Kat can't be here. She's too tempted. We must

sacrifice the air-conditioning to save our friend!"

I smile. I know Leela's half-joking, but I can tell that she's also trying to be nice. Also, it's the first time Leela has referred to Kat as a friend. I like it. "Okay. We must leave. But not tomorrow. He already rented a boat for us. But the next day for sure."

"Fine," Kat grumbles. "We leave Tuesday. But where to?"

"Venice?" I say.

"Venice," she repeats. "Good. I like Venice. Although my parents left me in the hotel with a babysitter when I was a kid because there was too much walking and I wouldn't stop complaining. It was still a nice hotel, though. A Westin, I think? Maybe we can stay there?"

"There is no budget for that," I say. "I'll start looking for a hostel."

Kat nods. "Now just to review: I'm not allowed to have sex with Alain, even a little. Right? What about clothes-on making out? I've been having some great fantasies about what I can do to him on the glass table on the terrace."

"And let's keep it a fantasy," I say.

Kat puts her hands on mine. "Just tell me one thing."

"Yes?"

"Is he a good kisser?"

I look her in the eye. "Very slobbery. Plus, he has terrible breath."

She lets out a groan. "Liar, liar, pants on fire."

VENICE, ITALY

The Basics: The canals of Venice are a wonder to behold.

There are no cars in Venice. There are no roads. Want to get somewhere? Walk, take a boat, or swim. Just kidding. Don't swim. The water's disgusting.

This place takes canals to a whole new level. They're in and around all the crumbling houses and buildings. Water, water everywhere.

"Are the apartments built into the water?" Leela asks.

"I think they're little tiny islands," Kat says.

"Whatever you do," I respond, "DO NOT FALL IN."

"I should have brought my wet suit," Leela says.

"The one you peed in?" I ask.

"That's the one," she says, laughing. "I marked it."

Instead of buses, there are water buses. Instead of taxis, there are water taxis.

"Do you think there are water Ubers?" Kat asks.

"Ha," I say.

There are also men in striped shirts and straw hats paddling fancy-looking gondolas and offering tourists rides.

And people everywhere. I have never seen so many tourists. It's like Venice is a piece of bread crust and we're all a bunch of pigeons.

All the stores seem to sell sparkly costume masks, pretty Venetian fans, and colorful bowls, wine glasses, and jewelry in something called Murano glass.

"I'm hungry," I say. "Let's drop our bags off and find somewhere to eat." We haven't eaten since our extended and delicious breakfast of scrambled eggs and fresh fruit and Nutella on ciabatta at Alain's. It was hard to say goodbye. To the food, the accommodations. And for Kat, to Alain.

"I'm starving," Leela says, dragging her duffel-suitcase behind her.

"Perfect," Kat says, adjusting the strap of her Louis Vuitton weekend bag on her shoulder. "Oh, and guys? I wouldn't mind doing some shopping. You know I only brought clothes for three days."

Kat decides that she can't take another hostel and gets us a room at the Westin.

"Are you sure?" I ask when we check in. "It's super expensive."

"I'm one hundred percent sure," she says. "My treat. Please don't make me sleep in another hostel. I'm all hosteled out."

Our room has two single beds, and we ask for a rollout. It also has a real shower and air-conditioning.

"Thank you, thank you, thank you," says Leela.

"Yes, thank you," I say. "This is spectacular." Between staying at Alain's and Kat paying for this hotel, I might have enough money to make it to August second.

"Ah," Leela says, turning the AC on high. "That's the stuff."

The plan is to stay here for two nights and then go south to Rome for the last few days.

Alain told Kat to take as much time off as she wanted. Of course he did. He's crazy about her. The heat between them on the boat was out of control. We really did have to get out of there.

We unpack, we change, we pack our day bags, and we go.

Three hours later, we take a gelato break. This time I try raspberry and dark chocolate. Mmm. It's just as good as I imagined.

I'm flipping through my *Travel Europe* to see where we should go. "Okay," I say. "We start with the Piazza San Marco. And then we'll go to some of the museums."

I should check on my family first, though. Make sure they're okay.

I connect to the *gelateria*'s Wi-Fi and see a picture from my sister. It's my mother. Her hair is in a ponytail, and she's smiling at the camera. She's holding a box of frozen waffles.

Huh?

There's a frozen food section behind her.

Oh. She's at a grocery store.

She's at a grocery store?

My mother is at A GROCERY STORE?

This should fill me with happiness. It really should. And I am happy. I am. My mother is getting better. I'm going to be free. My sister isn't miserable.

I sink a little into my plastic chair. It makes me happy. But also makes me feel like crap.

"Omigod," Leela says, staring at her screen. "Matt is still in the South of France. What's wrong with him? Are our exes going to stay on the boat for the rest of their lives? They're so annoying."

Our exes? *Our exes?* She wouldn't let me have a relationship with Jackson but now she's claiming my breakup? It's too much. It's all too *much*. Something inside me snaps.

"Stop. Checking. Matt's. Posts!" I yell.

"Excuse me?"

"Just stop it! You have to stop!"

She looks like I slapped her.

"You're the one who's checked your phone every five minutes this entire trip," she says.

"I'm checking on my *mother*. I'm not checking on some

guy who cheated on me and obviously doesn't give a shit about me."

"Stop bossing me around!" she says. "Don't tell me what to do!"

"You need me to tell you what to do," I yell back. "Or you'd be lost and drowning in your own mess!"

She looks away, her face flushed.

"Whoa, Syd," says Kat, looking uncomfortable. "Calm down."

"I don't want to calm down! Leela, you've been miserable this whole trip. And I'm trying to cheer you up, but nothing works. And I really, really need a break. I'm always doing crap for everyone else and I'm tired. And you made me give up Jackson because you want me to be miserable with you, and that pisses me off!"

The words feel good as they leave my mouth. I don't want to calm down! I'm pissed off! At Leela. At my mother. At my sister. At everyone.

Leela and Kat are in too much shock to respond.

"I need to take a walk," I say. "I'll meet you guys later." I take my mini-backpack and storm off, down one of the tiny streets. My heart thumps as I walk faster and faster.

How is it that I give up everything to take care of my mother for seven years and she gets worse and worse? And then I'm gone for four weeks and she's getting better? What the fuck? Is my mother better off without me? Did I *make* her worse? Is it my fault?

I turn on another street heading toward the Piazza San Marco.

Do I need to feel needed? Am I a horrible person?

In front of me is a bell tower. There are so many people. And pigeons. Actual pigeons. Is every pigeon in the world here? Is every *person* in the world here? Why am *I* even here? Maybe I've had enough traveling. Maybe I've had enough of Leela. Now that she and Kat are besties, they don't even need me. I could just go home. To my own room with my stupid glow-in-the-dark ceiling stars. Where I have more than one pair of jeans. And none of them have jam stains. And I have tap water. And 4G. And why the hell did I decide to buy snow globes? So many snow globes. So fucking heavy. So fucking dumb.

So many fucking tourists.

"Selfie stick?" a man asks. "Cheap price!"

"No," I bark. I need to get out of here. I turn a corner and get out of the square. Then I turn another corner and walk some more. Down a path and over a bridge, and then over another bridge.

Fifteen minutes later, the sun is beating on my back and I stop.

I don't know where I am.

I reach into my bag and look for my *Travel Europe*. It's not there. I left it on the table in the gelato place.

Merda.

I think of my friends' faces and feel bad I left them

there. They must be worried.

Okay. I just need to find Wi-Fi, then I can check my app. Then I'll text and find them. I walk around a bit trying to get online.

There's no free Wi-Fi.

Also I have about 3 percent battery. I didn't have enough time to charge it at the hotel.

My heart starts to thump. I turn around. Okay. I'll just go to the piazza. I'll find them there. I turn around again and walk the way I think I came.

No piazza.

Crap. I try to get Wi-Fi again but everything needs a password.

I scroll back to my messages. I look back at the picture of my mom.

She's smiling. My eyes tear up. I'm proud of her. I really am.

I scroll back to Jackson's last text.

I miss him. I wish he were here.

My phone dies.

Fuck.

My heart starts beating faster and faster. I am lost. I am sweating. I have nothing. Is this it? Am I finally going to have a full-on panic attack? Yes, that's exactly how this will play out. I will have a panic attack in the middle of some random street in Venice and I will pass out and fall into the water. I'll drown. Yup, I'll drown. They'll never find me because the water is so dirty. Everyone will think I took off.

360

Abandoned them. That I couldn't stand taking care of my mother. Or that I couldn't stand her getting better without me. Either way, they'll think I'm a terrible person. They'll be pissed at first, but then they'll be fine. Kat and Leela will become besties. My sister will cure my mom. Jackson will fall in love with a nice Canadian girl. Everyone will be happy and move on.

Meanwhile, I'll be decomposing in a canal. The fish will feast on my toes.

I feel light-headed. It's just like when I was at Anne Frank's house, or in the Tube station, or at the Arc de Triomphe. Any second now I'm going to faint and then it will be all over.

I breathe. I breathe again. Faster. It's coming. The end.

No. No, no, no.

I am lost. I am overwhelmed. But I am not being chased by a lion.

I keep breathing. I lean against a nearby building, close my eyes and focus on my breaths. In and out. In and out. Slowly. Slower still. *You're going to be fine*, I tell myself. *Everything is going to be okay.*

You are strong. You can do this. You've done this before. You can do it again.

I take another deep breath.

My head stops spinning.

I catch my breath.

I'm fine.

I'm fine.

I didn't faint. I'm not going to faint. I'm going to be okay. Everything's going to be okay. I will not fall into the canal.

I am not going to let the panic spiral. I am not going to let the fear win.

I am strong and I am brave.

I open my eyes. I push myself up. In front of me is a snow-globe display. Also a sign that says "Libreria." A bookstore.

I step inside and the cold air calms me down even more. I ask them if they have an iPhone charger I can use, and they say yes. I ask them if they have any English books, and they say yes, and point to the back. I ask them if they have free Wi-Fi and they nod and say *sì, certo*.

While my phone boots up, I buy a snow globe of a boat in the canal, a novel set in Venice called *In the Company of the Courtesan*, and a map.

I can do this. I can get home. I am a freakin' world traveler.

When my phone is on, I quickly send my friends a message.

Me: I'm OK. Sorry for freaking out. I'll meet you back at the hotel in an hour!

Then I look at Jackson's last message. Before I chicken out, I write:

Hi. I miss you.

I leave the store without waiting for responses.

I follow the map and start walking back to the hotel.

362

Along the way, I stop at a bench and sit. I open my book. I read. I breathe. I relax.

I show up at the hotel around eight thirty, just as the sun is setting. I knock.

Kat throws the door open. Her hair is in a towel. "Syd! You're okay!"

"I am," I say. It's nice and cool in here.

"We kept calling you but couldn't get through," she says.

"I can't get calls," I say. "Did you get my text?"

"Yeah. But that was a long time ago."

"Leela? I'm sorry for flipping out."

Leela stands and gives me a hug. "I think I deserved it."

"You did?"

"I force you to come on this trip and then when you meet someone I try to convince you he's a jerk."

"Maybe he is a jerk," I say.

"Maybe," she says, sitting down on the bed. "But I was an ass. I didn't want to share you with Kat or with Jackson. I just wanted things to be like they used to be, you know? Me and you. I didn't mean to mess up you and Jackson. I mean, I did, but I didn't." She sighs. "I'm sorry."

"I texted him," I admit, sitting down beside her.

"What did you say?"

"I said . . . hi. I miss you." My face flushes. "Lame?"

"Did he respond?"

"I don't know! I've been offline."

363

"Well, get online!" Leela orders.

I do and wait to see if I have any messages. One pops up.

Jackson: Hi. I miss you too. I know you can't be here but I wish you were.

There's a picture of a beach.

"He's in Corfu," Kat says, looking over my shoulder. "I know that beach. He's definitely not with Matt in Cannes anymore. And he still wants you to meet him."

"But I can't go to Greece. We're already in Italy, and we're flying out of Rome."

"We could go to Greece," Leela says. She hesitates. "Or you could go to Greece."

"Me?" I ask.

"Yeah," she says. "You. On your own."

My heart beats faster. "Huh?"

"Kat was telling me about Sorrento—"

"I was there when I was fifteen," Kat says.

"And it sounds kind of amazing and I was thinking that I could go with her there if you want to go meet Jackson in Greece. It's just six days."

"But . . ." I'm not sure what to say. "You two are going to travel? Just the two of you?"

Instead of feeling jealous, I feel a spark of hope. Of possibility.

Leela puts her hand on mine. "Go see Jackson. I'll meet you in Rome."

"But how will I get back to Rome?"

"You'll figure it out," Leela says.

I hesitate. "Are you sure?"

"Yes," she says. "Absolutely. Now come on. The pizza isn't going to eat itself."

CORFU, GREECE

The Basics: Do you like sandy beaches? Gorgeous sunsets? Old fortresses? If so, you're going to love Corfu!

Do you love ouzo shots? Drunken backpackers? Having a plate bro-ken over your head? If so, you're going to love Corfu.

We all take the nine-hour overnight train south. Leela and Kat get off in Termoli.

"This is us!" Leela says, giving me a big kiss. "Have an amazing time and I'll see you in Rome."

"Thank you," I say.

"I love you."

"I love you, too!"

"Me, too!" Kat says. "Group hug!"

We all wrap our arms around one another.

"Send me pictures," I tell them.

"No," Leela says. "I'm not going to bug you at all. And I

366

think you were right about the phone thing. We should both turn them off. Disconnect to connect, right?"

"It sounds so cheesy," I say.

"But it's true."

"Okay," I say, nodding. "I'll see you next week. And Kat, I will see *you* in September. Be good." I give her a knowing look.

"I miss you already," she says, making a sad face.

Leela and Kat step off the train, waving.

And now it's just me.

I get off the train at Brindisi at eight a.m. My boat isn't until ten. Jackson is going to meet me at the dock in Corfu.

Once I figured out how to make it happen, I'd responded to his 'wish you were here' text with:

Yeah? OK then. See you tomorrow.

Jackson: !!!!!!! Don't tease me. Are you being serious?

Please say you are.

Me: Not teasing. If you want me.

Jackson: I WANT YOU.

I smile to myself, buy a coffee to go, a bottle of water, and a chocolate muffin, and take a taxi to the docks.

It's starting to get hot. I tie my hair back and take a long sip of water.

I find some Wi-Fi and email my mom and sister.

Hi! I'm going to Corfu for a few days with some friends. Will be trying to stay offline as much as possible, but if you need me I'm at the Agapi Hotel. Love you! See you next week!

I message Kat and Leela my details, too.

I see a group of American girls and walk up to them. "Hi," I say. "Mind if I join you? I'm traveling by myself."

"Of course," one says. "Where are you going?"

"Corfu," I say.

"Us, too," the girl says. "Then we're flying to London. We're doing a semester abroad in Paris. Got any travel trips?"

"I have a ton," I say.

And with a whistle, we're on our way.

Seven hours later, I see him when I get off.

Jackson, Jackson, Jackson.

He's wearing his sunglasses and his hands are in his pockets. He runs toward me when he spots me.

He lifts my bag off my back and kisses me hard.

"It's you," he says, smiling.

"It's me," I tell him, smiling too.

He carries my bag on his back and takes my hand.

We take a taxi across the island to the western area of Agios Georgios. Jackson had been staying at a hostel called the Pink Palace, where they give you ouzo shots and break plates over your head, so he thought this other two-star hotel was quieter and more romantic. We hold hands at check-in, and fall onto the bed as soon as we're shown our room. The entire room is white. The walls, the furniture, the bathroom tiles, the bed. It's plain, but clean and modern.

It's also right on the water, which has a dreamlike white sandy beach.

We sit and talk in the blazing sun. We swim and laugh in the blue-green ocean. We hike over cliffs and find deserted beaches. We watch the sunset melt pink and purple across the sky. We spend a lot of time in our room. *A lot* of time.

He still snores. But I stay awake and listen and know I will miss the sound when he's gone.

We don't talk about the future.

We enjoy the island and each other.

We go into town and walk by the stands, and we try on cheap hats and shirts and dresses. I buy myself a pale blue sundress, my sister a snow globe, and my mom a silver bracelet.

I don't check my phone at all.

Tip: Toilets in Greece will often have signs asking you to put all paper waste in the garbage bin instead of flushing it down the toilet.

If you're sharing a room with a guy for the first time, you will probably ignore said sign. We won't judge you. We may have ignored it too.

"So . . . " Jackson says. It's August 1, our last night. We're sitting at our regular table sharing a plate of *gemista*. Tomorrow morning, we leave. I fly to Rome, where I meet Leela.

He flies to Athens, where he connects to Toronto, and then to Vancouver.

Luckily, I found a flight to Rome for only seventy-nine euros. I am now completely out of money.

"This is it," I say. "Our last night. For real this time." My throat tightens.

"What should we do?" he asks.

"Oh, I know what you want to do," I say, letting my foot find his under the table.

"No," he says, suddenly serious. "About us."

"Oh," I say. "Us."

"Yeah."

"I don't know," I say. "You live in Vancouver. I live in Maryland. We don't go to the same school. And I've never had a long-distance relationship. I'm actually pretty crappy at keeping in touch."

He nods. "I've never even *had* a relationship."

"My longest was two months."

"This is my longest." He motions between us. "It would be tough."

"I don't want to worry about you hooking up with some Ava."

"How do you know I hooked up with Ava?"

"You did?"

"*Way* before Matt did."

I shake my head. "I don't want to worry every time I see a picture of you with some Kardashian girl."

He blushes. "You saw that boat picture, huh?"

I make a face. "I did."

"Nothing happened."

I wave my hand. "I just don't want to worry about it. I don't want to worry about you."

"I don't want you worrying about me. I have enough people worrying about me. And you have enough people to take care of."

"We would never see each other," I say. "I've spent all my extra money on this trip. And even if I raided my dad's airline points, I can't leave my mom every few weekends to see you." Or maybe now I can. But just because I can, do I want to? I have enough trouble keeping up with my family and friends and commuting to and from school. I hadn't had time to read a novel just for fun all school year.

Even if my mom no longer needs my help, do I want to tie myself down again?

"I'm broke too," he says. "I had to take a bunch of loans for school. I used all my extra cash from working at Sadie's to pay for this trip when I was supposed to be paying off the bank."

"What's Sadie's?"

"A convenience store on campus."

"I didn't know you had a job."

"There's a lot we don't know about each other still. Although now you also know that I make terrible financial decisions."

"Maybe," I say. "But I'm glad you came."

"What a summer," he says. He sighs.

"So what does this mean?" I ask, my throat closing up.

"That we should just enjoy the moment?" he asks. He reaches for my hand across the table.

I nod. I'm going to miss him.

But, oh, what a summer.

My flight from Corfu to Rome leaves at eight fifteen a.m.

His flight from Corfu to Athens leaves at nine a.m.

We go to the airport together. It's small and quiet. We hold hands.

We check our bags. I'll have to pick mine up in Rome. We go through security.

I'm gate thirteen. He's gate nineteen.

By the time we get to my gate, they're already boarding.

"So," he says.

"So."

"I'll miss you," I tell him. My eyes prick with tears. Crap.

He pulls me into a hug.

I sob.

"This is stupid," he says. His voice is shaking. "We can still talk, can't we? And text? And see each other? I want to see you again."

My heart thumps. "How?"

"I don't know," he says. "We can't just end this. Do you want this? I want this. If you want this we can make it work somehow, can't we?"

I pull back. Tears are spilling down my cheeks. "But what about . . . *everything* . . ."

He puts both hands on my cheeks and looks me right in the eyes.

I look right back into his.

"You won't have to worry about me," he says.

My heart aches. I just don't know.

I kiss him again. And keep kissing him until everyone else is on the plane, and it's my turn to board.

My heart is pounding all the way to Rome.

I get my luggage and then check in again for my flight home.

I have two hours to kill until I meet Leela.

I find a seat at a café, and connect to the Wi-Fi.

A message from my sister pops up.

Addison: We can't wait to see you. Picking you up from the airport! Mom says she's going to drive at least some of the way!!!! Fingers crossed . . .

I stare at the message. My mother is going to try to pick me up at the airport? Seriously?

I put my phone down. I sink into my seat. The truth is, I'm not sure I believe she'll really get better. She might get better. But she might not. Am I strong enough now to handle it either way?

I think so. I hope so.

I take a deep breath and let the hope expand inside of me.

Then I pick the phone back up and respond:

Fingers crossed!

Because who knows? Anything is possible.

Next I spot a few messages from Leela.

Leela: See you soon. I'm in a shuttle on my way to the airport. Hope you made it okay. I can't wait to hear everything . . . Love you.

Leela: Also, um, Kat went back to the villa two days ago. Yes. THE villa. She told me she was going to tell you . . . I told her she should go. No regrets, right? And OMG you're going to be so proud of me. I stayed in Rome by MYSELF. And last night I kissed a HOT ITALIAN BARTENDER NAMED LORENZO. HE HAD A SCOOTER. GO CHECK MY INSTAGRAM.

Oh wow. We are so not getting any sleep on this flight either. Too much to catch up on.

The next text is from Kat, sent two days ago.

Kat: Did Leela tell you? I'm an idiot. I know. But . . . I have to do it. 🙈 Will you still love me?

Of course I will.

Then, finally, there's a text from Jackson.

I miss you already.

All around me, people come and go, hurrying through the terminal.

I miss him too. And maybe it's wishful thinking, but I go onto Google Maps and take a screenshot of the distance between Maryland and Vancouver. Forty-two hours by car, sixty-seven by train, eight by plane, and two hundred and

sixty-five by bicycle. I send it back to him with a note.
See you soon.

Tip: Make sure to wrap all of your souvenirs carefully in bubble wrap!

Otherwise your snow globe of the Leaning Tower of Pisa will probably break, dousing your jam-stained jeans and all of your knickers in water, glass shards, and sparkles.

The end. *La fin.*

Meanwhile, back at Blue Springs Summer Camp . . .
Coming soon . . .

JUST A BOY AND A GIRL IN A LITTLE CANOE.

Acknowledgments

Merci, grazie, and thank you to:

Jen Klonsky, editor extraordinaire, who believed in my one-sentence pitch and trusted me to pull it off. Thank you for your patience and support and excellent editing! I'm thrilled to be working with you! So many exclamation marks!!!

All the amazing people at HarperTeen, including: Bess Brasswell (yay! I missed you!), Alison Klapthor, Alexandra Rakaczki, Stephanie Hoover, Gina Rizzo, Lillian Sun, Michelle Taormina, and Catherine Wallace.

Laura Dail, my champion for over fifteen years. Tamar Rydzinski, the queen of foreign rights. Jessica Tarrant and everyone at Orchard UK. Lauren Walters, my amazing assistant, incredible designer, and super reader. How did I function before you?! Katie Hartman, who on many nights stayed up way too late reading this book, but told me how to sound younger and cooler. Avery Carmichael, whose notes were great and who made me laugh. A lot. E. Lockhart, best critique partner I could ask for and amazing friend. Angela Church, for her help with the accents, yeah?

Mitali Dave, for her quick read and advice. Adele Wash for her Aussie expertise.

To the people who helped me craft and understand Sydney and her mom: Judy Batalion, close friend and support system since high school and brilliant author of *White Walls*. As always, thank you for your invaluable insights and edits. Dr. Alicia Salzer, for her thoughtful read and her many explanations about panic attacks, caring for a parent, and agoraphobia. Bonnie Altro, friend and now therapist for REALS. Thank you for your excellent notes. All mistakes made are my own!

More love and thank-yous to family, friends, writers, and others: Elissa Ambrose, Aviva Mlynowski, Larry Mlynowski, Louisa Weiss, Robert Ambrose, the Dalven-Swidlers, the Dattilios, the Goldsmiths, the Heckers, the Finkelstein-Mitchells, the Steins, the Wolfes, the Mittlemans, the Bilermans, the Greens, Courtney Sheinmel, Anne Heltzel, Lauren Myracle, Emily Bender, Targia Alphonse, Jess Braun, Lauren Kisilevsky, Carolyn Mackler, Caroline Gertler, Stuart Gibbs, Jen E. Smith, Robin Wasserman, Rose Brock, Aimee Friedman, David Levithan, Adele Griffin, Leslie Margolis, Maryrose Wood, Tara Altebrando, Sara Zarr, Ally Carter, Jennifer Barnes, Alan Gratz, Penny Fransblow, Maggie Marr, Jeremy Cammy, and Farrin Jacobs.

Special shout-out to all the people who actually saw London, France, and more with me over the last two decades: Shobie Riff Farb, Shaun Povitz Sarno, Sari Decklebaum, Micheal Bilerman, Matt "Rico" Milberg, Bonnie Altro, Matt Altro, Sam Blaichman, Jess Bortnick, and Robin Wasserman (I still can't believe you agreed to come with me! *Merci!*).

Last, but never least, thank you to my amazing husband, Todd, who I backpacked with when I was nineteen, and my always-adventurous daughters, Anabelle and Chloe. Where to next, guys? You know, they call ice cream *gelado* in Portugal. . . .